Love
in
Exile

Love *in* Exile

Bahaa Taher

Translated by
Farouk Abdel Wahab

Arabia Books
London

First published in Great Britain in 2008 by
Arabia Books
26 Cadogan Court
Draycott Avenue
London SW3 3BX
www.arabia-books.co.uk

This edition published by arrangement with
The American University in Cairo Press
113 Sharia Kasr el Aini, Cairo, Egypt
420 Fifth Avenue, New York, NY 10018
www.aucpress.com

First published in Arabic in 1995 as *al-Hubb fi-l-manfa*
Copyright © 1995 by Bahaa Taher
The moral right of the author has been asserted
Protected by the Berne Convention

English translation copyright © 2001 by
The American University in Cairo Press.

ISBN 978-1-906697-01-3
Printed in Great Britain by J. H. Haynes & Co. Ltd., Sparkford
1 2 3 4 5 6 7 8 9 10   14 13 12 11 10 09 08 07

Cover design: Arabia Books
Design: AUC Press

Contents

Translator's Acknowledgments

I would like to thank the following friends for help with various aspects of the translation: Heather Felton, Margaret Litvin, Rusty Rook, and Katherine Strange (University of Chicago) and Neil Hewison and Kelly Zaug (The American University in Cairo Press).

1

Just Another Conference

I DESIRED HER IMPOTENTLY, like one afraid of incest.

She was young and beautiful. I was old, a father and divorced. Love never occurred to me and I didn't do anything to express my desire.

But she told me, later on, "It was written all over your face."

I was a Cairene whose city had expelled me to exile in the north. She was like me, a foreigner in that country. But she was European and with her passport she considered the whole of Europe her hometown. When we met by chance in that city, "N," to which I was tied by work, we became friends.

Tied by work? What a lie. I wasn't doing anything, really. I was a correspondent for a newspaper in Cairo that didn't care if I corresponded with it; perhaps it was keen that I not correspond.

At noontime, during the lunch break that punctuated the long workday for those who worked, we would sit together, drinking coffee. She would tell me about herself and I would tell her about myself. Silence brought us closer when we looked past the glass wall of the café to that long rectangular mountain, lurking on the other bank of the river like a long-tailed crocodile.

But when I began to desire her, I became a chatterbox. I barricaded myself behind a wall of words so as not to give myself away. My chatter just kept coming, massive, entertaining, and ceaseless, like a weaving-crazed larva unable to stop spinning his cocoon.

Perhaps I was—and how would I know now?—unconsciously weaving snares around her. She would look at me with her beautiful eyes widening as she smiled, asking me, "Where do you get all these words? It is *my* job to do the talking, so how is it that you outdo me?" But that afternoon I couldn't. The threads of words were scattered and broken. There were long gaps of silence during which I looked absently at the river while she sat there bent over her empty coffee cup, turning it in the saucer. I could only see her thick head of hair and her straight, jutting nose. She raised her head suddenly; looked at me when I fell silent and said, "Go on, go on," but the words just wouldn't come.

Outside the café we walked to where I parked my car. Today, as usual, I would take her to the door of the office where she works. I would leave her and pretend that I too am going to work.

When we got to the car she said, "I'd like to walk a little, do you mind?" She walked next to me, her steps slower than usual. After a few steps she stopped and said in a firm voice, "Listen, I don't want to see you again. Forgive me, but I think it would be best if we don't meet. I think I've fallen in love with you and I don't want that. I don't want that after all I've seen in this world."

I knew what she had seen in this world, so after a moment of silence I said, "As you wish." I watched as she hurried away.

But that was not the beginning. In the beginning everything was different. That day I was reluctant to go to that press conference. I knew ahead of time that certain things would be said which if I were to report, would not be published by my paper in Cairo. And even if the paper published the article, it would shorten it, dilute it, and jumble the paragraphs in such a way that the reader would not be able to figure out what happened exactly or what the story was about. I thought, on the way, about going to the airport. It was the day the Egyptian plane usually arrived in the city, which was frequently and unexpectedly visited by Egyptian officials. Maybe one of the ministers would arrive and make statements that would make the editor-in-chief so happy he would put it on the front page and finally be pleased with me. "Minister So and So states, 'Our economy has gotten out of the bottleneck.' The Minister says, 'We will discuss European cooperation in our spurt of development . . .'" The car actually turned to the airport route. The editor-in-chief really likes that "spurt of development." It appears every week in his articles. For many long years the spurt has been ceaselessly squirting out of the bottleneck in his articles. So, why don't I make the editor-in-chief happy, if I can? Why go to that wretched press conference this beautiful summer morning? Am I, as my ex-wife Manar put it, "fond of misery"? Why even go to the airport? How do I know that a minister will come or that the editor-in-chief is impatiently awaiting my report? It's best if I just shut up completely. This way I'll spare him from the awkward apologies, "I swear to God, my friend, your letter arrived too late," or "We actually put it in there but at the last moment news from the presidency came and 'ate up' all the space," or "You know? I am conducting an inquiry on so and so in the foreign desk because he did not show me the letter. I have actually turned him over to Legal Affairs," and so forth. So why bother the editor-in-chief or myself? The salary will keep coming, that's what matters. Let's enjoy the beautiful day.

I drove the car along the highway, crossing a wood en route to the airport, then turned on a packed dirt path between the trees and parked in the shade. The wood was cool and quiet and the new leaves which had a short while ago begun to re-adorn the trees were radiant green, almost diaphanous. They gathered in a precariously delicate dome, swayed by the light wind causing the sun rays to sneak through the scattered gaps, forming yellow waves coursing quickly on the grass and then disappearing, only to make another surprise appearance. The successive waves as they passed stirred up the little yellow and white wildflowers that adorned the land in the summer. The first time we went abroad on a one-week tourist trip to Bulgaria, I was dazzled by that ornamental pattern on the ground and so was Manar. She asked me while we were in the forest, "Is it forbidden to pick them?" I said, "I don't think so." So she started gathering a bouquet, arranging it by color. When she was done, she looked at the flowers in her hands and said in a disappointed tone, "But they were beautiful in the ground!" And indeed the little flowers had just died, folding their little petals over their yellow round hearts, their stems lying limp on the sides of her hand. I said to her, "I think these wild flowers live only in the ground." I held the wilted bouquet and threw it away keeping one flower, a yellow one, bigger than the others, which had kept its shape, its petals intact, and I stuck in it Manar's hair telling her how beautiful she looked. And indeed she was beautiful with that flower in her black hair. I kissed her and we laughed again, happy as we used to be because, for the first time, we were walking in a forest with endless green. But in the evening, at the hotel, I had to pay the price. In what strange part of her mind did she keep those little things? The things that I forgot right away? That ability to engender meanings that no one can think? I was apprehensive that night when she asked me half in jest, "Did you come to Europe before behind my back?" But I played along, saying, "Of course. Many times. Secret missions. Why do you ask?"

She said, "How did you know that these flowers lived only in the ground?" I fell silent and that also was no good. The jesting tone turned into one of light disapproval as she said, "Besides, what is this manner in which you deal with people here?"

"What manner?"

"This exaggerated politeness with hotel workers, waiters in restaurants, store clerks, and people in general. Do you have an inferiority complex towards these Europeans?"

"But have you noticed, Manar, that I deal with people in Egypt differently?"

She pursed her lips and began to shake her head right and left as if uttering the verdict after due deliberation as she said, "No. But here I notice that you overdo it a bit. I think it is an inferiority complex towards Europeans."

I was about to reply but I held off and said, "You may be right. I'll think about it." I had learned a long time ago to ignore her little, hidden tantrums. And I was . . . Enough already! Be fair. She also must have been ignoring your little hidden tantrums. The problem was not the wild flowers. So what was it, exactly? Had there been a mistake from the beginning? What was it? All I remember is that I was in love with her and that she said she loved me. I mean, she must have actually loved me at one time or another. Otherwise, why did we get married? I was the poorest among the editors who hoped to marry her when she came to work with us at the newspaper. Like the others I was captivated by her cheerful face, her ever-present smile, and her straight talk while she looked directly in the eye of whomever she was speaking with. She captivated me more than the others. I used to exert a great effort to talk to her in the normal way I talked to other women editors. I always took pains to look away from where she was seated in the big newsroom. It was she who began to walk over from her desk to mine to consult me as a senior colleague about a story she was writing or to have me look at the story before she sent it to the typesetters. Then she began to talk to me about her problems at home; they were pestering her to get married and parading her before suitors as if they were showcasing a commodity. She will never marry this way; she herself will choose. Why is choice the right of man alone? Her words frightened me. I said to myself she would never be that frank with me if I were the one she chose. But I took a chance and I proposed. She told me as we walked, holding hands on the

Corniche, "Mother said, 'Have you found nobody but this penniless journalist for whom you forgo an officer and a doctor?'" Manar surprised me when she proudly said as she squeezed my hand, "This means that Mom likes you and approves of you!" Before long I realized that Mom was the one who mattered. She felt somewhat ashamed in the presence of her father whom I liked from the first instant because of his simplicity and kindness. But Manar was ashamed when he would sit with us in the living room in his pajamas or galabiyya when we were engaged, or when he spoke proudly about how his boss praised the style in which he wrote the memo that day, or about how he had bought a watermelon on his way back from work after the vendor had sworn that it was the best quality. When he sliced it open at home he discovered that it was white inside, whereupon he went back and returned it to the lying vendor because he never gave up his rights and didn't allow anyone to cheat him.

Manar would blush noticeably when he told those stories and I'd notice a glance of wordless reproach in her mother's eyes. But after we were married, her mother had no qualms rebuking him in front of me. Manar would cry bitterly because after he retired he used to go out in the street in his galabiyya and sit for hours at the barber's, or grocer's shop, or on the doorman's bench. She would say through her tears, "Have pity, Father; our reputation, Father." He would promise her in his awkward embarrassment that he wouldn't do it again. But when he died Manar's grief over him was beyond anything anyone could imagine. She kept crying for months and talking to him all the time as if he were sitting with us asking him how he was doing over there and why he had left her? Didn't he miss her? I would ask myself whether besides grief, there were some pangs of conscience. What happened afterwards confirmed what I had suspected. Gradually, she began to talk about her father as a high-ranking official with a strong personality, feared by everyone at the office because he was firm and strict when it came to what was right, even though he never harmed anyone. She herself, with the passage of years, became convinced of that, demanding sometimes that I be firm like her father. When they laid me off work and there was not much to preoccupy me, the first time I stayed at the barbershop long after he had finished cutting my hair, chatting with him about nothing in particular I was dismayed and frightened. I hurried back home then sat at the desk to plan my book.

Manar had gradually begun to take after her mother. She would accuse me, for instance, of spoiling our two children and yet would be angry and come to their defense if I tried to punish one of them. Punishment remained her exclusive right and it usually came after we had gone out on a Friday. She got used to constantly discovering the mistakes the two of them had made: some display of "bad manners" as she would put it. The punishment: no allowance or no visits to friends and relatives. When she saw me playing chess with Khalid she accused me of distracting him from his studies. If I carried Hanadi and went around and around with her as she laughed, she would say, "This is the game that gave her a stomachache last week." When she noticed that Khalid loved poetry and that I encouraged him to read, she said the boy should not be led down the road to failure when he was such a genius in math, and when . . .

No. Stop it. Enough already once again. Where are you going with this? That she domineered the children? So be it. Where were you? Why didn't you do something to get closer to them? Weren't you out all day long at the newspaper or the Arab Socialist Union or abroad? What are you blaming her for, exactly? Besides, what's with that barber story? What does it have to do with anything? I was looking for the reason, for the seed of the mistake, my mistake or her mistake. But what have these things to do with the matter?

I was surprised by my face in the rearview mirror, frowning and absent and I was taken aback. I said, no, I am not going back to that, not in this beautiful place nor this sunny morning. I am not going to succumb today to this empty wandering where a scene with Manar surfaces from anything I see or just surfaces for no reason. Then one scene leads to another and hours pass this way. No, not today. If the serenity in this forest cannot save me from that, anything would be better than staying here.

I started the engine.

When I entered the hall at the hotel, the press conference hadn't yet begun. They had placed two tables together on a dais with three chairs and arranged about thirty chairs in the hall, even though there were only six or seven journalists who sat, scattered and silent. Perhaps, like me, they came because they couldn't find anything else to do. Who did you want to come? Who cares now, here or anywhere else? Who cares about a conference held by a committee named The International Doctors Committee for Human Rights about human rights violations in Chile? What Chile and what rights? The time of horror, my friend, was over when they slaughtered thousands in the capital's soccer stadium there. The time of shedding tears over Allende was over when the military killed him. They killed him three years after Abd al-Nasser died. They fought Abd al-Nasser saying he was a dictator. Why was Allende the one who was elected? The wolf said to the lamb: if you haven't muddied the water because you are a dictator, you have muddied it because you are a democrat. However you choose to look at it, you are still my lunch.

Who remembers Neruda now? I don't remember reading Neruda's name in any newspaper in my country since grief killed him after the military pounced on his country ten years ago. They finally silenced him so he wouldn't sing, wouldn't say: *On the shores of all countries my voice rises/ Because it is the voice of those who have been silent/ Because all who have not known singing / Have sung today through me.* In the old days, as a young man I read Neruda's poems in our daily newspapers, even in the evening newspaper. Back in the days when the papers said that a people's victory in any country meant freedom for us; the days when we cried over Kwame Nkrumah and Patrice Lumumba; the days when Radio Cairo sang for Port Said, Algeria, Malaya, and peoples *like good tidings bringing forth flowers from the depths of massacres!* Yes, nothing less than *flowers from the depths of massacres!* I remember back then a friend whose eyes would well up with tears when he read for us the poem, "*Children in my country starve to death and the fish in the sea drink coffee.*"

Nowadays no one cried over that. No one cried because the masters of our world dump coffee beans into the sea or bulldoze mountains of eggs. People now are more rational, emotions calmer. Tears well up only from watching too much television, including your own tears, hypocrite. You and your International Doctors Committee!

In my hand was a booklet I had taken at random from several booklets placed on a literature table at the entrance of the hall. I began to leaf through the pages. The dais was still empty even though it was time for the conference to begin. My eyes passed over some lines on the opened page of the booklet: "as for methods of torture in the prisons of Chile, they are the same as those described by the Committee in its earlier publications about that country and other countries in Latin America and other continents. The most commonly used method in Chile is that of electrical shocks in a manner known as 'the grill,' by placing moving electrodes on the victim's body chained to an iron bed covered with oilcloth. The shocks in this method cause severe pain in the muscles and nerves and their effects last for years. The person to whom they have been administered will suffer malfunctions in the muscle movements, continual insomnia and nightmares. The patient will suffer abnormal conditions during which he imagines that he himself was administering the electric shocks to his own body and relives the first torture ordeal and his pain . . . . There is the electric shock method called 'the needle' which is . . . ."

I stopped reading when I heard movement in the hall and saw a tall gray-haired man come forward and sit at the dais. He began to look around the hall calmly, unperturbed by the scant audience. When he started speaking English, I guessed from his accent that he was from Germany or one of the northern countries. He said that his name was Muller and that he was a doctor. He apologized for the delay in starting the conference and said he would mention the reason in a little while. He stated that the Committee that he represented and which was comprised of doctor volunteers from different countries was concerned with human rights in general but focused in particular on health and medical aspects. He said that the Committee had found in Chile some very serious cases among political prisoners, who number in the thousands. He began listing numbers about the conditions of patients in prisons, about torture by beating and electricity, sleep deprivation, rape, and other methods. He read the names of some who had died under torture.

We began to ask some routine questions seeking to clarify some details and figures. Suddenly, however, someone stood up. He was a local journalist whom I knew. His paper, *The Fatherland,* constantly attacked refugees from Chile and other countries and called for their repatriation or deportation. It kept publishing one article after another about the refugees saying that they caused overcrowding, spread crime, and polluted the environment and that the country should be saved from this danger. The journalist addressed Dr. Muller in a provocative tone, saying, "Don't you think, despite everything that is said about Chile, that it is more stable than many countries? Don't you think that the number of those dying in prison is by far fewer than those killed in civil wars in countries neighboring Chile?"

An angry grumbling noise rose in the hall. A woman journalist sitting in the chair in front of me didn't bother to hide her anger and asked in an audible voice, "Did you also invite Chile's generals to attend this conference?" Others commented on what she said. Dr. Muller tapped the table twice with his finger and said calmly to *The Fatherland*'s reporter, "I am not a politician, sir and our organization is not a political organization. We are physicians talking about cases that we have investigated carefully and verified. And yet I would like to remind you that before the military coup d'état no one was dying in Chile, not in guerrilla wars and not in prisons. This is how you should compare, if you want to."

Then Dr. Muller looked at his watch and said, "Pardon me. We've rented this hall for one hour and we are running a little late because we had a problem today in presenting the translation of a testimony in Spanish which I am anxious for you to hear." He pointed to the front row and a man and a woman got up and sat next to him as he continued, "A professional interpreter was supposed to come but he excused himself at the last moment. A friend, Brigitte Schaefer, volunteered to do the interpreting and I thank her."

Brigitte was wearing a two-piece uniform like that of flight attendants and had a pink scarf around her neck. She addressed us as she sat between Muller and the other man smiling awkwardly. She said, "Please forgive me if I am a little slow, because this is the first time I've worked as an interpreter." All the journalists' eyes were on her because she was very beautiful. One of the journalists said, "We'll forgive you with great pleasure. Please, take the whole time." The rest of the journalists laughed but Dr. Muller once again tapped with his fingers saying in a serious tone bordering on reprimand, "As I told you, this testimony is particularly important for our organization because it also involves medical personnel. But I prefer for you to listen for yourselves." Then he motioned the man to speak.

For the first time I turned my eyes from Brigitte to the man sitting to her right. From where I sat, I couldn't make out his face, for he had bent down his head so low that it came close to his arms, which he had clasped in front of his chest. The only thing I could see clearly was his smooth black hair. He began to speak in a very soft voice and it seemed that Brigitte asked him to raise his voice for he repeated his words without raising his head. She began, after each of his pauses, to translate into English, which correspondents in this country used.

He said his name was Pedro Ibañez, age twenty-six, and that he worked as a cab driver in the capital Santiago. At the beginning of the year, he was standing with his cab in the taxi stand in front of the main station waiting for his turn. He saw a man coming out of the station carrying a suitcase heading for the stand. Before he reached him, a driver whom Pedro had not seen before approached him trying to take the suitcase, pointing at a cab in the stand. The passenger refused to give him the suitcase or to go with him. Instead he went to Pedro's cab, which was the closest to him. After Pedro started moving in the direction of the address that he had given him, he noticed that another cab was following him. He saw in the rearview mirror the same driver who had tried to take the suitcase and he saw other persons with him. The passenger also noticed and began to look over his shoulder. He seemed disconcerted, as if trying to overcome his fear. Pedro was also afraid as the passenger asked him to go faster, faster, looking forward and backward the whole time. Then he suddenly said to Pedro, "Listen, they're after me. They're from the National Security Administration." Pedro was now genuinely afraid. He knew what the National Security Administration was. He thought of stopping the cab and letting the passenger out but he was not sure what that would lead to, either. When the man asked him to leave the main street and to go into a side street, he went along. Pedro said that he regretted it afterwards, that it was a bad idea, for it was difficult for the passengers in the car giving chase to do something in the crowded main street, but once they were in the quiet side street they had an advantage. Pedro speeded as much as he could to get away from them but their car was new and fast. The passenger noticed that and stopped looking backwards, then sat back in his seat telling Pedro calmly, "Listen, I am sorry I got you into this." Pedro never found out what "this" was. When the other car pulled up next to the cab at a traffic light, the passenger suddenly opened the door on the other side then jumped out and started to run in the street. He ran only two steps. Pedro said that when the shooting began, he slid down in his seat to duck but he felt the bullet that entered his side at the same moment and saw the passenger falling down in the street with blood gushing from his head.

Pedro was speaking in a monotonous voice and Brigitte was translating in the same monotone as she shifted her eyes between him and us in the hall. But I noticed that her face was gradually hardening and her voice rising a little when Pedro was pointing to the spot where the bullet entered his side. Dr. Muller urged him on with a gesture from his index finger pointing at the watch. Pedro nodded his head apologetically. He had forgotten his shyness and began looking at us. I noticed his big eyes under which were two broad rings like eyebrows upside down. I asked myself if it was insomnia.

Pedro's tone changed from the moment that Muller urged him on. Words were now rushing out of his mouth in a disjointed manner. Brigitte was having a hard time following him and at times apologized to us and asked him to repeat. The narrative was no longer neat. Once again he started to explain, this time pointing to his chest saying, "The bullet entered my chest and I, of course, didn't know the passenger. Sorry, I mean the bullet entered my side and settled in my chest as they said at the hospital, in this place. But I had not seen this man before he rode in the taxi and I think he died. No. I am sure he died because I saw with my eyes the blood and pieces of his brain on the pavement before I lost consciousness. When the officer asked me in the hospital I was very thirsty. I shook my finger like this: 'I don't know him.' The officer yanked out the blood IV from my arm and he jerked the oxygen mask from my face. The officer said, 'I'll let you die because you are Capetillo's friend. Why did he pick you specifically, of all the taxi drivers?' Of course the doctor was standing there when that happened and the officers were from the NSA—the National Security Administration. And after he yanked the oxygen mask, I actually began to die. I mean I lost my breath completely. It was the first time I heard the name Capetillo. I didn't hear his name and my brother didn't hear his name. When I tried to tell that to the officer, a lot of blood gushed from my mouth and I lost consciousness again. But the following day they began to interrogate me again when I regained consciousness. That day there were three from the NSA and they asked me about my family: Are we socialists? Are we of Allende's party?

Originally, of course, I am from the countryside, but we didn't get any land when they distributed the lands of the rich to the peasants in the countryside. Neither my brother nor I got any. That's why nothing happened to us when the rich returned after the coup and took back their land . . . I mean we didn't go to jail with the peasants who had taken the land. But I couldn't say that. I couldn't reply. I was very tired. One of the officers reached out and turned off the oxygen again. I felt the blood in my throat and my mouth. I could hear it gurgling in my throat but I couldn't spit it out of my mouth. The doctor brought a contraption, which he placed in my throat and began to pump out the blood. He filled many bottles with it. The doctor advised me to speak so I would live but he didn't turn on the oxygen. All he told the officer was that I couldn't speak." Pedro spread his hands in front of him and said to us, the journalists in the hall, in a loud voice and eyes wide open, "How can one speak without oxygen?"

The Fatherland reporter laughed and the other journalists looked at him angrily and one of them said, "Shhh" but he kept looking forward indifferently without looking at anyone. Pedro sensed that he had made some kind of blunder, so he became more confused and started to talk again, his head bowed down.

"I think it was on the third day . . . no, on the fourth day, when they brought my brother Freddie. They said that they discovered that Freddie was a socialist and that I was a liar. Did I say that my brother was a student as the University? They yelled in my face, 'You have to say everything you know about Capetillo.' But if I didn't know Capetillo what could I say about him? That day also I couldn't move. As I lay on my bed I saw them strip Freddie's clothes off. I saw them putting a large towel in his mouth. They tied his feet and wrists to a metal bed next to my bed. All I could move were my eyes. I shouted saying that Freddie didn't know Capetillo, that I did not know Capetillo . . . I shouted but no sound came out of my mouth. I saw them putting the electric things on Freddie's body. The doctor placed his stethoscope on Freddie's chest then shook his head for the officer and backed off. But the doctor remained standing there when they turned on the electricity. I heard Freddie's gasp despite the towel in his mouth . . . I saw his naked body rising high and arching so tightly that the whole bed moved with him. At that moment I could speak, so I said, . . ."

But we at the press conference were not able to find out what Pedro Ibañez said at that moment. Suddenly Brigitte stopped her quick, breathless translation. She kept looking at us, her eyes wide open, her face growing longer as her lips quivered. At the beginning Pedro, who was talking with bowed head in his tense Spanish, did not notice. I could only make out a few words, "Freddie . . . NSA . . . Capetillo . . . the doctor." Brigitte kept staring at us, pursing her lips. When they parted in spite of her efforts she pursed them again. She didn't cry or emit any sound; she just kept looking at us with her wide blue eyes. Finally Pedro too felt the silence so he raised his eyes ringed with two black crescents. Muller was also looking at her from the other side of the table. He reached out and placed his hand over hers, which was resting on the table, but she pulled back quickly as if she had been stung. She murmured something that I couldn't make out as she got up and moved away in quick steps then disappeared in a corridor opposite us.

Muller followed her with his eyes for a moment then turned towards us and said, "Pardon me, but the time we had for the press conference is up anyway. All I can say is that our Committee has investigated the incident and weighed all the details. Pedro was able to escape from the military hospital a few weeks later and his friends helped him to escape Chile afterwards. Then he was treated in Canada for serious complications to his chest because of the bullet and the torture. As for his brother, Freddie, the student Alfredo Ibañez, he died under torture. You will find all the details in the booklets at the entrance of the hall. We thank you for any cooperation with us if you publish something about these incidents, and . . . "

The woman journalist sitting in front of me got up to take a picture of Pedro who was shyly and awkwardly looking at the doctor and at us. After she took the picture she sat down saying loudly, "God damn this profession!"

Bernard, the journalist who sat at the far end of the hall, said as he got up from his chair, "Which profession? Journalism, National Security Administration, medicine, electricity, or taxi driving?" Then he kicked the metal chair and said, "Or the world?"

The clanking of the chair continued for a few moments then subsided.

2

A Distant Past . . .
A Dead Past

I STOOD AT THE ENTRANCE OF THE HALL leafing through the other book-lets. On the cover of one of them was a picture of Pedro Ibañez and next to it the picture of a young man who looked like him and who I guessed was Freddie. Like Pedro he had a large mouth, and thick hair and thick eyebrows above his dark eyes. He was wearing a white shirt, unbuttoned at the chest, trying to look older with his tightened, dignified lips, and the earnest look in his eyes. I wasn't surprised when I saw most of the journalists leaving without casting a single glance on the booklets. They were leaving hurriedly as if they were running away from the whole place and the whole story. I knew that before lunch we would all have forgotten Pedro and Freddie and Chile and that those who had to send cables or news stories to their newspapers would look for other top-ics. As I stood there a hand patted my shoulder and I heard someone say-ing, "I've been looking for you."

Surprised, I turned around and said, "Ibrahim!"

Yes. It was he, Ibrahim al-Mehallawi after all these years. He was thinner now and his hair had turned gray, though I noticed that he was as handsome in his middle years as he had been as a youth. I tried to smile as I extended my hand to shake his but he suddenly put his left arm around my shoulder and embraced me hard. That gave me a little start. Ibrahim sensed my aloofness and moved back a step, saying, "Its been years since we last met, hasn't it?" Then he looked at my perplexed face and said, smiling, "I know that you know a lot of poetry by heart. Don't you remember Ahmad Shawqi's line 'Death has erased all traces of enmity between us'? Many things have died, my friend, during these years and enmity no longer makes any sense."

Somewhat embarrassed, I said, "Of course, of course. Are you still working in Beirut?"

"Yes, I'm here on a business trip. I arrived only yesterday."

"I'm sorry I didn't notice you at the press conference. I would've . . ."

Ibrahim leafed through the booklets and put some of them in a small leather briefcase and said, "Believe me I didn't see you either, nor did I expect you to be here. I didn't think your paper was interested in news about Chile."

I noticed that I was still holding the booklet with Pedro's picture, so I returned it to its place on the table, saying, "Is any other paper interested? Pedro Ibañez would be lucky if any newspaper in the world published five lines about his story. As for our own newspaper, as you know, all world news is covered in less than five lines. We've progressed."

Ibrahim laughed softly as we moved away from the entrance of the hall and said, "Yes. I can't ever forget my surprise when I saw the paper for the first time after this progress. I was in Baghdad when I came across a copy and read the front page headline, printed in a large square: 'Arafa to Sabtiyya and Dalal to Supply.' I stared at the headline for a while, thinking there were some typos. It was only after I read the story that I figured out it was talking about appointments and promotions of some officials, high ranking or low ranking, only God knows. Only from the context was I able to guess that by Sabtiyya they meant Customs. Did you imagine at any time that our revolutionary paper would progress like that?"

I waved my hand saying, "Please, let's not open that door. Do you have time for a cup of coffee?"

"Sure. We can even have lunch if you don't mind."

His warm and friendly attitude surprised me somewhat, but as we walked, exchanging news about our mutual friends, I made an effort so he wouldn't sense any indifference on my part. I was actually happy to see him even though we had never been close friends, even when we were first colleagues as editors on the foreign desk in our youth. He was a zealous Marxist who said I was an idealist and a dreamer. I thought he was dogmatic and out of touch with the people. In those days I was reading Sati' al-Husari and the Arab nationalists and believed with Abd al-Nasser that our great state would be established tomorrow. I actually hung above my head in the large newsroom where we had our desks, this quotation from his famous speech on the day the union with Syria was announced: "A great state which protects rather than threatens, preserves rather than wastes." The calligrapher of the paper wrote it for me in beautiful Kufic script and I placed it under the map of the large fatherland, the Arab world. Ibrahim made sure I saw his smile as he looked at the sign, pretending to be lost in contemplation.

Thereupon I'd get furious and we'd argue and quarrel. But of course I was sad when they arrested him with the other communists in 1959, and I missed him. Then when he came out of detention and back to the paper some affection developed between us, as happens to old colleagues, until we had a falling out before he left Egypt. When the ordeal of the seventies came and overtook me and I was promoted to the post of consultant whom nobody consulted, he was working in Iraq, then he went to Syria until he settled in Beirut a few years ago working for a newspaper published by one of the resistance organizations there.

As we walked through the streets of the foreign city that had brought us together unexpectedly, each of us was trying to overcome his awkwardness, we made valiant attempts to speak like two old friends who had met after a long separation. But the silences were embarrassing because we didn't want to go back to any real discussion about the past.

I began to tell him about the landmarks of the city, which he was visiting for the first time. We crossed a wide square on our way from the hotel to the river. The square was surrounded by buildings in the new Roman style and their entrances were flanked by towering columns. In the middle of the square was the statue of a bald man riding a horse and pointing to the horizon in a dignified manner. I explained to Ibrahim: This is the museum; this is the university administration building; this man led a battle to liberate the country from the French in the nineteenth century. I tried to speak in as much detail as I could so the conversation would continue. Ibrahim was following what I was saying, murmuring "Yeah, yeah. Really?" When there was nothing else to say, we gave in and walked in silence.

Finally I said to Ibrahim, "Sorry for the long walk. I love this café and I always park my car near it."

Ibrahim paused a little at the entrance of the café then said, "But you're right. I really would have regretted it if I'd left town without seeing this place."

I didn't know whether he said that just to be amiable or because he actually liked the place. As for me, I really liked this oval-shaped café jutting into the river like a shell cast on the rocky tongue of land. A long path lined on both sides with beds of well-tended flowers led to its quiet location on the riverbank.

There were only a few customers, so we easily found a place at an open window overlooking, across the wide river, the mountain, which at that time of the year was covered with green forests and gardens. In the midst of the trees were scattered white houses with red tile roofs that jutted like graduated pyramids as they went higher up until at the very top they appeared like tiny red triangles in the midst of the trees.

As we sat down, Ibrahim said softly, "All this peace and serenity!"

I surmised that Beirut came to his mind at that moment but I said nothing. I left him absorbed in contemplating the river whose clear water was rushing, creating successive shimmering silver waves and following some white swans floating in circular motions, raising their lofty heads, looking at the windows in silence. The ducks, with their brown bodies and shining violet necks, were not content to look at us as they floated anxiously under the windows; they began to move their beaks with successive calls until a lady sitting near us relented and started throwing bread crumbs to them.

Ibrahim kept shifting his gaze between the river and the mountain for a long time then said as if following his train of thought, "How lucky you are to live here!"

"Yes, how lucky!"

Ibrahim felt there was something in my tone and looked apologetically at me, saying, "I mean . . . "

He didn't finish the sentence. When the waiter came I asked Ibrahim if he wanted a beer and he said, "Not at noon. We agreed to have coffee."

We ordered coffee and I said, smiling, "I never heard you turn down beer at noon or in the afternoon."

He said curtly, "Age." Then he pointed at my head saying, "Speaking of age, how come your hair is still black till now? We've all turned gray; how did you escape it?"

I also pointed at my head and laughed briefly, saying, "Arrested development!"

Ibrahim laughed in turn and said, "If arrested development could fend off gray hair, my hair would not be white and you would have seen me and our dear people from the ocean to the gulf having regressed to being little babies. All of us suffer from arrested development."

I shook my finger, cautioning, "Such talk should not come from a person as optimistic as you."

He shook his head, looking again at the river, "Yes, such talk should not come in such a place. Let's try to forget. How are the children, Nasser and Hanadi?"

"You mean Khalid and Hanadi. Khalid is in his third year at the College of Engineering. He will visit me soon. He will represent Egypt in an international youth chess tournament in London and he'll stop over here on his way. Hanadi is finishing junior high school, but I haven't seen her since last summer. I write to them and we speak a lot on the telephone."

Somewhat awkwardly, Ibrahim said, "Of course I heard about what had happened between you and Manar. I avoided mentioning anything about it so as not to bring back bad memories. But I was truly saddened when I heard of the divorce—I always held you and Manar in great esteem despite our differences of opinion. I liked her courage in defense of women."

I said with exaggerated enthusiasm as I stretched out my hand, "And I too hold her in great esteem, naturally. And I believe that the Woman's Page which she edits is the only thing still readable in our newspaper after its progress."

Somewhat perplexed Ibrahim asked, "Then why? Sometimes you told me about some disagreements you were having, and I remember that I always defended her and held you responsible. One thing was recurring in these quarrels and I used to blame you for it . . . I think you objected to her doing extra work at the paper."

"Yes. I believed she should spend more time at home with the kids."

He shook his head, unconvinced, and said, "Why didn't you believe that *you* should spend more time at home with the kids? You were out most of the time, in the paper or the Arab Socialist Union or on journalistic assignments in the country or abroad. Why wasn't she entitled to do like you?"

I said to myself, here we go again. The Arab Socialist Union and the

paper. Are we talking about Manar or about you, Ibrahim? You're dragging me step by step to start settling the account, aren't you? But I
responded matter-of-factly, "You might be right. I thought motherhood
was more important that anything else, even more important than father-
hood. I may have been wrong there. But anyway, that was not the reason."

"What was it then?"

I sighed, saying, "For years I've been asking myself that question,
Ibrahim."

He said in disbelief, "You mean you don't know why you divorced
Manar?"

I shook my head, "There were many squabbles, things that happen to
couples as you know, but they were not the real reason."

Ibrahim knit his brow, saying softly, "Usually the real reason is
another woman or another man but I haven't heard anything about that
in your and Manar's case, even after all these years."

Then he was silent for a moment before saying, "Perhaps you
were . . . "

He hesitated a little so I asked him with an eagerness that surprised
him, "Perhaps we were what?"

He looked me straight in the eye as he said, "Perhaps you were, I mean,
I think that you and Manar were looking for a perfect love that was impossible in this world. That's why you were quarreling over the slightest disappointment that kept you far away from this impossible perfection."

"Perhaps."

I turned my face to the window to suggest that I didn't want to talk
about it anymore and asked myself again, is that me and Manar or you,
Ibrahim? Are you not now talking about yourself specifically? Was that
quest for the impossible the reason you left Shadia in your youth and still
haven't married? But who am I to say that? If I don't know myself, how
can I judge others? But he is asking me the reason. You say another man

or another woman. How easy and clear that would have made things! You say search for perfection? But we lived together for many years and accepted life as it is. We didn't expect it to give us what it could not. And yet, the end in my mind is an impenetrable fog. Landmines exploding in the dark. Quarrels repeated every day, insults exchanged, temporary reconciliation, remonstration for what happened in the past, and pledges for the future before a new landmine explodes and we're back at square one without knowing why. I thought a lot. Oh, how I thought! I told myself perhaps it had something to do with what had happened to me at work. I was only one step away from editor-in-chief, then Sadat came and everything was lost. I became the consultant no one consulted. But Manar was not so weak as to give up on me for that reason. She had principles. Money had not been an important thing in her life from the beginning. When we got married we had nothing, then, thanks to Manar, we were able to get over the hard days when my salary and hers were not enough to live on and raise the children. She never complained and didn't change when our income increased and we had more than we needed. She made no demands. It was I who tried to compensate her for the long days of deprivation. So how is it that we couldn't get over the period of failure, when my ascendancy in the paper had stopped, and after I began my speedy decline to be limited to a small column once a week on an inside page filled with advertisements? Did we also, despite the principles and the slogans, worship success and "arriving" like all the others with us in the paper and outside the paper? Admit it. Admit that, filled with defeat and anger, you became impatient, ready to quarrel at the drop of a hat with Manar and everyone else. Why couldn't she have also become impatient and disappointed? Did she realize also that the disappointment meant that she was forsaking me at a time when I needed her more than ever? Perhaps, for in the beginning it was she who initiated both the quarrels and the reconciliations. I realize now, with perfect clarity, that my clinging to Abd al-Nasser's dream at that time was not just faith in the principle of which I was totally convinced all my days, but it was clinging to my personal dream, to my days of success and glory and arriving. And I understand now that Manar, whose situation in the paper was frozen like mine and on my account, came to consider Abd al-Nasser her personal enemy.

After they cut down the woman section to one-fourth its size, she remembered that it was he who caused the 1967 setback, and the detention camps, and all those things that so many people were talking about after he died. Manar forgot her profuse tears when he announced he was stepping down and her pained scream, "Did we need this catastrophe after the loss of Sinai?" She forgot her joy when he reversed his decision to step down and forgot how she had fainted and had a long breakdown after his death. Her attacks on Abd al-Nasser and my desperate defense of him became just an excuse to vent the tensions, nothing more. The leader turned into an old domestic toy with which we hit each other in our quarrels, then put aside only to pick up again after a while. I thought, when I wrote my book on Abd al-Nasser and published it at my expense, that we, he and I, would regain some of what we had lost. I answered all the accusations leveled against him with documents and all the evidence I had lived through. But the book was issued and with it secret orders were issued to newspaper stands and bookstores to hide it, so no one saw it. Even those colleagues and writers who I thought would care and to whom I had given the book did not comment on it. No one attacked it and no one supported it. Rather, a deathly silence, and the remaindered copies that came back to be piled at home provided the tombstone. In this new defeat, Manar never sympathized with me as she had before. She would point to the books piled in the corners and grumble that they would gather dust and insects. But admit also, the books were not the reason nor was politics the reason. Don't you remember that at one time we pledged not to talk about

Abd al-Nasser or Sadat or about anything else that we disagreed about? So what happened? Neither she nor I had figured out that talking politics had nothing to do with the chasm which opened between us and that when we stopped talking about it, the quarrels came quick and violent without our knowing why. It may be my fault or hers, but the disagreement which arises from a small sprout, with a known seed, soon branches out on its own, recalling insults and shortcomings of the past, and when I said something and when she said something else, and what I promised her as we walked on the Corniche during our engagement that I would. Then words, words, and more words until we find ourselves in a thick forest of "I said, you said" where we would stumble in the midst of its thorny branches, bleeding together without knowing a way out. The only solution was to get away from one another. Why? What's the reason?

A hand was patting my hand and I came to, saying, "That was not the reason . . . "

"The reason for what?"

I didn't answer. Ibrahim continued in a soft voice, "I'm sorry. Please believe me. I didn't know this issue still affected you so much."

"What issue? You're wrong," I said in protest.

Ibrahim said, feeling somewhat uncomfortable, "For quite some time now your thoughts have been far away from here. You were also moving your lips and . . . "

He didn't finish his sentence but I was boiling in anger inside towards Manar and Ibrahim and the whole world so I said, "Listen Ibrahim. Let's lance this boil and get it over with."

He looked perplexed as he said, "What are you talking about?"

"Your suspension from work. Yes, it was I who requested that; it was my responsibility."

Ibrahim continued to pat my hand saying, "Forget that. I forgot it. Didn't I tell you, 'Death has erased all traces."

But I pushed his hand away somewhat harshly, saying, "But I have not forgotten. I will tell you secrets that you didn't know . . . "

Ibrahim's face turned red and he waved his hand impatiently, saying, "What secrets do you want to explain to me in 1982 about things that happened in '69? What's the importance of that now? I told you I have forgotten about it."

"And yet you must know that the article you wrote about the March 30 Declaration in which you said that the government imagined the right wing could be faithful to the revolution and that it could carry out the reforms . . . "

Ibrahim interrupted me, grumbling, "I told you these things are over. March 30 Declaration, really! Go now to any street in Cairo and ask people about the March 30 Declaration. If you find in all of Egypt ten people who remember what that Declaration was about, come and let's settle the score."

Then he seemed to be exerting and effort to smile as he said, "O brother, how far away from those days we are now! Bring back that time then suspend me from writing as much as you like. Would it make you happy if I said that I was wrong when I wrote that article? You were right in all you said about Abd al-Nasser back then. I was wrong."

Then he remembered something and his smile broadened as he said, "And by the way, do you know your nickname in Cairo now? We heard in Beirut that in Egypt, since your book on Abd al-Nasser, they have been calling you 'Widow of the Dear Departed.'"

I feigned a smile, saying, "Yes, I've heard the nickname. But at least you know that I defended Abd al-Nasser before he died and after he died. I didn't change my position. I stood by him out of conviction."

Turning his face away from me again, Ibrahim said, "Yes but that did not prevent you, during his era, from ascending in the paper like a rocket and going abroad on all the press assignments at a time when traveling abroad was more difficult than traveling to the moon."

Shaking, I said, "What? Was I promoted because I was dissembling or because of nepotism?"

"I didn't mean that."

"Then what do you mean? I thought I was a journalist who could write. I thought I was also the first journalist to enter Port Said in 1956 while bombs were falling on it and that I didn't write about the war in Yemen from my office; I was with the troops in the mountains. But naturally that doesn't matter now."

Ibrahim raised his hand in front of my face, saying, "There's no doubt that you wrote out of conviction. The question is . . . "

But I was not in control of myself. I was shaking as I spoke. "Please tell me what you mean by that. Didn't many journalists change their skins to stay in their posts? Didn't they compete in cursing his policies whose praises they had been singing, just to please Sadat? Did I do like them?"

"Of course not. I am truly sorry. I told you I didn't mean to . . . "

"No, you mean it. Besides what happened when you and your friends took control of the culture sector in the country? Didn't you fire me from the People's Culture Committee?"

"I beg your pardon. Who did that?"

"You, the communists."

"These are delusions."

I knew that my voice was loud and that eyes were staring at me in the café but I didn't care, "These are facts. I loved that man and I still do. He wanted to change life in our country but you and others fought him."

Ibrahim threw up his hands in the air. He too was getting agitated as he said, "No, this is too much. How did we fight him and where did we fight him? In detention camps of the Oases or the Barrages? Or maybe we were the ones who fought him in Yemen and Sinai without knowing it. Look at matters as they are, my friend. We were never the reason for what happened. We are even defending him now in spite of all that happened to us."

"After the opportunity was lost."

"Who lost it?"

Before I could answer, Ibrahim raised his hand in front of my face quickly and said, "Listen, can we stop this discussion? I have apologized to you and I am apologizing to you again. Forgive me, if I hurt you. I admit I was wrong."

Then he began to tap the table with his index finger, saying, "All of that was in the past, a distant past, a dead past. Don't you understand?"

I noticed a cup of coffee in front of me so I reached out a shaking hand and when I took a sip I found it cold. I focused my eyes on the river and for a long time I didn't see anything. But I came to when I became aware of motion and noise on the still surface. A swan was supporting its weight on its tail, rearing and quickly sweeping the waves with its wings, leaving behind two parallel lines of white froth. Some gray ducklings that were floating in a line behind their mother were frightened and dashed towards the rocky barrier at the bottom of the window, shrieking in their thin voices and shaking their still unfeathered tails. As for the swan, it quieted down finally and began to glide on the water majestically, looking slowly right and left.

I gulped down the rest of the cold coffee and, to break the silence, I said, "Listen, Ibrahim, I am also sorry. Please forgive me. What happened just now makes no sense when you're my guest. First of all, you didn't tell me what brought you here?"

"I am writing something for the paper and . . . "

He fell silent for a moment before adding, "And by the way I'd like to thank you because you haven't done what my Egyptian friends do who meet me abroad and ask me eagerly and with interest how things are in Beirut. As if they don't read enough about it in the papers."

"Perhaps I also would have asked you if it hadn't been for this warning, even though a great poet told us a long time ago about what's happening in Lebanon."

Ibrahim asked incredulously, "A poet?"

"Yes. He told us years ago of what is happening now when he said:

From Beirut we are a tragedy

Born with artificial faces and artificial minds.

The idea is born a whore in the market

Then spends her whole life patching up her virginity.

"'Then spends her whole life patching up her virginity,'" Ibrahim repeated. "What a truthful image! All whoring ideas now call themselves principles and screw the truth." Then he raised his finger cautiously as he said, "But not in Beirut alone. Who is that poet?"

"Khalil Hawi."

He knit his brows, saying, "I don't know him. Is he related to George Hawi?"

"How would I know? All I know is that he's a poet and I like him."

It occurred to me that in the past we knew the politicians thanks to the poets. We knew the rulers Sayf al-Dawla and Kafur because of Mutanabbi, not vice versa. But today we want to know the poet through the politician. We kill our poets with silence and we kill them with forgetfulness. I wanted to ask Ibrahim, 'If it is true that poets are the nation's conscience, what is the fate of a nation that forgets its poets?' But instead I looked at my watch and said, "But there's another important question we haven't asked: how are we going to eat? It's now after two, which means that they've closed the kitchen here and in all other restaurants in town."

Ibrahim shook his head, saying, "But you didn't think, I mean, we didn't think of the important question in time!"

We ordered some light sandwiches and some pastries they served in this café and I promised Ibrahim to make up for it with a substantial meal at dinnertime. As we ate we started talking about our colleagues in the paper and what happened to them during these years filled with change. We talked about those whose stars had risen unexpectedly and about those who had been removed, all in line with Sadat's electric shock policy. Ibrahim asked me, "But how did you, specifically, end up in this country?"

"I think it was my office," I said, laughing.

"What office?" Ibrahim asked in surprise.

I made a gesture with my hand in a circular motion indicating the space around me and added, "The office, the room where I sit in the paper. It was a large office befitting a deputy editor-in-chief. Many of those who were on the upswing coveted it but I was there, large as life, and they didn't know how to kick me out of it. I think my removal had been predetermined from the day of Sadat's coup, but they were surprised to find that my name was not on the list of the secret organization within the Arab Socialist Union, or on any other list. Those days I was an elected member of the Journalists Union Council so they tolerated me grudgingly. They promoted me to editorial consultant so I wouldn't do anything. But I stayed there in place. When they opened a bureau for the paper here, that suited me just fine."

I didn't tell Ibrahim that I welcomed the removal to get away from Egypt altogether after the divorce.

But throughout our conversation about the paper and the colleagues I was thinking of Shadia, the enigma that neither I nor anyone else understood all those years; beautiful, graceful Shadia, the most beautiful female editor since we started working. She fell in love with Ibrahim and Ibrahim fell in love with her. I used to tell myself that was what they meant by natural selection because Ibrahim was also attractive, with his imposing athletic build and his penetrating brown eyes. He attracted attention instantly, even though he never paid attention to his wardrobe on the assumption that elegance was an empty trapping of bourgeois life. Shadia remained faithful to him throughout the years of detention and rebuffed many attempts to get close to her. She even accepted the persecution that she suffered at the paper as a friend of one of the "enemies of the revolution" as they used to say back then. As soon as Ibrahim got out of the detention center they broke up. Other colleagues and I tried to mediate but to no avail, and neither she nor Ibrahim gave an explanation of what happened. Then Shadia surprised us all a little later by marrying the paper's cashier whom we called Uncle Abd al-Latif because of his exaggerated dignity and his slow movements and gestures. Shadia had her first child exactly one year later, then surprised us again when she requested to be transferred from editing to administrative work and landed a job in bookkeeping. Afterwards the Shadia that we knew vanished. She put on weight and no longer cared for her appearance at all. She constantly, winter or summer, wore something a bit like an unbuttoned coat with large sleeves over her dress with a scarf covering her hair. She kept telling the colleagues with a happy laugh that she did that because Si Abd al-Latif was a very jealous man. I saw her going from office to office, pregnant or with a swollen belly as if pregnant, standing for a while at the doors of each office asking for news of the editors and employees in the paper, then spreading news from one office to another, saying through the pealing laugh that she had learned, that she adored gossip. I couldn't believe that this was Shadia, the editor who used to sit at her desk quietly most of the time, but who lit up with enthusiasm when she talked about a liberation movement in Africa or developments in emigration to Israel or the miracle of the economy in Japan. It seemed that she had totally forgotten those things and I kept wondering whether a defeat in love could do that to a person.

I never posed that question to Ibrahim. But, sitting in the café in this foreign city, silently drinking coffee after our light meal, and after he had expressed a desire to stay in that place for some time, I couldn't help it.

I asked Ibrahim, as if I had just remembered something, "By the way, and since you've asked me about Manar, I also will ask you a question that has puzzled me a lot: why did you and Shadia break up? Why did you leave her or she leave you?"

Without turning his face from the window, Ibrahim said, "And I will answer you the way you answered me: do you think knowing that will do any good now?"

Then he turned towards me, adding, "And yet I have a friend who says one shouldn't hide anything after the age of fifty. It doesn't make any sense to keep secrets or to hide anything. Yes, I truly loved her. In my whole life I've never loved another woman as I loved her. When the years of detention just continued I wrote her from prison saying that I released her from her commitment to me. And up to that point no harm was done, but . . . "

Ibrahim seemed hesitant for a few seconds but then he hurried to add, "I also wrote to her saying that if she wanted to wait for me, she was free to amuse herself by going out with any man that she wished to go out with . . . "

In shock, I said, "No man says something like that to a woman in our country, Ibrahim."

"Nor in any other country, my friend. But that's what happened. If you ask me now why I wrote that unfortunate sentence, I'll answer you that I don't know. Did I actually want to free her from committing to a person without a future? Perhaps—and perhaps there was some other reason. One changes in prison. Raging emotions outside get extinguished inside its walls. Her letters to me, though short, were burning with love and longing. The lines I wrote her were extinguished ashes, lukewarm and perfunctory. She must have gradually figured out that my love for her had died. She was courageous and noble when she clung to me all those years. Perhaps she also had hopes that things would change when I got out of prison, but after the forgiving and the long wait she saw somebody other than her old lover. She saw the actual author of those lukewarm lines. And Abd al-Latif was there. She felt his secret love for her as every woman did. She knew that the cashier couldn't even in his wildest dreams hope that the gifted editor would requite his love. For him she remained an idol as unattainable as the stars. I think it was that kind of worshipful love that she needed at the time, that she was ready to sacrifice everything for its sake. Perhaps if she had waited a little longer . . . "

Ibrahim did not finish saying what he was thinking. I mumbled, "Yes, why do we destroy ourselves with our own hands?"

He didn't seem to have heard me. His face now looked profoundly sad, but he shook his head and tried to make light of things as he said, "But why do you ask me about Shadia alone? What happened with her was repeated with others. I didn't succeed in having a committed relationship with any woman. In my life I have known some women. When I knew a liberated, cultured girl, I found myself unconsciously longing for naiveté and innocence, and when I met a simple girl, after a while I felt bored and unconvinced. I would also find myself needing a mind to converse with and so on. I think I wasted my life looking for one woman who combined all these qualities, one that hasn't been born yet."

"Or perhaps you needed to have some humility."

"Perhaps. But it's too late anyway. At my age, women don't preoccupy me much. It would be better to talk about things useful for work. I'll stay here only a few days and I have work that you can help me with."

I leaned towards him, lowering my voice, "Then I will tell you about the first thing that will be useful for work and we won't be far afield. Do you see that girl over there, sitting at the window, reading a book?"

Ibrahim looked at her. She was playing with a lock of her short blond hair, totally immersed in reading and looking like a student wearing jeans and sneakers. Ibrahim turned his gaze away from her and said nonchalantly, "She's too young. I told you I am no longer interested in women."

"But believe me, *she* is very interested in you. I noticed her sitting in the lobby of the hotel where we had the press conference, just as immersed in reading."

"But why?" Then it suddenly dawned on him and he laughed, "Unbelievable! Even here?"

"Especially here. You came here as a reporter of a Palestinian newspaper and a leftist one to boot and you expect Democracy to let you hide from its eyes?"

Continuing to laugh, Ibrahim asked, "Do they follow you too?"

"No, I am a journalist from a meek, peace-loving country."

Ibrahim cast another casual glance at the girl then shrugged his shoulders and said, "We've gotten used to this in every country, and since I do nothing except write, it doesn't concern me. You'd better talk to me about other things. What about the country and the people here, for instance?"

I wanted to be evasive so that we wouldn't have another argument, so I told him that I didn't know many people here because they didn't like foreigners and they don't mix with them. He answered with his old, unshakable conviction, "You don't mix with the people. If you came to know some leftists, for instance, you'd see a different picture of life." He refused to believe me when I told him that I saw no difference between left and right, that when they came to power they were equal in exploiting the countries of our poor world and in extorting us with debts. Ibrahim kept shaking his head disapprovingly, repeating that I was living in Europe without seeing it, and that in Europe, in spite of everything, hope remained for the future.

Ibrahim continued, excitedly, "I am not even talking about science or civilization but about humanity itself, my friend. Tell me, please, how many doctors do we have, at Muller's age or younger, who volunteer to defend the oppressed in the world or even in their own country? And how many engineers or lawyers or journalists? I'll tell you something. In the hospitals and the camps in Beirut I saw nurse volunteers from Sweden and Holland and England and many other countries in Europe who knew what was awaiting them in the midst of the civil war and the insane killing. One of them—you must have read about her—lost her limbs to Phalangist bullets in Tell al-Zaatar, but her colleagues stayed there."

"But there must be more Arab nurses than them . . . "

Ibrahim bowed his head and said, "Yes and there are also Arab journalists like me who have gone there because they believe that this is their cause. So they are not doing anybody any favor by going there. We went there only to defend ourselves and some of us are also employees on the payroll. But I am not talking about that. I am talking about those who volunteer, those who give themselves to others, in deeds rather than in loud speech. I am talking, if you will, about the humaneness, which you don't see here, but which I see over there every day. Yes, I know ten or twenty or thirty Arab doctor volunteers, a hundred, two hundred, a thousand freedom fighters. But is that, my friend, the Arabism that you were dreaming of?"

I sighed, saying, "I have enough worries, Ibrahim, so please be quiet. If you ask me, 'Where are the Arabs?' I'll ask you, 'And where are the Workers of the World who united?' Let's not disagree again."

Then I said to change the subject, "But an idea occurred to me after what you said: why don't we exchange places; you come to live here in Europe with the left that you like and I go to Beirut?"

Frowning, he said, "And why didn't you do that from the beginning? I don't want to live here, but why don't you come to Beirut?"

"I had no choice. You know that our paper does not have any business in any Arab country since the peace treaty with Israel and I need my salary to raise my children. I don't have any other income."

But I sensed that Ibrahim was not following what I was saying. He was looking at a certain spot in the café. "If you really don't know anyone in this country, come and I'll introduce you to its most beautiful woman."

I followed the direction of his eyes and I saw Brigitte and Dr. Muller seated at a table close to the entrance. I turned my gaze away from them and said to Ibrahim, "You certainly don't mean what you're saying! Leave her alone, Ibrahim. What happened to her with that miserable translation is quite enough!"

He got up, saying, "Sorry if I don't have time for such sensitivity. I am a journalist and I work here, and I want to talk to Muller and this beautiful woman."

As Ibrahim went towards Brigitte and Muller, the "student" followed him with her eyes without raising her head from the book. I turned my eyes to the window. There were some light clouds spreading in the sky, covering the sun but not quite blocking it, but the water of the river had lost its sheen and its wavy surface had turned the color of mercury. The swans and ducks had settled down peacefully near the riverbank. A strange still had settled on the whole place but it hadn't settled on me.

All the things I had talked about with Ibrahim started to mesh, not explaining anything or shedding light on anything, but intersecting, intensifying, and leading to dead ends. We had resurrected the past, and lo and behold, all the riddles were as alive as they had been long ago. Did I find out, for instance, why he had separated from Shadia? Admittedly, he did what he did, so why didn't he explain to her upon his release from detention that he had not meant to insult her? Why didn't he explain and why didn't she forgive? Why did she have to destroy herself after that? Where is that rot that gnaws at us and causes destruction? Why did things go bad between Manar and me? I mean the truth, not the details that happen thousands of times every day between husbands and wives. I remember well that desert of silence I lived in with Manar for months and months before the divorce, avoiding eye contact and avoiding being in the same place with Khalid and Hanadi. We were two warriors who had surrendered to the enemy, too ashamed to look each other in the eye. But who or what was the enemy? What had she discovered in me or I in her? I now see her on that distant night, farther away in time than the publication of my dead book. We had been invited to dinner at a friend's house. I stood waiting for her as she was preening in front of the mirror. When she was done she felt the necklace with the gold heart pendant. It was an old gift that I had brought back after one of my trips abroad. She said in a tone of annoyance, "I think all my friends are tired of seeing me with this necklace; each one of them has sets of jewelry that go with their different outfits and I have nothing but this necklace."

Without meaning to, I blurted out, "No one has been spared the open-door policy." Did she deliberately choose to talk about the necklace? Did I deliberately choose to talk about the open-door policy? I don't think so. But she turned towards me suddenly with bloodshot eyes and said in a soft voice with trembling lips, "Please don't talk about the open-door policy and don't take that lofty position. You, you in particular, were the first to adopt the open-door policy before the expression had even come into existence. It was not I who asked for the Mercedes or this apartment in Garden City. I was content with our little house in Giza and didn't ask for anything."

I said, "But I was trying to make you happy, Manar, you and the kids. You know I paid everything I had for the car and the apartment. Did I steal to do that?"

Her whole body shook as she spoke, "No, you did not steal. You only saved the hard currency from your revolutionary journalistic assign-ments and when you came back, you changed it on the black market and then you bought and bought." I said I only did what others were doing. She screamed as she took off the necklace, "Then don't lecture me about the open-door policy or anything else. Please don't lecture me."

I was seized with anger saying, "Yet I haven't noticed that you turned down anything I bought. Why did you accept the car and the apartment without uttering a word?"

Brandishing her index finger in my face with every word, she said, "I did not ask for anything. I did not say, 'I am a revolutionary.' I did not tell stories about my poverty in the village and the suffering of the peasants and the justice that the revolution will bring about." Then she came closer to me, saying, "And I did not attack the open-door policy!"

I replied. What did I say? It doesn't matter, doesn't matter. But was that a warning that she had freed herself from something or other? Perhaps. Shortly after that, Manar began her own schemes. She began to save her own money and buy silver from Khan al-Khalili and sell it when the price went up. She told me one day in a casual manner that she had bought a quarter of a taxi. That was the first time I'd heard that you can buy fractions of a taxi and that was before she owned the whole taxi and before she bought on the installment plan, from the Journalists Union, a parcel of land they advertised in Hurghada and another one in the Pyramids area.

But once again, what are you blaming her for? Manar never demeaned herself when she did that. Don't you remember back in those days respectable female colleagues selling, right in the paper's offices, imported clothes, sunglasses, and small electrical appliances, and respectable male colleagues engaged in so-called suitcase commerce, smuggling clothes and other goods from Beirut to Cairo? What am I blaming her for? I am not blaming her; I am just asking: How did she end up doing that when all her life she was not interested in money or acquisitions? Was she taking her revenge on me? Why? It was you who gave her the pretext anyway. She was only doing what others were doing and you were only doing what others were doing. You were also buying and buying. Why? And when did words become just words? Revolution, Arabism, socialism, and justice? Words for articles and symposia but not for living. I was only doing what others were doing! To convince others with our words, of justice, equality, revolution, and sacrifice. And yet we were living better, in more luxury, so we would get the inspiration! Neither I nor the others saw any contradiction in that. But Manar was watching me with indictment in her eyes when I met with my friends and spoke the resounding words: Did you see? The uprising of January 18 and 19 . . . . The people are moving! The end is near. Did you see? The Shah and Sadat in Aswan, imagine! Egypt wants to bury Europe's nuclear waste in the desert. Imagine! Words and words and words which we said as we felt our expensive neckties and looked around us as if spies were recording every word we said, as if each word would bring down the regime! What if we had actually lived the revolution we spoke about? What if we had gone back to our villages or to our poor neighborhoods to live with our families without speeches or slogans? Would everything have actually died? And what did we do the night Sadat visited Jerusalem? We deemed that we had done our duty entirely when we met in the café and argued and screamed and cried. Screw it all! Screw it! What does it really have to do with the revolution? What good are these thoughts now? What is the connection between this gentleman sitting in the café overlooking the river and the green European mountain, and the hungry, poor child who walked two hours a day wearing torn shoes in the dust, the mud, the heat, and the cold to go to school, dreaming all the way of paradise because it had lots and lots of food? What does it mean to continue this lie of a life? Who am I? And why don't I go down right now to the bottom of the river, to watch from deep in the water the undulating bellies of the white swans and pray that the current would carry me very far away, away from the swans, the ducks, the trees, the mountains, and people; far away to a gap buried in the midst of the rocks where I would sneak and lie low and where the moss and weeds and snails and fish would cover me and hide me forever? If only I could totally vanish!

3

This Evening I Want to Talk

I BRAHIM PATTED MY HAND, startling me. "What's the matter?" he said. "I'm afraid," I responded without thinking.

Ibrahim laughed, thinking I was speaking in jest. "Well then, don't sit by yourself. Come and join us. Dr. Muller asked me to invite you," he said.

Ibrahim introduced me to Muller and Brigitte in a few words and we exchanged a few sentences about my work and life in that city and what I thought of it. I tried to be focused as I spoke, but English proved elusive as it usually did when I was tired or pensive, so I opted for silence.

Ibrahim turned to Muller continuing a conversation he had started earlier, "Of course I have documents about specific cases that I can show you."

While Ibrahim was opening his briefcase to take out some papers he told me in passing that they were cases of some Palestinian and Lebanese men that had been abducted by Israeli patrols from Southern Lebanon with the help of Saad Haddad's army.

When he took out the papers he began to sort them out before giving them to Muller, saying, "Some of these abductees have been tortured in Israel and some have disappeared entirely."

Muller looked up after glancing at the papers and, nodding, said, "Yes. These are cases that fall within our mandate, but only tangentially. Couldn't you submit these papers to Amnesty International? They have more visibility than we do."

"We have actually submitted them to Amnesty International, but your testimony as physicians especially in the torture cases . . . " Ibrahim said.

I no longer followed the conversation. We were seated at a table that was far from the window so I couldn't see the river but I kept looking with rapt attention at the sky and the distant mountain. What reminded me now of that child? What opened all these wounds? Or have they been open all along and it's just that I have sometimes been distracted from them? And how about that other wound which cannot ever be forgotten and from which nothing will successfully distract me: I, too, have created misery for two children that are my whole world or were my whole world. What good can any justification do about that, you deserter? Does it really torment you as it should or are you still too absorbed after all? Too absorbed in the child within you that has been defeated for more than forty or fifty years? If only I knew where the real mistake is or when it started!

Brigitte turned towards me and said in a soft voice, "What are you thinking about?"

Without giving it much thought I said, "That this life is a lie."

She leaned back, mildly surprised, and said, "I didn't think that was the problem. I thought it was too real."

Once again we were silent. She began to smoke and shift her eyes between Muller and Ibrahim who were engrossed in conversation. I noticed that the expression that had come over her face at the end of that press conference with Pedro Ibañez was still there in her wide eyes. Her blue irises were moving quickly and her eyelids were constantly twitching, and she was trying to overcome this by smoking and maintaining a smile on her lips. I discovered as I looked at her closely for the first time that her features were somewhat large. Her nose was long and jutting and her mouth a little too wide, and yet everything about her face appeared proportional and beautiful, with her broad brow and her thick and shiny golden hair, parted in the middle and ending in a straight bun pulled behind her head under which her white high neck appeared. I also discovered as I looked at her that her smile was not feigned, rather her face was naturally smiling. I tried to figure out where that feeling came from but I couldn't pinpoint it.

Muller was telling Ibrahim, "We must send an investigating committee. Actually, we are a poor organization that operates on the donations of its members and most of them are old like me. Which means that even if we secured the funding there would be a problem finding volunteers for the missions, I mean volunteers who are young and capable of doing the work."

Ibrahim said, "Couldn't you do that by collaborating with another organization?" Ibrahim began to cite names of organizations and committees that had branches in Lebanon. It seemed that he was determined not to leave Muller without getting an answer. There was no room for us in this conversation, so I turned to Brigitte and said in a soft voice, "I understand from what Muller said at the beginning of the press conference that interpreting is not your profession."

She brought her face closer to me and said, whispering like me, "If it were my profession, I wouldn't have ruined the conference." Then she gestured with her hands apologetically as she smiled.

I said, "But what you did was the only human thing at that meeting."

The smile disappeared and her face hardened somewhat as she said, "No. I am no better than the others. It, it was just a moment of weakness."

I said in disbelief, "But why do you apologize for that?"

She shrugged her shoulders as she said, "All there is to it is that I don't like pretense. I don't want you to understand something untruthful about me. You did say you hated lying, didn't you?"

I tried to change the subject so I pointed to her blue uniform and asked her, "Are you an airline stewardess?"

"No, but I am a different kind of stewardess. I'm a tour guide."

I was struggling to keep the conversation with her going, for her sake and for my sake, so that we wouldn't go back to silence and brooding. I asked her, "Do you like it?"

She smiled again and said, "I didn't choose it but it was the only job available to me in this country. And, incidentally, I know several languages." I searched for something else to say but I couldn't go on anymore.

Once again I leaned back in my chair in silence like before. She kept looking at me curiously then she also withdrew and lit another cigarette.

Muller broke off his conversation with Ibrahim and turned towards her somewhat angrily. "Enough smoking, Brigitte!" She turned to him and patted his hand saying, "Don't be cross, Doctor. I don't smoke at all at work." Then she laughed, adding, "You know smoking is not allowed on tourist buses at least."

Once again I noticed that when she laughed or smiled or even merely moved her lips, delicate parallel lines appeared on her face at her chin and at the corners of her eyes. I said to myself that perhaps that was what gave her face its constant smiling expression. I looked at her closely, wondering where the other expression that I couldn't pinpoint came from. Muller was now speaking to her in German of which I understood a few sentences. I was able to make out his saying, "Is it punishment? That's not good, Brigitte."

Ibrahim turned to her and spoke to her in an intimate tone as if he had known her for a long time, in the manner of journalists when they try to entice others to speak, "Brigitte, are you German or Spanish?"

"Neither the one nor the other. I am Austrian," she said.

Ibrahim said, "But it is obvious that you have perfect command of Spanish. Pedro was sometimes talking very fast and in a soft voice most of the time but you always kept up with him. Where did you learn Spanish?"

"At the University."

Then she fell silent for a little while and said, "And it's also my husband's language."

I thought her voice changed slightly as she said that and I also thought I noticed some mild surprise on Ibrahim's face when she spoke of her husband. But he continued in his normal tone, "Your husband, is he from Spain or Latin America?"

There was a note of defiance in her voice, the cause of which I couldn't determine, as she addressed Ibrahim, "He is neither from Spain nor from Latin America. He is an African from your continent, from Equatorial Guinea."

"And they speak Spanish there?" Ibrahim asked.

I knew he was asking just to say something, but Brigitte said, as the tension in her voice rose, "You're a journalist and from Africa to boot and you don't know whether they speak Spanish there or not?"

Then she backed off immediately and apologized, "I am sorry. I didn't mean what I said. It's a small country anyway and I haven't met many people who know anything about it."

I intervened in the conversation to rescue Ibrahim, whose face had turned red, and said, "So, tell us something about that country. I confess that I don't know anything about Equatorial Guinea. Have you been to it?"

She knit her brow and appeared reluctant for a short while but she quickly overcame her hesitance and said, "I intended to go but I was divorced before I did."

Then Brigitte laughed awkwardly and silence prevailed again. I felt tenser and I wanted to get up but at that very moment Ibrahim said, "I heard you say that you are a tour guide. This is my first visit to this city, so what are the things you advise me to see?"

Brigitte reached for her purse on the table and took out a business card, which she gave to Ibrahim, saying, "You can come to our company at this address and at the times indicated on the card. And you can also book by telephone, and if I'm the guide at the time you come, I will guide you with extra special care."

We all laughed perfunctorily but Muller said with a sly look in his eyes, "I think Mr. Ibrahim would have preferred that you guide him without the company."

Maintaining that perfunctory laugh, Ibrahim said, "Yes, without the company and without the guiding also."

But Brigitte's smile disappeared suddenly and she kept shifting her glance among the three of us, then focused her eyes on Muller in a fixed stare and said in a tone that she tried to keep matter of fact, "See, Muller? Didn't I tell you? Here we are laughing and jesting as if nothing had happened. No one has poked his fingers in Pedro's wounds and no one has killed his brother Freddie. So why the pretense then?"

She was looking at Muller alone as if she had forgotten us and her face regained that other expression which I hadn't been able to pinpoint before: that total hardening of her features and her eyes, a mask which fell over the face and covered it. What kind of mask is it? Is it one of grief or cruelty? It is neither one nor the other, so what is it? But at that moment she propped up her head with her hand and turned her face away from us. I thought to myself: Finally the mask is about to fall off! She is going to cry now!

Muller also apparently expected that, so he reached out his hand towards her saying somewhat confused, "Brigitte!"

She turned towards us, her eyes somewhat red but without any trace of tears. In her earlier defiant tone she said to Muller, "Don't worry." Then she pointed at me and added, "All there is to it is that I wanted to prove to this gentleman that whoever suffers, does it alone. I did not suffer, none of those who attended the conference suffered. Pedro alone suffered."

She began to tap the table with her fingers as she looked at Muller, "No matter how many medical committees or press conferences, Doctor."

Muller, sounding somewhat desperate asked, "So you think we should stop working?"

Brigitte turned her eyes away from him and said in a soft voice, "No, I meant something else."

Then she looked towards Ibrahim and me and said, "I did not mean you in particular, I am sorry."

The atmosphere became heavy and awkward, so Ibrahim, looking at me and gesturing with his head that we should leave, said, "But why do you say that? We are the ones who should apologize, really."

He put his hands on the arms of the chair ready to get up, saying, "My friend and I were about to leave, anyway."

She stretched her hand towards us and said solicitously, "But you can stay a little longer, I mean, please."

Once again we settled in our place somewhat awkwardly. Yet Brigitte, who had insisted that we stay, ignored us and bowed her head and was silent again. Muller's face displayed a tension that I could not understand as he watched Brigitte. It seemed to me as she clung to the chair and pulled her body up that she was exerting great effort to get a grip on herself. I said to myself as I looked at her: Why are you resisting crying, Brigitte? Why don't you cry and get it over with? Perhaps, like me, you have lost the ability to cry? I know I lost it some time ago but when did I do that? Perhaps the last time I cried was years ago, after the divorce when I closed the door of the room I had booked at the hotel and held the divorce document and began to read those strange sentences which severed everything between Manar and me forever. "I, the marriage and divorce notary of the neighborhood of ———— . . . . There appeared before me Mr. ———— with his wife and consort ———— . . . the divorcee of full legal age . . . one first irrevocable divorce . . . he is not entitled to consort with her unless . . . Number 10960." At that moment the crying came on its own, hard and incessant. Moments of misery got mixed with moments of joy: our stealthy kisses during our engagement; her pale face the day she gave birth to Khalid as she lay on the gurney on which they took her from the birthing room; her limp hand holding my hand and telling me with a smile despite the exhaustion, 'I knew you wanted a boy!'; her waving to me at the arrival gate and standing on tiptoe saying, 'Hurry up, don't buy anything from the duty free store. I don't want anything, get out quickly'; her determined face as she said with finality, 'I'll take the children. Besides, when did you ever care about raising the children?' Everything in one moment in the midst of the tears. However, that time I was crying over myself; I was pitying myself and pitying Khalid and Hanadi. I do not mean this kind of crying, but rather crying for any Pedro or any Alfredo. I mean my crying as a boy over Umm Sabir the martyr and the policemen that the English killed in Ismailia, like crying over Jamila Buhayrid whom the French tortured in Algeria, like my tears over Lumumba the day they killed him in the Congo and the people's tears in the street that day. I mean those things that have gone away, very, very far away, things that happened many centuries ago. I mean, since when did I lose the feeling? But let's say I am old, so how about you, Brigitte? Perhaps you are right: those who suffer do so alone. So why the pretense?

She, however, was now smiling her normal smile as she pulled another cigarette from her pack and apologized, "Forgive me, Doctor."

The doctor shrugged his shoulders and once again they exchanged a few sentences in German. When they were done, Muller turned towards us and said in a reproachful, almost sad tone as he pointed at her, "She knows that I consider myself responsible for whatever happens to her in this city. Her father was my best friend. In our youth we went together to war in Spain and since that time we have been inseparable. He wanted

Brigitte to study law like him but she opted for literature and she asked me to convince him." Then he turned towards her saying, "Who knows, Brigitte? Perhaps if you had studied law you'd have been with us back home now. Perhaps you'd have worked with your father, and perhaps continued to work in his office after his retirement."

Brigitte said, "But I am happy with my work here, Doctor Muller. I prefer it a thousand times to poring over law books and writing briefs. And I prefer staying here to going back home."

Ibrahim asked her half in jest, "Aren't you homesick?"

She answered with a smile and a decisive hand gesture, "Absolutely not."

So he turned towards me and asked, "And you?"

I answered him in Arabic, "Please leave me alone, Ibrahim. That's all I need right now!"

Ibrahim, vivacious once again, did not argue with me but turned towards Muller and said, "When you took part in the war in Spain you were with the Republicans, right?"

Muller nodded and Ibrahim heaved a sigh of relief. He looked at the Doctor as if he were seeing him for the first time. I was on the point of wagering with myself that he would ask him about that war, which took place dozens of years ago, as if it were still going on. In our youth, that war which we did not live through and which we only knew by reading about it, meant many things to us: the dream of a new world, one united against dictatorship and injustice, the dream which collapsed leaving behind a few symbols: Hemingway and *For Whom the Bell Tolls*, Malraux and *L'Espoir*, Picasso and *Guernica,* and Lorca's poems, the symbols that fixed our imagination in our early youth. I said to myself: perhaps Ibrahim will now ask Muller if he met Hemingway during the war! But he surprised me when he asked him looking towards me, "Then perhaps you can give me a better picture about the situation here." He pointed to me saying, "My friend claims that the left has died in Europe and in the world. Is that true here?"

Muller laughed perfunctorily as he said, "I am afraid I can't enlighten you about these matters. I lost interest in politics some time ago."

Brigitte said, "And didn't you find that to be better, Doctor?"

Ibrahim did not pay any attention to her comment and said in protest, "But why? Most likely you were a Marxist when you went to fight in Spain."

Muller shrugged his shoulders again and it seemed that he was thinking what to say. Something occurred to me so I said to Ibrahim, "Perhaps I can clarify something. I remember I was here in Europe in '68 during the invasion of Czechoslovakia and I followed the waves of resignations from the Communist parties. Many at the time thought . . . "

Ibrahim interrupted me saying in disgust and anger, "The invasion of Czechoslovakia. These European comrades are really sensitive! How many died in that invasion? One? Ten? Have you heard of a single capitalist that resigned from capitalism when the machine guns killed thousand of communists in Chile's stadium and in the streets? Or before that when rivers in Indonesia turned dark with the blood of those they slaughtered there? The invasion of Czechoslovakia, really!"

I said without emotion, "You see? You are agreeing with what I mean. The blood of poor nations is not important even if it is the blood of millions, but Czechoslovakia is something else."

I was speaking to change the atmosphere of the gathering but it was Muller who became agitated for the first time when he addressed Ibrahim and said, knitting his gray eyebrows, "I didn't witness the invasion of Czechoslovakia, sir, but I witnessed the invasion of Hungary before that. I was there by chance working as a volunteer doctor before the events began. I saw the tanks and I saw the dead. The poor Russian soldiers didn't even know they were in Budapest. Their commanders lied to them and said they were fighting the English invaders in Port Said, in your country . . . "

I was not following the discussion, however; none of that mattered to me anymore. I saw Ibrahim doing what he had been blaming me for earlier. He was talking enthusiastically as he used to a quarter century ago about things that had happened a quarter century earlier. I heard him speaking about the Port Said war, waving his hands, his face turning red as if the English warships were laying siege to it at that very moment. I saw the old doctor no less agitated than Ibrahim, speaking of Budapest with a light spray coming out of his mouth. I heard the names of Nasser, Stalin, Nehru, Khrushchev, and many other names. Nkrumah's name came up also in the discussion but I didn't know in what context.

I turned my attention to Brigitte. At the beginning her eyes flashed with interest as she followed the conversation then gradually that interest fizzled and disappeared behind the smoke of her successive cigarettes. From time to time she looked at Muller and the expressionless stare that puzzled me appeared in her eyes and the contagion of that stare spread to the doctor engrossed in the discussion without his eyes meeting hers. I felt some kind of tension spreading through his voice and his body, an almost unnoticeable tension but one that Brigitte also felt and turned her face away from as if in remorse. What is between her and him? Why is she rejecting that paternal attention that he has been desperately trying to impose on her since we sat together? What has this got to do with me? Why is that strange contagious atmosphere, which I don't understand and which is adding to my chagrin, spreading to me?

Muller suddenly wrested me away from myself as he said, "I beg your pardon for this question and please don't misunderstand me. My friend says that you are a Nasserist, and despite everything I admired Nasser during his revolution. But don't you think the time of these nationalist revolutions is gone?"

But what is this doctor talking about now? And why are they all looking at me so curiously as if I am going to solve a problem for them on
which destinies hinge? What's the importance of my saying anything in
this foreign city to these two strangers or to Ibrahim who doesn't like me?
What do I have, really, to say? I can, if they want, talk to them about
Manar; that's the only thing I can think about. No, not even that. What have
I learned about Manar after all these years that we lived together? I apologized, "Forgive me, doctor, but now I am like you. I lost interest in politics
some time ago and perhaps I never was knowledgeable about it. I was an
intruder. At one time I thought I understood but now I know I was wrong."

Ibrahim who was now getting really angry, said, "And those theories
you used to argue with me about in the newsroom and Sati al-Husari and
the nationalism that set history in motion and all those ideas? And telling
me time and time again that they have built their strength in the West
thanks to the nation state and that they are fighting our unity so that we
wouldn't become strong like them? Why don't you say all of that instead
of mumbling 'I don't understand, I don't know, I was wrong'? Why do
you take pleasure in insulting yourself? Or are you hiding behind these
insults an attitude of being above it all, as usual? Or is that true and you
consider yourself already dead? If that is true, then why don't you get up
and throw yourself into the river?"

Muller said with a mixture of surprise and alarm, "No need for all this
severity, Mr. Ibrahim. Maybe your friend doesn't feel like talking, so
why the severity?"

I said to the doctor, "Don't worry about it. We have been used to this
manner of discussion for a long time." Then, turning to Ibrahim I said,
"Nothing of what you said is true. All there is to it is that today I have
discovered something quite important, perhaps thanks to Pedro Ibañez,
or perhaps you were the reason, or maybe Brigitte or Manar. I discovered
that I am a liar."

Ibrahim said impatiently, "Here we go again!"

But I no longer felt anger towards Ibrahim. He was not able to provoke me. I was indeed far away from the discussion, from anger, and from the whole place. Suddenly I felt exhausted so I stood up and said to Ibrahim, "I am a little tired and must leave now. You want me to give you a ride somewhere?"

Ibrahim replied somewhat awkwardly, "No. I know the way to the hotel. But you, are you leaving now because I upset you? Please don't get me . . . "

I said, trying to smile, "Of course not. I'll come to your hotel tomorrow as we've agreed and we will continue the discussion. Tomorrow I'll be ready for you!"

While I was shaking Ibrahim's hand Brigitte stood up suddenly and said decisively, "Take me with you." She bent down to gather her purse, waved to Ibrahim, and gave Muller a quick kiss on his brow.

Brigitte sat next to me in the car and I followed her directions to take the shortest route to her house. She had asked me where I was going as we were leaving the café and when I said I was going home she asked me to take her to the nearest bus stop or taxi and didn't much object when I offered to give her a ride any place she wanted. I looked from time to time at her face in the rearview mirror and saw the mask, that total withdrawal to the inside and was on the point of saying something, almost saying, "Listen, daughter, your whole life is still ahead of you, don't let yourself become like me! Go back to your husband if you love him and if that was the cause of the worry written all over your face." But I held back, telling myself that I hardly knew her, that I shouldn't force myself upon her silence. When I finally stopped the car in front of the apartment building where she lived in a quiet neighborhood at the outskirts of the city, Brigitte invited me to go upstairs with her to have a drink. I told her that I was tired and wanted to go home to rest. I wasn't lying. She placed her hand on my hand on the steering wheel and said, smiling, "Then come, I'll make you a cup of strong coffee that will make the fatigue go away. Come, please." Her sudden smile lit up her face.

She was going ahead of me at the entrance of the apartment building lined with mirrors on both sides. She walked in quick steps and I saw five or six reflections of her to the right and to the left, in her blue uniform, tall and erect, and I saw myself behind her with my slow steps and my dark clothes: two complete opposites. I said to myself sarcastically: Spring and Fall, day and night. Come, Ibrahim. Here I am taking pleasure in insulting myself.

Her apartment was on the tenth floor, a large one-room apartment, or it seemed large because the few things scattered on the sides left the whole middle part empty. After the vestibule, there was a large sofa to the left, which I guessed she turned into a bed at night. Next to it were two small chairs around a small bamboo table covered with a small tablecloth with a yellow and red rose pattern. At the end of the room there was a black screen covered with the picture of a young woman wearing a white kimono with gilded hems and hiding half her face behind a rose-colored fan. A white paper globe containing a large light bulb hung from the ceiling. Brigitte left me and went behind the screen that hid the kitchen and bathroom. I heard the sound of water from a faucet and from there she said to me somewhat loudly, "I'll be with you in a minute. Please make yourself at home."

I walked around in the almost empty room. In a corner next to the large balcony I found a small shelf with a recorder and some tapes of easy listening music next to which were some books. I read the titles. Most of them were detective novels in German and English, with frayed covers. On one cover was the picture of a slain, goggle-eyed young woman and on another cover was the picture of a man holding a smoking gun and hiding his face behind a hat. But I also found in the midst of these books a book of Heine's poems in German and another of Lorca's poetry in Spanish. From behind came Brigitte's voice apologetically, "You won't find anything of interest to you in those books."

I turned towards her as she approached the small table where she placed two cups of coffee. She had taken off her jacket and shoes and kept on her light white blouse and the blue skirt and was wearing a pair of slippers.

As I sat on the chair opposite her, I pointed to the room and the woman in the kimono and I said, "Where did you get these Japanese ideas?"

"I didn't get any ideas, Japanese or Chinese. When I moved here I had nothing at all. This was the cheapest way to furnish the place," she said with a light smile.

As she reached out her hand giving me my cup of coffee, I asked her, "Are you really happy here as you said? Don't you really want to go back home?"

She nodded, agreeing with what I said like a pupil reciting a lesson she had memorized, "Yes, I am really happy here and I don't want to go back home."

Then she looked at me and asked, "And you? When your friend asked you this question you refused to answer him. So, are you happy here?"

"No, I am not happy here."

"Would you be better off if you returned to your country?"

I thought a little before answering her. Rubbing my forehead I said, "It's not easy. Like you I am divorced and my family lives there. But you are young and you could start anew if you went back, but I . . . "

I couldn't continue so I fell silent and she said after a while, "I am sorry. I didn't understand a thing. Perhaps what your friend said is true. You do take pleasure in tormenting yourself."

"Perhaps."

Brigitte sensed that I did not want to talk, so she said as she leaned her head on her hand, "Don't worry." Then she asked me. "Would you like to drink something?"

"Aren't we drinking coffee already?"

"Then with your permission I will have a drink."

She left her cup almost untouched and disappeared behind the screen then returned with a tall glass that she kept shaking in her hand and once again sat opposite me. For some time only the clanking of the ice in the glass could be heard. Suddenly, however, I found myself saying to her without thinking, "Something puzzled me while we were sitting in the café, something about Dr. Muller. Sorry for the question but, I mean, when you were talking together there was . . . "

Then I stammered and didn't finish what I wanted to say. She took a large gulp of her drink then put it on the table and fixed her blue eyes on my face, smiling broadly and moving all those delicate wrinkles on her chin and around her eyes, she said, "There are many things between us. The first thing is—he was my mother's lover."

I was taken aback like someone stung, murmuring, "I am, I am sorry for the question. Why did you tell me that? I never imagined that . . . "

She interrupted me without changing her smile, "And why not? Didn't you say that you hated lies?"

"I didn't say that. I said I discovered I was living a lie."

She got up and started pacing in the room continuing to shake her glass and speaking to the accompaniment of the clanking ice, "I thought you said that. I saw something in your face."

"But once again, please, why are you divulging this secret or other secrets to me? We've barely met. I even doubt if you know my name."

"Didn't you ask me about Muller?"

"Yes, a casual question, a mistaken question. But I didn't want to learn any secrets. We're strangers."

She stopped and looked at me for a little while before saying, "But that's better, as you know. People don't disclose their secrets to friends but to strangers, on a train or in the odd café. But that is not the issue now. The issue is I want to talk. This evening I want to talk. Don't you have that desire once in a while?"

"I talk the whole time, but with myself. There is an incessant dialogue in my head."

"I have the same thing but I am tired of it."

Brigitte went towards the sofa but didn't sit on it, rather she sat on the floor covered with gray carpeting, then leaned her back to the sofa and stretched her empty arm on it. She just barely touched the glass with her lips then placed it next to her on the floor and undid the braid wound behind her head and began to unbraid it slowly. The sun was bathing her as she sat there and I saw through the balcony some delicate white clouds once again drifting calmly towards the golden disk that was close to setting. Brigitte began to speak softly as if she didn't care whether I heard her or not but what mattered was for her to talk.

"Yesterday Muller came. I hadn't seen him in many years and everything came back anew. Once again, against my will I became Brigitte the little child. We lived . . . I mean we still live in a little town in the west. I was an only daughter. As a child I didn't know my father as they described him to me in his early youth. I didn't see that enthusiasm that led him to the war in Spain a long time before I was born. I only saw what twenty years passing had done to him. I was told that he was a capable lawyer but I knew that he only accepted difficult cases, lost causes mostly. He accepted defending the poor and labor unions for meager fees merely to undo an injustice or to establish one legal right or anoth-

er for the unions. It occurred to me later, when I grew up, that he wanted to make up for the defeat in Spain by achieving victory by law for all
the oppressed in the world or at least in Austria. But that resulted, unfortunately, in many more defeats. His luck with the law was no better than
his luck with war. All that happened was that clients with important cases
and fat fees began to avoid him, then they actually boycotted him. And
look at him now, after all the years he has worked, living in the house he
inherited from my grandfather, with nothing but the tiny old pension and
a small financial aid sum from the union. And yet I still remember when
I was a child how he was totally engrossed in his failure of a job, as if he
had forgotten my mother and me. He devoted all his time to his office or
the court or his office at home, poring over volumes and writing briefs.
I loved him very much. I felt even when I was a little child that he was
defeated, and I pitied him as if I were his mother, not his daughter. I took
coffee or juice to him in his room then sat for long stretches of time
watching him as he read and wrote and as he constantly rubbed his forehead. When he noticed my presence he would ask me in surprise what I
was doing there, why I didn't go to play or sleep. Then I would go to him
and kiss him on the cheek and ask him to tell me a story so that I could
go to sleep. He would seem to resent my keeping him from his work but
he would put his arm around me and begin to make up little stories in
which justice and goodness always triumphed. I always remember a
pigeon being chased by an evil fox but it enlists the assistance of the
flock of pigeons and it beats all the fox's schemes. Yes, my father did not
succeed at war or at law but it was impossible for his poor animals to be
defeated! As for Uncle Muller, he was different. Muller was always a
successful doctor and used to come to the house a lot when my father
was there and in his absence. Actually, he came more when my father
was not there. He brought me candy and carried me and kissed me. He
asked my mother, who was unwell, 'How's our Frau feeling today?' He

would hold her wrist and her hand and feel her chest and take her inside to continue his examination or they would send me out on one pretext or another. I was, as far as I remember, eight years old when I confronted Muller. I opened the door for him when he came and when he offered me candy, I threw it and began to hit him in his belly and his legs with both my fists, shouting, 'Go away! Go. I don't want to see you. I don't want the candy that you bring. Go. I don't like you!' He stood there speechless. My mother was also standing behind me with her hand on her mouth, her eyes growing wider. Afterwards Muller no longer came but my mother went out a lot." Brigitte fell silent for a little while then added, "That was before my mother died. Before she went to the sanatorium where she died."

I was listening intently from the beginning, anxious not to miss a word she said. My senses, which had been torpid and numb a little earlier, awakened. Something in the tone of her voice got to my heart, filled me with sadness and pity for her. I was on the point of getting up and sitting next to her on the floor to tell her also about everything that pained me, without lies or pride or hiding behind words to preserve that façade which hid the collapse and waste. I didn't do anything, however. I kept looking at her, frozen on the little chair. She had managed to undo her braid and let her long golden hair cascade over her right shoulder then she began to comb it with her fingers. But before I could find something to say, she surprised me by laughing as she looked me straight in the face, saying, "But that's a childhood memory. I have learned for some time now to forgive my mother, even to understand her. I could also have forgiven Muller."

I found myself saying after a little while, "He's very old."

As usual she repeated after me, "Yes. He's very old."

She reached for her glass that she had forgotten, raised it to her mouth then put it back down next to her and said somewhat loudly, "Listen, everything can be forgiven except lying to yourself and lying to people deliberately. It was you who said that, wasn't it? I mean, what do I mean? I want to say, if you make a mistake, be courageous. A person must at least try to act like somebody who has made a mistake, and not continue the deception."

I didn't understand what she was driving at exactly. Was she now talking about me or about Muller? What mistakes can I correct, and is there still time? But instead of that, I continued to talk about Muller. I said, "Perhaps he is atoning for his mistakes. He is trying now even at his age. He's trying to help others."

She said in disgust as if I had offended her, "Help others, really!"

"Isn't what he is doing now, this very moment, a kind of . . . "

She interrupted me rather angrily, "No, it's not kind of anything! I told you I was about to forgive him had it not been for these committees and ridiculous things."

She got up suddenly and began to pace in her almost empty room crossing her arms in front of her chest. Once again I was perplexed and felt that I was not in the right place for me, so I wanted to drop the whole story and the place and just leave. But she came and stood in front of me and she said calmly but decisively, "It was Muller who ruined my life."

I said in true consternation, "He was with you also? I mean did you and he become . . ."

She smiled thinly and interrupted me saying, "Lovers? No. What an imagination! Muller!? I told you he helped me in his way and ruined my life. I mean, if you cannot help a drowning person, why do you pretend that you are reaching out your hand to him? Why do you hasten his drowning? And why do you keep pretending once and twice and a hundred times until you make a vocation of it?"

The sun had set but she didn't turn on the light. And in the semi-dark room she began telling her real story. Once again she paced as she talked, then returned and sat next to me, then got up again and sat on the sofa or in her favorite spot next to the sofa on the floor, all without stopping talking. She was letting out before another human being whom she met by accident at the time that she wanted to talk, all the dialogue that kept taking place for years in her head. Once or twice I saw tears glistening in her eyes, but that evening also she did not cry. At least she did not cry in front of me until I left her apartment after that long day.

She turned on the light before I left and we were both startled as if we both were waking up from a dream. At the open door I held her shoulders and kissed her on the forehead.

She leaned in and also kissed me on the cheek saying, "Thank you. You don't know what a beautiful gift you have given me!"

Then as she shook my hand she said, "Today is my twenty-seventh birthday."

4

Fragile as a Butterfly

As a young man learning to read foreign literary works at the Faculty of Arts, the sentence that Tolstoy used at the beginning of *Anna Karenina* puzzled me: "All happy families are alike, but each unhappy family is unhappy after its own fashion." I asked myself: Why does he begin his great novel with this platitude?

Now towards the end of my life, I realize that he was right. I don't know much about happy families and whether they are alike in their happiness or not. But I know that misery is a scar on the soul, that if it begins in childhood, it lasts the whole lifetime. I understand that no two scars are alike, but I also ask myself: Even if these scars are not alike, aren't these things engraved on our souls signs by which we know each other? Aren't we also alike?

Why did Brigitte choose to tell me all that she told me? Was I really that unknown passerby that she wanted to tell all her secrets to in order to get rid of them, or was there deliberateness and choice? And why was her story, far removed from my world and from everything I knew as it was, able to penetrate my heart so deeply? Why did I grieve so much for that defeated father and for lonely Brigitte and her African husband that her words made me see and pity? I understood your world, far removed from my world. Perhaps you too could see, as I have, a world far removed from you, a small village that has nothing in common with your village, a poor village in the deep south of Egypt, in which an only child

lives also with his father. And yet I know that I won't tell you; and with
equal certainty, I know that I won't be able to escape those two eyes, the
eyes of that child pursuing me since the morning. The travails of that
long day are of no use. It is no use that I toss and turn in bed looking for
a sleep that doesn't come. It is no use my asking this child what's the use.
What's the use of your pursuing me to the twilight of my life? What lessons would I learn now? And what's the use of learning lessons now that
it's too late? Or is it that you don't want to teach me anything, but you
are claiming one right or another. But what right?

Yes. I see you. I see you as you come to me, always an only child, a
child whose mother died of malaria when he was four. The first thing he
remembers is her face that night, a face like white wax washed by incessant sweat and teeth that chatter. She shudders and asks for water. He
sees his father raise her head so she can drink and the shuddering stops
suddenly and her head rests on his hand. To this day he sees her pupils
swimming slowly on the whites of her eyes. To this day he sees his father
laying her head down, whereupon her very small yellow face shows
from her long black gown, and his father standing up, placing his hands
on his small shoulders, looking at him in surprise, saying, "It's over, my
son." He is terrified when he sees women rushing into the room, wailing,
with their flailing arms holding their black head covers, and he buries his
face in his father's galabiyya.

Then you always come to me on your first day at school. How proud
he was that day having put on a suit for the first time, his father accompanying him to the school far away in the city. He remembers how
happy he would be, early on, when one of the teachers would tell him to
go out of the classroom and ask his father to bring some chalk or ink for
the pens or to carry one of those big maps that they hang on the chalk-
board. I'd even be happy when my father would ask me to help at the
end of the week after all the pupils and teachers were gone. He lifts his

galabiyya and ties it around his waist and roll his sleeves up to his shoulders while I carry the water buckets and we make the rounds of all the classrooms and he moves from one classroom to another mopping the floor with his wet rag as he crouches on the floor. When did I begin to feel ashamed? When I grew up a little bit? When one teacher yelled in my face as he looked at his watch, saying, "Why hasn't your dopey father rung the bell, boy? Go wake him up!" When the pupils taunted me if we had a fight during recess? Back then we, the poor, were just a few souls scattered among the sons of landlords and officials in the city who took pleasure and pride in insulting us. Hostility intensified the better you did at school. Some of the boys managed to hide their poverty. But how could I have done that? And how could I have hidden my high scores in all subjects? But even after my father was pensioned off while I was still at elementary school, my nickname survived generations of teachers. When a new teacher came and as usual began to read out the names of the pupils then asked the inevitable question: "What's your father's occupation?", several pupils volunteered before I could answer, "He was the school custodian," whereupon the teacher would know and I would know that there would be nothing to prevent him from calling me names and punishing me in ways that he wouldn't dare mete out to the children of other fathers.

How many times I fought with pupils who insulted me because of my father! How many times I beat them and they beat me and I bloodied them and they bloodied me without ever daring, not even once, to tell my father about the cause of my injuries! And how exceedingly proud I was afterwards, at the paper and the Arab Socialist Union and in front of Manar when we first met! I told everyone about my father, the school custodian who denied himself and saved every penny to give me a university education. But did these big harangues heal the early wounds? Did they remove the humiliation? Perhaps. When the President was one of us, the poor, when he took our side, when poverty was not something to be ashamed of. But didn't I feel the same old shame when I had to fill the family information and list the father's and grandfather's occupation when Khalid thought of applying to the military academy after he graduated from secondary school? Why the pretense then? Why the lying? The paradise of the poor is over; there has never been a paradise of the poor. That also was a lie that we should forget.

I take pleasure in insulting myself, really, Ibrahim! But Ibrahim is right! How can sleep come when you are tormenting yourself with these ideas? Why don't you think, for instance, that you've been determined to declare your poverty and to overcome in yourself the humiliation you've felt because of this poverty? You haven't done like others you know who spent their lives trying to escape from their poor families and hide their modest origins. Why don't you remember that when the coup at the paper took place you refused to go with the flow? Why don't you remember what you said to the person who suggested to you, "Send a telegram of support to the President! The President likes you and he knows that you are quite a writer. Write an editorial against the power centers!"? You dismissed him politely, saying, "I am not sending a telegram and I am not writing an editorial." You knew that he was going to convey what you said and you wanted him to do just that. You didn't deliver an eloquent speech; you only wanted them to know that you were not for sale. So they knew and you paid the price. And why don't you remember that you resisted the fall after Manar left you? That you resisted collapsing in the face of the humiliation of defeated love? That you refused to complain or to take advantage of your wounds? That you have tried under all circumstances to save yourself from falling into the well of self-pity and then to make that a justification for every fall?

Doesn't that earn me forgiveness, Ibrahim? Shouldn't I be forgiven because I have tried, Ibrahim? But what is the importance of all of that now? When does that child permit me to have peace with him? When will he leave me? If only sleep would come!

But it doesn't. I doze off a little then I am overcome with dreams from which I awaken in panic without remembering what they have been about. I sit up in bed again and I resist a desire to get up and smoke. I use the doctor's warnings to prevent myself. I am visited by his frowning face after he examined me and took my blood pressure the last time, when he asked me calmly not to return to his office again if I continued to smoke. I remember the splitting headache I had in my last blood-pressure episode and my desire to smoke subsides but sleep is far off.

How about poetry? I have tried it on nights like this one. I recall all the verses I have memorized until sleep overcomes me. Shall we begin with Arabian pre-Islamic poetry? Tarafa ibn al-Abd whom you adore? Go ahead:

Khawla has remnants in the gravel-plain of
Thahmad which show up like the remains
Of tattooing on the back of the hand

Is it "the back of the hand" or "the inside of the hand"? It doesn't matter. Go on. Skip the description of the she-camel. Go directly to:

So if you seek me in the circle of the people you will meet me
And if you hunt me in the wine-shops, you will catch me

What comes next? . . . Ah:

And my drinking wine and my pleasures did not cease

And my selling and my squandering my acquired and inherited wealth

Until the clan shunned me, all of it, and I was isolated like a mangy camel

Yes, exactly, Mr. Mangy Camel! That's you all right. The clan shunned you even though you didn't go to the wine shops or the circle of the people! Or perhaps because you did not go to the wine shops or to

the circle? That way we will not get anywhere. That is not Tarafa's night,
anyway. It wouldn't do under the circumstances. Skip all pre-Islamic
poetry otherwise you would be likely to stumble on the verse:

Truly did Nawar not know that I am a firm fastener

Of the knot of cords and their severer?

So that Nawar would not lead to Manar. Let's go to Mutanabbi, but
there is

Insomnia compounded by insomnia . . .

Forget him also now. He is not likely to bring sleep. Who then?
Buhturi? *I saved myself . . . .* Too much bluster at night! Salah Abd al-
Sabur? *My neighbor strung from her balcony a cord of melody*? But we
will immediately reach *and the morning came but no smiles* and all that
sadness. Amal Dunqul? He will lead us directly to *Do not make peace* and
we will spend the whole night with that which we want to escape. We
would like a calm poet. Zuhayr? Umar ibn Abi Rabia? Kuthayyir Azza?
Sayyab? Ahmad Shawqi? Who? Who? A soothing poet, a kind poet . . . .

But I am entering a long hall lined on both sides with bald-headed,
bare-chested men smiling slyly as I pass quickly in the middle. There is
something important that I must do but I don't know exactly what it is. I
am climbing a minaret or a tower. I am climbing fast but a huge hand is
pushing me down. I shout in protest, "I must save her. I must save him!"
There is a small boat in the midst of tumultuous waves and overhead birds
that look like vultures are hovering and diving at the boat like a dire warning. A person appears on a high rock wearing an official uniform and holding something that resembles a scepter that he points in a commanding
manner. He rebukes me saying, "It's too late!" I turn my eyes where he is
pointing his scepter. I hear a scream and I see many ambulances coming.
I run. I don't know if I am running away from the ambulances or running
after them.

@

Still in bed, I reached for the alarm clock and silenced it.

In the morning I took my blood pressure medication with a glass of juice.

I was very tired but I called Ibrahim at his hotel to tell him that I'd arranged an appointment with a journalist and that I'd pass by for him at the hotel to go together.

I had indeed made an appointment with Bernard who was the first to come to mind when Ibrahim asked me to introduce him to fellow journalists in town. My relations with journalists did not go beyond casual meetings at conferences or official receptions. It didn't take me long to find out that things here are different from back home, where after you've met someone once or twice you invite them to visit you at home. I found out that journalists and others in general here did not welcome social relations that were not useful. As I was not an important source of information and was not connected to influential circles, they didn't make an effort to get to know me. I considered this solitude part of the punishment time I was doing in exile, though I didn't know when it would end.

And even though Bernard also had not invited me to his home, he was different from the other journalists I had met. Even his appearance was different. His attire always met the minimum requirements of acceptability but it was a far cry from the formal elegance that characterized prominent journalists, whom I always saw wearing high collars, designer neckties, and jackets from haute couture boutiques and such. To the contrary, Bernard's jacket always seemed a little too large, perhaps to hide his big belly. I have never seen him on one of the television programs on which journalists normally appear. I don't think he could overcome his spontaneous way of talking to offer his views on the screen in that studied manner that didn't upset anybody as the others did. I also don't think he had the time for that sort of thing. I knew he was a widower and that he had adopted a Vietnamese boat-refugee child and was raising him by himself since his wife died.

On our way to the café where I had arranged to meet Bernard, Ibrahim once again began to arrange the papers that he carried in his little leather briefcase and seemed to be in a taciturn mood, uncommunicative. I, on the other hand, had lost the morning stupor, which was replaced by that false energy generated by coffee and lack of sleep. I couldn't control my desire to talk about serious and not so serious matters, but Ibrahim replied curtly and turned the conversation in the direction of the job he had come to do. He asked me about the inclinations of the newspapers in town and which would be likely to help him with his task. And even when he was asking about that, it was obvious that he was thinking about something else. His first disappointment in the press came when we met Bernard.

We met at the café across the street from his office. It was a journalist's hangout, and its owner, Elaine, hung photographs of famous writers, in some of which she stood next to them and in others she placed her hand on their shoulders. Most prominently displayed was a large oil painting, which looked old if not authentic, of a somewhat stout woman wearing see-through clothes and holding in her right hand a long white bird feather and in the other hand balanced scales.

As soon as I introduced Ibrahim to him, Bernard said, "Coming from Lebanon? You must have the latest news."

Ibrahim looked long at him and I thought he wouldn't respond but finally he said, calmly, "What would you like to know about Lebanon?"

"What everybody would like to know. To understand the reason for this long civil war and to know what's going on over there."

"But there is no mystery there. You know that Israel is amassing an army in the south and is arming the Phalangists in the north so the war will continue, don't you?"

Bernard shook his head, saying, "It's not that simple. The Lebanese are not just puppets moved by whoever wishes to move them. There must be something wrong with Lebanon itself."

Ibrahim did not comment on that. Instead he began to tell him about the Israeli patrols that kidnapped Palestinians and Lebanese from the south. Then he pulled out the papers that he had arranged of his briefcase and said to Bernard, "Take this for instance. This is the case of the Lebanese driver, Said Dakir. The soldiers stopped the ambulance he was driving in southern Sidon and considered him a terrorist because the car he was driving belonged to the Palestinian Red Crescent. They blindfolded him and put him in a military car, which took him to Israel, and there they beat him with clubs and rifle butts until they shattered the bones of his legs and he couldn't walk anymore. He was also subjected to torture by electricity, exactly as you heard yesterday from Pedro Ibañez. Here are the photos of the marks of torture by electricity around his nipples and there are of course marks in the others places. And here is a neutral medical testimony about his case."

As Bernard leafed through the papers, speed-reading the lines, he said, "Yes. These are obvious cases. But they are written very poorly."

Ibrahim said in disbelief, "Really? The Lebanese colleague who translated these papers into French told us that French was his mother tongue!"

Bernard said, "Then he is a hopeless case, as a son. But that's not the problem. I could easily rewrite them in a way that would make them publishable but that won't solve anything." Then handing the papers back to Ibrahim, he added, calmly, "You won't find one journalist here willing to publish this."

Ibrahim said, "Why? I'm giving you specific cases with names and testimony from neutral sources."

Bernard interrupted, "I believe you one hundred percent and yet I cannot publish this."

Disappointed, Ibrahim said, "But why?"

Looking at him through his thick glasses, Bernard said slowly, "You know why. If we say that armed soldiers kidnap unarmed citizens from another country, that's a serious accusation."

Ibrahim interrupted him, "But I give you the proof of what I am saying and I give you real names."

Bernard hesitated before saying, "Not enough. I told you I believe you, but how would the editor-in-chief believe me? What would I do or what would he do if we received an official refutation and we were told that these are commandos and that we are encouraging terrorists, or more seriously, what if we were told that by defending these terrorists we are anti-Semitic?"

Ibrahim mumbled as if talking to himself, "Anti-Semitic? What has the world come to? I knew I'd meet some difficulties, but not to that extent."

Bernard laughed as he looked at me and said, "Why do people get dejected so easily?"

Ibrahim waved the papers in his hand and said, "Because of what we see."

Bernard fell silent for a moment then said, "But you know that a journalist, like a doctor, should keep a distance from the cases he is treating. They should not be his worry night and day, if he wants to live."

I said in jest, "Ibrahim is a committed journalist."

Bernard said, "Even a committed journalist has his own life, his joys and worries. I know a journalist who considers himself committed like Ibrahim. He is swamped from the morning by the world's news and problems; the wars, the famines, the crimes. He cares a lot and he grieves, but what really breaks his heart day and night, is that his son, whom he loved and raised, grew up and had a family of his own and soon forgot his father completely. He doesn't even bother to call him on the telephone once a week or even a month to ask how he's doing or even to find out whether he's alive or dead."

Bernard's voice was now full of bitterness. It didn't seem that he was talking merely about a journalist he knew. I asked myself if he had a biological son.

Bernard, however, regained his composure and said as he turned to Ibrahim, "You see? This is a very small problem but it might preoccupy a journalist more than the war in Lebanon. Calm down. Ever since we sat down together you've been very tense, even though you definitely know the problems in our profession. So let's think of a solution for these papers that are tormenting you."

At that moment the café owner, Elaine, short with dyed blond hair, was approaching us carrying two cups of coffee. She placed one in front of me and one in front of Ibrahim, smiling broadly and saying, "Good morning, gentlemen."

Then she said to me, "Here's your medicinal coffee as usual, sir, decaffeinated coffee." Then she turned to Bernard and asked him, "Another glass, Monsieur Bernard?"

Bernard looked at the glass in his hand to see how much was left before he made up his mind, then told Elaine almost regretfully, "No, I must go back to work. But I think I asked you about your husband. If he is here tell him we would like to see him, if we could."

Elaine, still tending the table, said, "Of course he's here, but he is in the kitchen. Lunch must be prepared for the customers, as you know. Should I tell him?"

"Yes."

Elaine left and Ibrahim and I looked quizzically at Bernard who told me, "I have a surprise for you two. I am going to introduce you to an Egyptian like yourselves. But that is not the surprise, of course. There are many Egyptians here. The surprise is that he is a colleague in the profession!"

I was surprised when I saw him coming towards us with the white kitchen apron. He made a few tentative steps before reaching us then went back and took off the apron, hung it on a clothes rack and dried his hands on a towel before heading back to us again. I had seen him several times before. The first time I saw him I guessed that he was Egyptian even though he was blond and his features were not much different from Europeans. There was something about his appearance, that indescribable something that makes people from the same country recognize each other. But the times I had seen him in the café earlier he had not shown any interest and had not tried to initiate a conversation with me, so I said to myself that perhaps I had guessed wrong. What really surprised me now was finding out that he was Elaine's husband. He was much younger than she and I said to myself that the age difference couldn't be less than twenty years.

He shook our hands. His hands, which had been soaked in water for a long time, were still moist despite his efforts at drying them. Bernard, pointing at him, said, "Mr. Yusuf." After the introductions he pulled out a chair and sat on its edge awkwardly. Bernard said encouragingly, "Come on, Yusuf. Get to the point straight away. These two gentlemen are journalists and from your country."

Yusuf said, "It's not easy. It needs time."

Bernard said, "Sure. What we need now is for you to tell us briefly. Don't you want to be a journalist? You must learn how to be concise." Bernard then turned to me and said, "In brief, Yusuf wants to publish an Arabic newspaper here and would like to consult you."

I looked at him, somewhat perplexed, "Just like that? Publish a newspaper? Are you a millionaire?"

Yusuf laughed and said, "No, but I have a millionaire."

"Even if that's true, it is not enough. Do you have prior experience in journalism?" I said.

Overcoming his shyness, he said, "Yes and no. I mean I haven't published a newspaper before but I was a communications major at Cairo University several years ago."

"Why did you leave Egypt?" I asked.

Yusuf laughed softly and said, "Is this investigative journalism or just an investigation?"

I said apologetically, "No, it's just curiosity. You don't have to answer if it bothers you."

"Doesn't bother me at all. I was a junior in college and I had been sentenced to six months in jail because I had taken part in a demonstration against Sadat and I mixed it up with the University police. So I ran away to Libya after the verdict and from Libya I came here."

Ibrahim said with a faint smile, "So, my friend, we are in the same boat."

Yusuf wagged his finger, saying, "No, I am not in the same boat with anyone. What I've seen since I left Egypt is enough to . . ."

Then he fell silent. And Ibrahim asked, "But how did you arrive at 'N'?" then paused and said, "No, I am not taking part in this investigation. You're right, Yusuf. It's as if we are putting you on trial."

That was indeed the only time that Ibrahim intervened in the conversation. His eyes followed us but I noticed that he was somewhat distant.

During that time Elaine was hovering in the café, putting tablecloths and silverware on the empty tables but stealing glances at us from time to time. Yusuf was also following her with his eyes as she moved from table to table. Bernard said, "Of course I understood everything you said in Arabic. But is everything all right? Did you come to an agreement?"

I said, "We've just been introduced to each other."

He laughed as he pushed his cup away, "I am afraid there's no time for anything more!"

And indeed Elaine was approaching us and she laid her hand on

Bernard's shoulder, asking, "Are you done? They are asking for Yusuf in the kitchen. He's the chef as you know!"

A smile lingered on her lips but a stern look appeared in her eyes as she said, "Isn't that so, Yusuf? They need you over there."

Yusuf did not reply but got up saying to me, "I'll call you, Ustaz. I know your name and I'll get your number from the directory."

He nodded a goodbye as he moved away with Elaine following. When he disappeared I asked Bernard, "Is this story true or is it just one of those dreams? Is there actually a millionaire?"

Bernard replied slowly, nodding in emphasis, "He's not just a millionaire. He's also an Arab prince, and not just any prince but a progressive prince to boot."

I repeated, savoring the sentence, "Not just any prince but a progressive prince to boot."

Bernard said, "I am not kidding. He's a prince from one of the Gulf countries. Yusuf worked for him at one time. And now he wants to publish a newspaper in Arabic here. He's asked Yusuf to look into the matter."

"And why wouldn't he publish it in London or Paris?"

"Perhaps because there's a glut of newspapers in London and Paris!" Bernard said.

"What does he want from me?" I asked.

"Yusuf says the prince knows you as a journalist, that he likes you and has advised him to consult you."

I said, slowly, "The progressive prince knows me? How interesting!"

But Ibrahim, who had remained silent for quite some time, suddenly exclaimed, "And what's wrong with that? Why should it matter to you whether he is a prince or not? So long as he wants to publish a good newspaper, why don't you help him? Even the Marxist organization with which I work received donations from princes and wealthy people; should we turn them down because they have not come from the proletariat?"

In exasperation I said, "You are free and so am I. I don't want to have anything to do with this kind of newspaper, with progressive or reactionary princes!"

Shaking his head, Bernard said slowly, "Once again, I understood all this conversation in Arabic!"

I laughed nervously as I said, "Sorry, Bernard. My friend was trying to convince me to work with the progressive prince!"

Bernard said, "And I agree with him. What matters in our profession is one thing: to be able to say what you want to say. Think about it. If it's a serious project and if you can help and if you find that you're free to say what you want, why not do it? If . . ."

Ibrahim intervened, interrupting again, asking, "Isn't there a communist party newspaper in this town?"

I volunteered an answer, "Yes, there is. It's a tiny newspaper, read only by the party members and, as you know, there's only a few of them."

Ibrahim frowned, saying, "So it's a tiny newspaper! I reject this despair. The world has not died, the revolution has not died, otherwise what's the meaning of what's going on in Lebanon, in Nicaragua, and the Philippines? East and West, the world's on the move and tomorrow the whole world will change! Even here it will change. Don't make fun of a small newspaper!"

Bernard started whistling the *Internationale* in a comic way and moving his finger to the rhythm. Then he laughed as he looked at his watch and told Ibrahim, "I would have loved to drink a toast with you to world revolution, but unfortunately I have to go back to work for my capitalist paper."

When he got up he shook Ibrahim's hand warmly and said, "You are right. Try with the party newspaper. I'll also think of what else could be done to publish your papers."

We had plenty of time before lunch. Ibrahim wanted to go on a walking tour of the city so I accompanied him downtown. He didn't stop in front of the elegant stores that visitors usually found attractive. He also didn't stop in front of landmarks and statues. When I pointed out the large church in the main square and tried to tell him its history and how the practice of Catholicism had been forbidden in the city until the end of the last century, and how Protestants used to persecute Catholics, he nodded and said with a faint smile, "I read a little about the history of the city before coming here."

Ibrahim noticed the frustration in my face and said, "Listen, I'll tell you the truth. When I was younger and whenever I traveled anywhere, I always took my camera and took pictures of old cathedrals and statues and buildings. I also wrote the date behind the pictures. Now these things no longer hold any interest for me at all. Even the things I have already seen have gotten mixed up in my head. All I want to see now when I visit any city are the trees and the green. With old age I have come to look for everything that reminds me of my childhood, of the Nile, and the sycamores and the willows. I am a peasant, as you know! We can also go to your café by the river."

"We will go there for lunch if you like. But there is a small garden nearby which I like and which I call 'my secret garden.'"

On our way from the crowded downtown area, crossing a side street going towards the river, Ibrahim asked me casually, "Where did you take Brigitte yesterday, or where did she take you?"

"I gave her a ride home, " I said.

Should I also tell him if he asks me that I went up to her apartment? And what would he think if I told him that?

But Ibrahim didn't ask me. When we arrived at the front of an old building we entered through its arched gate and crossed a small corridor ending up in the garden which was in the middle of a plaza surrounded by houses that were at least a century old. It was indeed a beautiful secret garden that you wouldn't see from anywhere on the road.

Ibrahim paused at the entrance of the garden smiling and shading his eyes with his hand and looking around at the trees. Then he said in a casual manner, "Do you come here to love?"

I replied casually, "Wasn't it you who said yesterday that we're too old for that now?"

Ibrahim did not reply and proceeded to walk slowly as I followed his steps in the middle of walkways lined with high poplars with their thick green foliage and the chestnut trees that had begun to bear their round green nuts. He walked also taking in the beds of flowers on both sides of the walkways. There were roses showing off their red and yellow petals in the youthful flush of early summer and next to them were beds of pansies in different colors: white, violet, and brown and in the middle of each of them a round yellow ring of small dots like intricate ornaments. Ibrahim seemed totally absorbed taking in the flowers, and we didn't exchange a word until we sat on a bench in a corner overlooking the whole garden.

We sat in silence, each lost in his thoughts. It was Ibrahim who broke the silence when he asked me without looking in my direction, "How old is your son Nasser?"

I turned to him, somewhat taken aback, "His name is Khalid, as I told you. Soon he will be twenty. But it is really strange you asking me about him now. I was thinking of Khalid at the very moment you asked me about him. I was thinking that today is the day I usually call him. So what reminded you of him?"

"I remembered when I was his age."

I said with a heavy heart, "Certainly you were different."

"How?"

"Khalid's changed a lot lately. He was a normal young man who loved sports and reading literature and especially chess. It was I who taught him chess, but he started to beat me at it when he was fourteen or fifteen and that made me happy like any father."

I paused for a little while before adding, "He was also religious all his life. But now he's gone far . . ."

"You mean he joined the Islamist groups or something like that?"

"No, but he's overdoing it now. Even the way he talks now is different."

Then I was overcome with sadness as I told him, "Hanadi tells me that he no longer watches television and he wants her also not to watch it."

Ibrahim laughed and said, "On this particular point he is right. Our television is a tool for mental retardation."

Ibrahim most probably wanted to change the mood and when he saw that I was not responding he said, "Listen my friend. It's a phase. Would you be surprised to know that at his age or when I was slightly younger, I never left the mosque? I never stopped performing prayers and I did my ablutions repeatedly because I'd think somehow that I had lost my ritual purity. I asked God for forgiveness for sins that I had not committed. I asked for forgiveness merely because some forbidden thoughts occurred to me. I cried, praying to God to forgive me for these evil thoughts and promised to repent."

"We've all been through that."

"So, why are you so afraid for Khalid then? He also will find his way. Come on. Once again I am sorry that I am bringing up disturbing topics. Come on. Forget those thoughts. I'll tell you something that'll really surprise you! Would you believe that the garden in our house in the village was as well tended and beautiful as this garden? My father was very strict with the gardeners and didn't tolerate any negligence."

I tried to smile, saying, "I heard it was a palace, not a house."

"No, that's an exaggeration. It was a big house, a beautiful house."

Then he fell silent, adding, "But I never knew happiness in it." This time he was depressed.

"Even you?"

Ibrahim looked at me and spoke slowly, "What do you mean 'even you'? Yes, even I. I've heard you speak about your poor childhood and believe me, sometimes I've envied you! I asked myself why was I not you. Why I was not anybody else instead of being me? Sometimes these strange ideas come to me."

"Was your childhood that miserable?"

He continued as if he hadn't heard me, "I ask myself a lot these days: What are those coincidences that control us and make us? Was it really necessary for me to be born the son of the landlord of the village? Was it necessary that my father filled the house with books that he acquired and embossed his name on them in golden letters without opening any one of them, then saddled me with the task of reading them ever since I learned to read? Would my life have been ruined from day one? Would my eyes have caught the rot everywhere? Why haven't I enjoyed life as everybody else has?"

Ibrahim began his questions calmly then tension crept into his voice. I was about to tell him that these ideas were not "scientific" but I held off when I saw him rubbing his forehead with his hand and staring straight ahead as if looking now, in this garden, for answers to the questions that had tormented him for a long time.

Finally he started looking towards me again, repeating his question in a soft voice, "Why? Now I ask myself: When did my sorrows begin? Was my mother the cause? Perhaps she was the first sorrow that I experienced in my life without understanding what caused it. I can still see her there in our big house in the village, in the house of many rooms, filled with furniture and pictures and books, moving alone from one room to another, lifting things and putting them back in their place. She would give the many servants orders in a voice that lacked self-confidence, as if she were begging them, and then quickly take back the orders. She would tell the servant, 'If you are tired, postpone this chore until the afternoon, no need to hurry; the world will still be there.' She almost apologized for just being there. In the morning she kept busy applying makeup, lipstick, and eyeliner, and putting on a fancy dress and a lot of jewelry then staying at home. She just moved from room to room and sighed. As for my father, I have never heard him call her by name. He always addressed her as 'Hanim.' He would bow in front of her as she sat in her seat and kiss her hand, asking her very politely before going out, 'Does the Hanim have any orders for me?' and she would mumble, 'May you come back safely, sir.' But even when I was very young I knew that he was cheating on her the whole time. I was five when I saw him in the barn on top of a woman. I was filled with anger and ran back to the house and wanted to tell my mother. But when I saw her in her usual chair, almost sinking into it with her thin body, listening to the radio and staring absently, I was afraid. I felt, even at that age, that I could kill her if I spoke and told her what I saw. She was as fragile as a butterfly. Do you understand? What did my father do exactly to destroy her in that manner? Do you understand what I am saying?"

I said, "My mother died when I was a very young child but I understand, of course, that a mother is . . ."

I hadn't said anything more than that when Ibrahim raised his hand objecting and said, "No, I don't mean any mother. Please don't talk to me about Oedipus or Freud or any of that nonsense. What distressed me was injustice, not those imaginary complexes. What distressed me with my mother was the very same thing that distressed me when I saw my father and his men stealing from the peasants later on. I mean, when I grew a little older. When I saw them cheating the peasants when weighing the cotton or when doing the calculations. I was either finishing primary school or just beginning secondary school when I started to read and understood and when questions began to form in my head, the same questions that have tormented me all my life. I thought that the overseer had made a mistake when he counted the three *kantars* on the scale as two and a half *kantars* and I said loudly, 'It is three *kantars*.' The peasant was standing at the head of the line, cowering with a bowed head watching his cotton, which was swinging on the scale like a carcass. When I said what I said he exclaimed, 'It is three *kantars*, sir. The young master has ruled.' But my father who was watching from a distance looked angrily at me and said, 'You, boy. Why are you standing here in the dust? Go back home at once.' That day he took me to Cairo and placed me in a boarding school there."

Ibrahim fell silent and leaned back, almost panting. Then after a little while he said, "Please forgive me for disturbing you time after time. But believe me, I myself don't know why I am telling you all this."

"You haven't disturbed me at all, Ibrahim. All there is to it is that I am thinking of something else. I am thinking of that child who pursues us to the end of our days. Isn't there a way to get rid of him?"

Looking at the trees as if seeking an answer there, Ibrahim said, "If only I knew!"

5

What a Beautiful Man You Are!

WHEN I OPENED THE DOOR of the apartment a smiling Abd al-Nasser looked at me from his color photograph on the wall. I had in my hands the stuff that I'd found in the mailbox: issues of the newspaper sent from Cairo and a lot of junk mail. I looked through the newspapers but didn't find the Thursday issue in which Manar wrote her weekly column. I put the new issues on the desk in the living room on top of all the other newspapers.

I sat at the desk and began trying to reach Cairo by phone. As usual my heart beat faster as I dialed the number, looking at the picture of Khalid and Hanadi in the frame on the desk. I tried several times to no avail. As usual there was the busy signal even before I had finished dialing the number, or just total silence for a long interval after I had dialed, so I had to start all over again. I was used to that and I knew that the only way to get through was to keep re-dialing time after time. So I began mechanically dialing as I stole glances at the headlines of the newspaper in front of me. Suddenly and without the phone ringing on the other end, Hanadi's voice came as a surprise, "Hello. Dad?"

"Yes, love. How are you Hanadi?"

"Studying is killing me. It's very hot here."

"It's O.K. Hang in there, Hanadi. The exams are next week, right?"

"Yes. Pray for me, Dad."

"I am always praying for you. This year, though, we need a high score for the preparatory school certificate."

"Just how high, Daddy?"

"As high as you can. Let's say ninety percent, for instance."

"Really? I'd be very happy with sixty percent or even fifty. What's wrong with fifty? It's not as if I am going directly from preparatory school to university!"

"Well, if you don't start now . . . anyway, just study. Don't think of the score or anything."

"I am not thinking about the score. I am thinking about something far more important."

"Which is?"

"The gift you'll give me when I pass my exams."

"Like?"

"Like you should start saving right now. This year I'd like a membership in the Equestrian Club. I want to learn how to ride horses."

"Is it that very expensive?"

"Well, we're talking about five hundred, a thousand, as much as you like."

"A thousand? Really? All for sixty percent? What if it were ninety percent?"

"I would ask you to buy me a car, of course. Here, Dad. Here's Khalid the genius who gets 'excellent' and ninety per cent and such. Bye, Daddy."

Khalid's voice was deep and dignified as he said in formal Arabic, "Peace be upon you."

"And you too, Khalid. How are you, son?"

"I am fine, Thank God. And you, how's your health? I hope its fine, God willing."

"Very fine. Did you get 'excellent' this time Khalid?"

"Don't believe this jabbering girl. The results have not been announced yet."

"When will they be?"

"Next week, God willing."

"And you'll come immediately after they're announced, right?"

"After the results? No. You know, Father, I have to prepare for next year's project and other things."

"So when are you coming, Khalid? I miss you very much, son, and would like for you to spend two or three weeks with me before you go to your championship matches."

"I also miss you very much, Father."

"So, how long would it take you, Khalid?"

"Frankly, father, I don't know."

"Why, son?"

Khalid was silent for a few seconds before saying, "Listen, Father. Frankly, I have withdrawn from the competition."

"Withdrawn? Why, Khalid? You don't want to come and see me?"

"No, God forbid, Father. Actually it is difficult to say that I am not coming to see you, because I really miss you. But I don't like to lie."

"Lie? What's wrong, son? Are you tired? Is anything the matter?"

"No, Father. I am very well, thank God. But frankly, I read a *fatwa* that says that playing chess is prohibited. And I am convinced of it."

"Prohibited? Chess?"

Khalid was silent for a few moments before saying decisively, "Yes, Father. Prohibited."

After the conversation I stayed for a while leaning my arms on the desk then went into the kitchen to make the cup of coffee I had promised myself, but instead I sat on the stool there and began absently to look from the kitchen window at the buildings opposite and at the sky and the trees, my mind unfocused, unable to gather my thoughts. Finally I found myself murmuring softly, "Prohibited. Indeed, prohibited!"

Ibrahim was waiting for me in the lobby of the hotel and, smiling, he waved to me as soon as he saw me coming in. When I came close to him he stood up and alarm showed on his face as he asked me, "What's the matter? Are you ill?"

"No. I mean, the usual condition, hypertension. Sometimes it acts up giving me a splitting headache, as you know."

"But why did you go out if you're not feeling well? You could've called, I would've understood."

"Don't worry, Ibrahim. I took my pill and I'll be all right in a little while."

We had agreed at midday to take a night off from everything to go together to the cinema. Ibrahim had seen an ad for *Lawrence of Arabia* and he said he had seen it ten years earlier but would like to see it one more time because he liked the music a lot. Now Ibrahim was trying to dissuade me from going to see the film saying it would be best if I got some rest, but I convinced him that I was also in need of recreation, that *Lawrence* might be useful now.

"Well then, we'll talk about that later. Now you will come with me to see Dr. Muller who promised me yesterday to give me a complete list of all the organizations and societies I can correspond with," Ibrahim said.

"We agreed to take time off from work this evening, didn't we?"

"Yes, but I made this appointment with Muller yesterday, and it won't take long anyway," Ibrahim said, smiling.

It was a short walk to the other hotel. As Ibrahim was trying again to convince me to rest that night, I couldn't help it and I told him everything about my conversation with Khalid. I was fighting back the tears as I told him but he said, calmly, "Don't blame him, my friend. I told you he's now at the age of innocence. That does not mean that he doesn't love you or that he doesn't want to see you. What he believes in now is more important than his love for you and than his own life. Don't you remember the way you were? Were you thinking about your life when you entered Port Said during the English raids?"

"That was different. Back then there was a cause . . ."

Ibrahim interrupted me, "A cause you believed in. He too believes in his cause. So, how is it different? Almost at his age you wanted to sacrifice your very own life. He is now sacrificing something much less: he sacrificed a trip during which he could've seen you."

"It's different. I have this idea in my head that I cannot explain clearly to you or even to myself . . . I mean, what we were doing in our youth was for the future, for life. What I'm noticing gradually about Khalid is some kind of total negation of life. The future is only what comes after death. Yesterday you explained to me what we were like when we were his age. All that sense of guilt for this or that evil thought. Wasn't that before we discovered that we were neither angels nor devils? That we were humans who sinned and repented?"

Laughing, Ibrahim said, "I was telling you about my memories but I am not an authority on matters of repentance. Now, if you've forgotten, I am a Marxist. And in any case, you didn't stay with Khalid to . . ."

Ibrahim stopped and murmured an apology but I completed his thought, "I understand what you're trying to say. Had I stayed with him, I could've influenced him. But how could I have stayed? Manar and I have accustomed Khalid and Hanadi since they were children to persuasion and reason and freedom of choice. After the divorce, he chose to stay with his mother and sister. That was one of the reasons I left the country. It was difficult for me to be in the same city with my children but apart from them, making appointments like friends or strangers, like . . . "

I fell silent before my voice choked on the tears I was fighting back. We had gotten close to Muller's hotel, so I tried to calm myself before we left the dark of the road for the hotel lobby.

Muller was sitting in the lobby with Brigitte. They were drinking in silence and looked despondent. Ibrahim whispered in my ear as we came close to them, "It seems that something has happened here too, but what?"

Muller's face, which usually looked like a mask, was now sullen and tense. But when we sat down, he took out of his pocket a large white envelope and said, "I haven't forgotten you, Mr. Ibrahim. You'll find all the addresses here."

Ibrahim opened the envelope and I saw a long sheet of paper divided into columns, hand written yet arranged more neatly than any printed page. After looking at the sheet, Ibrahim said, "Thank you, Dr. Muller. We will not take more of your time," and started to get up, but Muller said, "Please wait. Perhaps the two of you can help me." Then he turned to me and said, "Perhaps you in particular can help me." Then he was silent for a moment before saying, "Pedro has disappeared."

"Who is Pedro?" I said.

Then I suddenly remembered and was ashamed of myself for having forgotten him before Dr. Muller replied, "Pedro Ibañez, at the press conference. He took his suitcases and left the hotel." Dr. Muller began to explain to us the trouble he had gone through to get Pedro an entry visa so he would appear at the press conference, for here they don't welcome refugees from Chile or anywhere else. Therefore, the visa permitted

Pedro to stay for only one week. And even though he knew that, he took his suitcases and left the hotel without a word.

Ibrahim said, "But why are you so worried, Doctor? Pedro is not a child and he can take responsibility for what he has done."

Muller replied tensely but spontaneously, "The problem now is not Pedro, but the organization."

I stole a glance to Brigitte and she returned my glance with a faint smile on her lips. Dr. Muller did not notice and continued to complain that he was afraid Pedro wouldn't reappear before the visa expired and the organization would face problems in this country. Perhaps they'd say that the organization was encouraging illegal immigration and then give it a bad name here. He was afraid that if that happened the organization's image would suffer in other countries as well.

Ibrahim, somewhat perplexed, asked, "But what exactly is the problem here, Dr. Muller? Why did Pedro flee?"

Dejectedly Muller said, "That's what I'd like to know."

Brigitte took a big gulp of beer then put her glass down and said, "But you definitely do know, Doctor. You know that ever since he fled Chile he hasn't gotten legal residency anywhere. You also know that in Austria he was staying at the holding center for those who fled their countries and that the center was more like a prison."

"They were investigating his case and ultimately they would have accepted him as a refugee. It was certain that he would have gotten out of the holding center," Muller protested.

Brigitte continued, her speech somewhat slurred, trying to stay cool, "And how long would he have waited, Doctor? Months or years? How long do you think a person can bear to stay in that holding center? You've seen them there at the camp closest to our town. Forget the cruelty of the guards. How long do you think a person can bear the hostile and hateful looks of our affectionate townspeople?"

Angered, Muller uncharacteristically snapped back, "He was running away from something worse. He should have appreciated what the organization had done for him."

Raising the glass again to her lips she said, "Yes."

Then she relaxed back in her seat. She was wearing jeans and a light white blouse. Her hair was loose and the way she slumped there made her a picture of exhaustion and resignation.

Ibrahim cast a quick glance at her then turned to Muller and said with sincere warmth and animation, "This is a matter that we should indeed work for, Doctor. To tell you the truth, ever since I attended that press conference yesterday I have been chagrined and felt guilty about this man. I will write about him in my small paper, but how would that help him? And now you are saying that my friend and I can help you. How?"

Muller said, "Yes," then turned to me and said, "As a journalist living here you must have contacts with persons who can help us look for him, naturally without the police."

Before I replied, Brigitte, staring at Ibrahim, suddenly exclaimed, "What a beautiful man you are!"

There was silence for a moment. Ibrahim blushed and Dr. Muller looked somewhat angry but he smiled for the first time as he said in a desperate tone, "Hans Schaefer's daughter."

Then he turned to us and added, "Just like her father since I knew him half a century ago. He surprises you with the strangest things at all the wrong times."

"But any time is the right time for a woman to tell a man how beautiful he is!" Brigitte retorted.

I commented, "I've always told Ibrahim that he's in the wrong profession, that he would've become an international movie star if he'd gone into cinema."

"Stop it," Ibrahim shouted angrily.

His face was flushed and scowling. Brigitte sat up in her chair and, addressing me as she looked at Ibrahim, continued, "No. Movie stars are like dolls, painted things accurately rendered to the square centimeter. What's beautiful about Ibrahim is that life in his face. If you look at him closely you'll find for instance that his mouth . . ."

Ibrahim interjected again but this time almost imploringly, "Stop, please. We're talking about something more important."

"Did I upset you? I am sorry," Brigitte said.

Muller, in a wise tone of voice, said, "At Ibrahim's age, a man is not happy to hear that he's handsome, but intelligent, perhaps, for instance . . ."

Brigitte replied skeptically, "You think so? I don't understand what you mean by age but I know intelligent men who are ready to give up all their intelligence just to hear . . ."

Then Brigitte placed the beer glass on the table in front of us and her face became quite serious, the way people who suddenly realized that they were speaking under the influence of alcohol did. She just abruptly fell silent. After a while she turned to Ibrahim with that serious look on her face and said, "I am sorry if I've upset you." But she couldn't help it and added, laughing, "But what can I do if you're really beautiful? I am not flirting with you or anything. I just want to tell you that you're beautiful."

She continued to laugh in short, intermittent bursts as she placed her hand on her mouth.

Ibrahim looked at his watch but I told him, "Don't look at your watch. Lawrence of Arabia is now riding a camel in the desert, having gone a long distance."

"It doesn't matter. Pedro is much more important, " Ibrahim said.

"But we agreed to take the night off from work, didn't we?"

"Let's take tomorrow off. Now, can we actually do anything for Pedro?"

Leaning her head back, with eyes closed, Brigitte said, "Please leave Pedro alone. Perhaps he'll fare better on his own than with any organization. Perhaps he'll take a break from interrogations and police pursuit for a few weeks or even a few months. Perhaps he'll take a break from being kicked out of one country to another. Just let him be."

Muller said in a stern tone, "I know what you think of our work, Brigitte. But tell me this: if there were no organizations like ours trying to help these victims, would the world be better off than it is?"

"I don't think it would be better off," then she looked at his face and added, "and I also don't think it would be worse off, Doctor." Her tone was quite calm, almost tinged with pity for Dr. Muller. The usual combative tone was now gone from her voice. It occurred to me that, after talking to me about him yesterday, she had erased any traces of bitterness towards him.

We didn't see *Lawrence of Arabia* the following night, or the one after that. The days left for Ibrahim were filled with work for him and for me too. I was writing my monthly report to the newspaper in which I had to include bizarre news "From the West." It was the only report that the paper published in full, thus justifying my salary to some extent. All I had to do was read the papers published locally and cull those news items that were also given prominent places in these papers. The ideal story of course was of the "man bites dog" variety rather than the other way around. I was quite lucky this time, for here was a news item that followed this script to the letter. The headline was "Food Eats Customer" about a man in a French restaurant who wanted to sniff a lobster to make sure that it was fresh before it was cooked and it bit off his nose. There was another story about a young man who broke the record of walking on his hands by staying upside down for twelve continuous hours. The young man said that he was trying to bring his record up to twenty-four hours, and so on. I tried to sneak in among those stories something about Pedro in the report even though I didn't know what good that would do. Finally I wrote down what happened at the press conference saying to myself that perhaps they would have a slow news day as happened from time to time and they would publish it. But I was also certain that I was lying to myself.

I also tried during those days to help Muller look for Pedro. Once again I sought out Bernard, who I knew had work-related contacts with refugee and immigrant communities. But, like Brigitte, Bernard thought I should leave Pedro alone. He told me that he was sure that the police had not lost sight of Pedro for one moment and that if they wanted to return him to Dr. Muller they would do it on their own. Bernard told me, "Most likely Pedro went with some of his compatriots from Chile or Latin America. They have a secret network to help each other. I can introduce you or the Doctor to some groups in charge of refugees but what good would that do? Even if they knew where he is they wouldn't tell us a thing. They'll find him a secret job in a restaurant or a hotel and he will live there for weeks and months without seeing the street for fear of being arrested by the police who keep an eye on him as I told you. They will let him be so long as he's useful to owners of restaurants and hotels and stores who need him and people like him because they work a lot and cost little. If they ultimately arrest him, it will be because he is superfluous or has been used up and is no longer good for anything."

When I told Bernard in alarm, "So let's find him to save him," he replied with a faint smile, "Really? You think you'd be saving him? Then come with me and I'll introduce you to dozens who are living this way, from Chile and all other countries on earth. They prefer that a thousand times to returning to their countries and they prefer it also a thousand times to holding centers." Then he asked me, "Can you or the Doctor guarantee you'll get him something better than what he himself is trying to get?"

I had no answer for him and yet Bernard agreed to meet Muller and continued to accompany Ibrahim, Muller, and me in the evenings during the week, to the societies that looked after refugees and to poor neighborhoods that offer shelter to illegal aliens. Nevertheless we didn't find a trace of Pedro until the week was almost gone.

During those days I also went with Ibrahim in the mornings to accompany him to his various appointments with journalists and political party leaders and some Arab residents in town. He wanted to write a series of articles after he returned to Beirut and began to collect some material that could help him. And throughout he was sharing the documents he brought with him about those people abducted in Lebanon and the people he met with would promise him very politely to study the matter but would disappear after that. From time to time we saw the "student" in the hotel lobby or suddenly at one of the cafés where we sat. Sometimes an athletic young man appeared with her and they behaved like lovers, hugging and kissing but without letting us out of their sight. Sometimes, however, she "deserted" her lover and he had to follow us by himself.

The only place that Ibrahim insisted on going to by himself was the office of the Communist Party. That day he met me at the restaurant after he returned beaming and his eyes glowing with pride, and said to me, "Finally, I've seen the real Europe. Finally I've come to know the Europe you haven't known! Can you imagine that here also they persecute the communists as they do in our country? Can you imagine that the police keep them under surveillance and tap their telephones and they give them a hard time in their jobs, which they find only with great difficulty? Can you imagine that they even deny them housing in the state-subsidized homes just because they are communists?"

I asked him in surprise, "How can that make you happy?"

"I found the comrades here to be extremely steadfast despite all the persecution!"

With difficulty I prevented myself from smiling, or thought I had since he continued in a reproving tone, "You are making fun of that? Listen, all this persecution fills me with hope, contrary to what you might think. Here they are a tiny minority. I know that quite well. And their newspaper is tiny as you said. But why do they fear them so much when they're such a tiny minority? There's not a single communist party in Europe that is bearing arms or will bear arms any day to topple the government. So why do they fear them? You want to know why? Because sooner or later they are the alternative to Europe's crisis and to the world's problems. They are the future. They are the inevitability of history."

In shock I said, "But, Ibrahim, even the most extremist communists would not say such things now! Not even the Kremlin itself dreams that can happen in the West. What has happened to your mind?"

That was the way we argued at lunch or in the car. We quarreled as we did when we were young. And even though we never agreed or anything, he was quite truthful when he said at our first meeting here that "death has erased all traces of enmity between us." Within a few days we developed some kind of real closeness and affection despite the persistent disagreement. It was as if somewhere deep down, neither of us took that disagreement seriously; we were arguing *pro forma*, feeling that we were ghosts from a bygone era. We knew that Abd al-Nasser would not rise from the dead and that the Workers of the World would not unite. But we never said that. We always said the opposite. I told him that the people would not forget what Abd al-Nasser did for them, that the people in our village would not forget it was he who built the medical center in a village half of whose inhabitants died of malaria in one day, a village that had known only a visiting doctor who went there once a month. They would not forget that he built two schools and distributed land to the poor and that he employed the sons of those poor in the factories that he built. Like Ibrahim I found certainty in little things. I told him that a few days earlier I had made a friend listen to a speech of Abd al-Nasser and his eyes glistened with tears! I reminded him that after all that was said against Abd al-Nasser the people still went out on the streets in 1977 carrying his picture and shouting his name. I told him that that meant his revolution would be revived by the people one day. I told Ibrahim many things and he listened to me, shaking his head stubbornly and repeating, "But he forgot his allies and embraced his enemies and they destroyed everything. Besides, who gave us Sadat?"

I would try to answer and the give and take and the agitation would begin anew. But once while we were in the thick of arguing, Ibrahim suddenly stopped and asked me, "Listen. What are you trying to convince me of? To change my way of thinking and join you? At this age? I'd rather commit suicide!"

I knew then that he was like me, clinging to his certainty so that his world would not cease to be, so that the dream for which we paid a whole lifetime would not come to an end! But towards the end of the week Ibrahim showed little interest in this kind of discussion. At the beginning he was mumbling a vague complaint. He told me once that I, even though my marriage had failed and even though I had gone through an ordeal, was more fortunate than he was because at least I'd known complete love once in my life. He reiterated what he had told me earlier; that there was some barrier standing between him and every woman he had known but that he didn't know what that barrier was. Besides, what good would it do to find the person that one had spent one's entire life looking for, but too late? Usually I didn't reply to his questions. I knew that I could help him better with silence than with words.

Two days before his departure we met for dinner at the restaurant overlooking the river. It was not the Ibrahim that I knew. He came a little late and sat down opposite me. He was pale and clasped his hands in front of him but that did not stop his fingers and hands from shaking. It seemed to me that his whole body was shaking as he nervously jiggled his legs under the table. I asked him as gently as I could, "What happened, Ibrahim?"

But instead of answering he asked me, "Can *you* tell me what happened? I mean why do we not know any real joy or even any true tranquility any more? Do you know how the order to deprive us of happiness was given?"

Keeping the same gentle tone as before I said to him, "A few days ago you spoke of coincidences that make us. You talked about your parents and you told me that what has tormented you all your life is injustice."

Somewhat perplexed he said, "I said that? How important is it? Is that the problem? I think injustice has tormented me as it has other people but that did not mean that their life came to an end. Life accepts justice and also accepts injustice."

"What do you mean by that?" I asked, cautiously.

"What do I mean? I don't mean anything. When I arrived here you asked me about Shadia, and since that time I've been thinking. But what is it that I wanted to say? Yes, I didn't want to be unfair to her. I did actually want her to leave me. While we were in detention, we didn't know when we would get out or if we would get out at any time. I thought she was a prisoner like me, sitting and waiting. I said I can at least set *her* free."

"But whereas that was your intention, Ibrahim, instead of setting her free, you destroyed her." I regretted that as soon as I said it. I wanted to apologize to Ibrahim, but he answered me without any irritation, totally impassively, "Couldn't it be that she has also destroyed me? Couldn't it be that I have spent my whole life looking for a Shadia that was and then was lost?"

He drank a whole glass of water in big gulps then filled it again and began to look at the river in silence. There was a lone, insomniac swan gliding slowly over the river's black surface, bending its long white neck, its beak buried in its chest. Ibrahim kept following it until it disappeared then, without looking in my direction, he said, "I love Brigitte."

"I know."

"Yes. I think you know. But what's to be done?"

"There's no need to tell you what you already know, Ibrahim. I think she's young and we've grown old."

"Why've we grown old?" And he turned towards me adding, somewhat angrily, "Why does time pass without leaving a mark on the soul? Without saying: here you stop loving and here you quit hope and here you stop thinking?"

Feeling his tension infecting me, I said, "Perhaps the marks are there but we ignore them."

Waving his index finger in my face he said, "Absolutely not. I don't find these marks within myself. I am still that child tormented by his mother's suffering. I am still living the same joy when Shadia said she loved me. I still see her shutting her eyes as she said it. I hear now the stinging of the whip on my body in prison and the first bomb in Beirut is still resounding in my ears. All of that is happening now, here on the bank of this river. So what does it mean when you talk to me about time? I mean, are you following what I'm saying? Death I understand, but what's the meaning of time? What does it mean that I tell you I love her and you talk to me about time? What's the connection?"

He fell silent; he was now taking quick, successive breaths as if he were choking. After a moment I said, "Listen. Did *she* tell you that she loves you? I heard her flirting with you that night when we met at Muller's hotel. Did she tell you later that she loves you?"

He shook his head slowly but emphatically.

"So, what are you blaming her for?" I said. He began to rub his forehead with his hand and said, "Did I say that I blame her? All I said is I love her."

He fell silent again before saying, "I've just come back from her house."

Something inside me twinged when he said that, but I didn't say anything. Then he began to speak in a soft, detached voice as if he were talking about something that happened to someone else. He was looking at the river through the glass window and occasionally looking at my face but I was almost certain that he did not see me. He said, "From the beginning, perhaps the day following our meeting at Muller's, I told her of my love for her. I couldn't help it. I couldn't think of anyone or anything else after she left that night with you. Even the word 'love' cannot adequately describe the thing that happened to me. What's that thing?

"The years of my entire life surged and all life was epitomized in one thing: I want this beautiful woman for myself. I want her here and I want her now. That will fix everything, all the mistakes and all the disappointments. Justice will be restored to the world. I was playacting when I was arguing with you or anyone else. I was lying. Even when I told her that I was ashamed to tell her of my love when she was that young and I that old, I wasn't being truthful. I felt that I was entitled to her, that there was nothing more natural in the world than that she would be mine. She spared me lying when she said, 'Why me? Many young women would love for you to flirt with them, so why me? I am not good enough for you!' She didn't want to say, 'You are not good enough for me.'"

Ibrahim smiled sadly as he stretched his hands towards me, "It had nothing to do with age or youth or anything else. I am ashamed to tell you this, but I have had relations with women younger than her. My problem with them was how to get rid of them, not how to pursue them. All there is to it is that she didn't love me. She was distant and hard to reach the whole time. But that night she was strange. She drank a lot and laughed. She said, 'I am celebrating my day off tomorrow.' She was more cruel than usual with Dr. Muller. Did you notice, as I did, that she'd always upbraid him in subtle ways and that his glances towards her are filled with guilt? Did he, like me, pursue her with his love? Why not? I will not blame him. What difference does it make if he was twenty, thirty years older than me? She called him 'Uncle Muller' as if she were insulting him, the word 'uncle' coming out of her mouth as if she were calling him names. She laughed for no reason and patted him on the hand. He kept his cool. He said to her, 'Don't have any more drinks, Brigitte.' But she said to him, 'What do you say we put an end to the list, Doctor? What do you say we stop at Pedro?' I didn't understand what she meant. But he blushed suddenly and gave her a long harangue in German while she interrupted him and answered him very coldly. When they were finished she looked towards me and said, 'Don't worry. Dr. Muller and I are used to these arguments just as you and your friend are used to them. But we are also friends, Dr. Muller and I. Right, Doctor?' He didn't seem to have heard her. He was sitting in his chair with bowed head, resting his arms on the arms of the chair. Then she got up. She was staggering and she said to me, 'As for you, your chivalry won't permit you to leave me like this. You will see me home, won't you?'"

Ibrahim fell silent for a moment and cupped his chin in his hand. I waited for him to continue but he was totally lost in thought. I couldn't control my eagerness as I asked him, "Then what? What happened?"

Startled, he came to and said, "Nothing happened."

"How?"

He whispered, grinding his teeth as if preventing himself from shouting, "I told you nothing happened. Don't ask me how. She was holding my hand in the cab, gripping it convulsively. Wasn't that what I'd dreamed of? As soon as we entered her apartment I took her into my

arms. I kissed her face and every inch of her and she was panting, her
eyes closed, trying to get out of her clothes while in my arms, whispering tensely, 'Yes, kiss me like that, like that, come on.'"

Then Ibrahim struck the table lightly with his hand and said, "So,
what happened? You tell me. Wasn't that what I had hoped for? Or perhaps it wasn't what I'd hoped for? She was trembling in my arms. She
was screaming in anger asking me what happened but I stood before her,
paralyzed, almost dying of shame and despair as she hit me with her fist
in my shoulder and asking me angrily, 'Why then? Why did you chase
me all that time?'"

"At our age, things like that happen, " I said softly trying to console
him.

He laughed nervously and said, "But you don't understand. What
happened was not impotence. I mean it was not my body that couldn't.
My body was quite ready, more ready than any other time, because I
wanted her so much. Another terror was paralyzing me, as if I felt that if
I touched her we would both die instantly."

"Wait a minute. Maybe I didn't understand. You say you wanted her,
and you were not physically impotent but you stopped? Why? I don't
understand."

"Nor did I. Nor did she. She thought I was making fun of her, that I
was playing with her, so she started throwing books and whatever she
could reach at me. She hurled insults at me saying I was crazy, a cow-
ard, and then looked at me in surprise. She saw copious tears coming
from my eyes and saw something in my face that made her stop her
insults and her fury. She came close to me, put her bare arms around my
neck and pressed my face into her chest, saying 'Don't worry. Forgive
me, please forgive me. Maybe it is my fault. I don't understand what's
happening, but maybe it's my fault.' She began to rock me on her chest
and talk gently to me as if she were talking to a child. Perhaps she also

was crying. That pity killed me even more than her earlier screams. I ran. I ran away. Believe me I was running in the streets like a person being chased. Nothing like that had ever happened to me before. So why did that happen to me with the woman that I desired like no other woman? Do *you* know?"

I shook my head and remained silent. Ibrahim smiled sadly turning his face away from me and whispered, "But I told you before. It is Shadia coming back to me at the end of life, coming back this time as a punishment."

His smile turned into a soft laugh as he grabbed my hand placed on the table with both his hands and looked at me for a long time before saying, "May God help *you*."

"What do you mean?" I cried.

6

Lorca's Drum
for the Poet's Blood

WHY THEN WAS I SO ANXIOUS that no day passed without meeting her? Why did I go to "our" café long before the time she usually came, my eyes fixed on the entrance? And why did my heart skip a beat as soon as I saw her in her blue uniform, walking on tiptoe as usual, her smile filling her face, filling the whole world around her? Why did I hide my embarrassment and my bafflement by talking at length about countries I had visited and people I had met, rather than talking about myself and about her? And why was I afraid of her straightforward gaze as she searched my face, behind all those empty words, for the truth? Why did Manar's picture fade and Brigitte's face become a constant fixture in my sleepless nights?

Despite that, the secret love that Ibrahim had guessed at was not everything. I, my own wounds exposed, wanted also to protect her, as if I were atoning for some sin or other, the nature of which I had no inkling of. I realized my helplessness. I knew that I couldn't repair what had happened in the past, nor heal those scars that her constant smile hid, nor make her cry. Perhaps she also felt that there was something else connecting me with her—something other than desire and love, that made her tell me her story in such a straightforward manner since that first evening in her apartment, enabling me to see her and know her. I saw Brigitte the child hitting with her little fists Muller's chest. I saw her at school, before her beautiful figure had developed, tallish for her age and

on the heavy side, wearing those thick prescription glasses, before contact lenses hit the scene, ashamed of her appearance and deeming her
nose too long. Outside the classroom at school she would be found in
remote corners, reading books. She loved the authors her father loved:
Hemingway, Lorca, and Goethe. She especially avoided boys. Back then
she didn't like men, as she told me, laughing. "That was before I discovered I couldn't live without them." One time, as she sat in the garden,
engrossed in a book, a student approached and dropped a letter in her lap.
She couldn't believe it; it was none other than Johann, that handsome
boy that half the girls in the school were after but whom none caught. He
also was shy like her. Did her aloofness and loneliness attract him to her?
Brigitte said, "We needed each other to discover ourselves and our bodies. When we held hands, we were able to go out to the wide world
through the narrow hole of fear. Then when we matured, we separated.
We're still close friends. After him I knew others. They were nice, but
none left a mark. At university there were the foreign students also. Girls
back then were whispering about African males. We only had six or
seven African students but they were very popular with the girls and very
unpopular with the boys, or so I thought. I mean, I thought they were
popular with the girls. Only when I knew Albert did I discover that for
the girls, it was just a matter of curiosity about the exotic, about that fer-
vid dancing for hours at the club, about that endless African joy as the
body danced. And, more importantly, curiosity to find out the joy of this
African sex that everyone talked about. Then after trying it, everybody
went back to their own corners: the girl to her Austrian boyfriend and the
African to his place in the forest.

"Albert was different. He was not the best at dancing. To the contrary,
he was most devoted to his studies. He also had his own worry: he did
not know when he was going back to his country.

"He had run away from the regime in his country and was pursued by it. He didn't know when the nightmare of that oppressive regime would end. He told me during our earliest meeting about that dictator who was in power those days, the one who ruined the country. He told me that before mad Macias ruled it, his country had been a happy oasis in that corner of Africa: everyone made a living and had a roof over their head. Everyone knew how to read and write at least, and those who wanted to pursue further education went to universities abroad. For the most part they went to Spain, the colonial power that had left behind its language. The local population of a few hundred thousand did not have enough manpower to develop and utilize the country's resources, so they imported workers from neighboring countries, from Nigeria and Cameroon, to help with the coffee and cocoa crops and mining gold and copper. When mad Macias took over, foreign workers fled, as did those of the local population who could. As for the thousands whom he put in jail, few of them survived. And in our country, Austria, there was a chocolate factory that used to import cocoa from there, before Equatorial Guinea stopped exporting even cocoa. In our town a few dissidents came together and put out leaflets and wrote to Europe's newspapers. I feared for Albert. Throughout our life together I feared for him after two of his colleagues disappeared without a trace.

"And so, I did not meet Albert in the dance hall but in the library. He was preparing a thesis on Lorca. At the beginning he needed my help to write his ideas in proper German, and I needed him to help me with Spanish. We sometimes went out of the library and strolled on the riverbank for hours, speaking a strange language that we had made up together, a bit of German that he didn't know well, a bit of Spanish that I was trying to learn, and a few words in English and French. We talked about Lorca and about Schiller, and about African authors that I had never heard of but whom he made me read and like: Achebe, Sembene Ousmane, Soyinka, and others. These are the ones I still remember. With him I discovered not only new writings but also a whole other world that enchanted me. And when I read a work I didn't like, he would get mad and tell me that I was like other whites, that I looked down upon others from above, even though I tried to hide it . . . I asked him, perplexed, how he expected me to understand in that poem those rituals and myths about which I know nothing? And he answered, 'And do I, the African, know your European myths? How do I know Oedipus and Faust? A person learns if he wants to understand.' It wasn't easy to learn, but I tried. And it wasn't easy to convince him of my love, but I tried. Love came naturally like walking or talking, when I held his hand on the street, when I kissed him on the cheek as a friend when we met. But when we exchanged our first real kiss on the riverbank, he asked me if I, too, wanted to try African men. I was barely able to prevent myself from slapping him, however I called him names in German, using obscenities I knew he didn't know, and left him standing there. I decided never to go back to that vain man. And when several days had passed without him coming to make up with me, when nothing was left in life except longing for him, I sought him out at his usual place in the library. I sat next to him in silence, opening a reference book with a trembling hand as my whole body called out to him, and he extended a reluctant hand towards me which I grabbed. He looked at me with a sad and guilty face, but he didn't say anything. Such was his pride.

"And yet Albert didn't care when he heard in or outside the university those crude words about Africans and blacks. He would say, 'These don't concern me in the least. You are the one I love and you are the one I care about because you are going to become one of us. As for the others, when I hear someone saying something like 'these African monkeys' or 'Why do these blacks remain here?' I know the quality of that person's mind and I don't waste my time even thinking about what he's said. I am not like the Africans who want others to recognize them. Let others go to hell. I want first of all to recognize myself. My worries are much bigger than dealing with these sickos. My worries are there, far away, with Macias.'

"I agreed totally with him. What does what others do or say matter, so long as he alone is my whole world? So long as I don't see those others when he's with me?

"But that was not enough for Uncle Muller. He also needed Albert to continue his own war. Back then Muller had started this human rights thing after he retired and closed his office. Albert and his friends used to go to him to help them with their battle against Macias. I can barely forgive myself to this day because it was I who introduced him to Muller. The Doctor formed a society to combat racism in our small town, which Albert and the other Africans and some foreigners studying at the university joined. Muller would invite his few Austrian friends and give speeches and organize demonstrations in public squares against racism and celebrate an Africa Day, and hold a symposium with such themes as "Towards One World," and so forth. And from that time the town changed. Before, life went on, but now, people were divided: they were either with his society, and these were ten persons at most, or against his society, and these were all the rest. Even those who used to hide their racism were now bragging that they were against the presence of blacks in town and were openly hostile to all people of color. It was an exciting opportunity for something to happen in the stagnant life of our little town, to have a big topic of interest to the people, a topic reminding them of the days of Aryan Fever and *Deutschland über alles* and those things.

"These days in particular he started to urge me and Albert to get married. We had been living together for some time and we were happy. Oh how happy we were! We spent the nights together in total harmony; we read at the same time, studied, talked, danced, made love. Everything in its time. A secret call from the mind and body and the whole being to which the other person responded, because that call came to both of us at the very same moment. And we had agreed. No, no; I am lying. There was no agreement but rather an understanding that we would go together to his country after Macias's fall and there we would get married. Then I would give him and his tribe ten boys—girls were not permitted. He would tell me 'boys who look like you' and I would tell him, 'No, boys as beautiful as you.' He thought I was mocking him and got angry but I kissed him and told him, truthfully, 'But I have not known beauty like your beauty, I haven't known anything more beautiful than your eyes glistening with love or burning with anger—I haven't known a mouth that's as perfect as the one made by those two full lips.' Albert laughed and asked me, 'Is it from Rimbaud?" and I said "No, it is you!"

"So how was all that lost when we got married? How was it lost when we were no longer just he and I, but he and I and Muller—and the world?

"My father didn't want us to get married. He told me in his way of speaking, 'But you're not a barmaid. This marriage would pass if you were a barmaid.' It was as if he could see everything. He advised us to wait just as we had decided earlier, to wait until Albert was done with the university and with Macias, then leave together. He told us what until that moment we did not understand well. He said that people in our country kept their eyes closed to our relationship as a passing whim, some kind of measured freedom that they permitted youth to have within limits. As for marriage, it's a crime, a stain on the whole white race that no one in our town would forgive. We didn't believe him. Once again my father lost the case and once again Muller won when he urged Albert, 'Come on. Let's teach them a lesson. Let's teach the folk in this town that the world has changed. They must understand finally that racism debases their humanity.' A lot of words that Muller kept feeding Albert, words like those he used in the leaflets of his ersatz society until he ultimately influenced him. As for me, it didn't make any difference. I told my father that even if the whole town shunned me, Albert was my town and I couldn't care less about anyone else.

"I was telling the truth but my father was right.

"After we were married no one visited us at home anymore, even those who used to before. At the university, students walked behind us in groups, not saying anything but the hateful glances in their eyes were unmistakable. We didn't care. When we went to the restaurant where we used to eat before, the waiter stood at the door, his arms crossed, and told us that all the tables were reserved. We saw most tables empty, but we didn't care. We laughed. We strolled in the streets of the town with his arm draped over my shoulder, responding to the jeering whistles by whistling back and singing loudly. When those sitting next to us on the bus or a movie theater got up, looking askance and with hatred at us, I threw down my coat on one seat and my purse on another, heaving a sigh of relief, and we didn't care.

"But did we really not care? Or was it that I, only, didn't care? I didn't notice soon enough that Albert had come to hate going out at night. I didn't notice that he spent long days on end in our small room, without going to the university. I didn't notice that he had begun to drink more than before. I came to understand later on what that meant. But in those days I was preoccupied with something more important; when Albert began to change, I also was changing; I was overcome with a new joy. I mean, when he began to receive only his African friends and stay with them in a corner of the room, drinking and speaking a language I did not understand, I was too preoccupied. His baby, which had begun to take over my body, also took my full attention, kept me from even studying for the end-of-the-year exams that were approaching. It was only later that I came to understand the meaning of that listless look in his eyes and those nervous laughs. I was totally engrossed in my own joy.

"And yet it would have been possible for everything to continue, to recover ourselves after a little while. It would have been possible that I would come to and figure out what was happening to Albert or that he would fall back on his old attitude of disdain of that stupidity and not care.

"Everything was possible until that Saturday night, when we went out together as we did in the old days to take a walk on the riverbank.

"It was a peaceful night. None of his friends had visited him and he hadn't had a drink. We were back as we had been before, talking about poetry and about Lorca. He agreed to my request and started reading out loud those beautiful lines from Lorca's 'Lament for Ignacio Sanchez Mejias.' I have never in my life known anyone read poetry like Albert, nor have I to this day been moved by anything like his way of reciting Lorca's pained lament of his friend, the bullfighter. His voice did not shake or change, it came out naturally from his strong larynx as if he were continuing the conversation we had before he read the poetry. Then gradually the whispering voice, the sad voice, turned into a plaintive African song in which the long vowels were lengthened even further to sound like deep continual moans, as if the lips never closed, to keep that anguish pouring continuously from that broad chest and from that roaring waterfall of his larynx. Little by little the cypress trees arrayed in an orderly manner on the Austrian riverbank disappeared and the solid stone houses that lined both banks dissolved to form a virgin forest, a hot forest embracing scattered cottages under a big silver moon. Suddenly Lorca takes off his hat and his Spanish garb to stand there, naked and black, beating the drums in that forest as he elongates his anguished groans over Ignacio, as

The dove and the leopard wrestle
at five in the afternoon.
And the thigh with a desolate horn
at five in the afternoon.

. . . .

And the bull alone with a high heart
at five in the afternoon.

  . . . .

Death laid eggs in the wound
at five in the afternoon.

  . . . .

A coffin on wheels is his bed
at five in the afternoon.

  . . . .

The wounds were burning like suns
at five in the afternoon.

  . . . .

It was five by all the clocks!
It was five in the shade of the afternoon!
Five in the afternoon.
Five in the afternoon.

"I was deep inside the forest, with the drums, with Lorca and Ignacio, with Albert, the world having stopped at five in the afternoon. Albert had his hand on my shoulder, his chanting carrying me to those sad distant drum beats. Together we were lost in that ecstasy because after a moment, just one moment, we will discover that elusive secret and will know why his grief for Ignacio has become all the grief in the world and why the sadness of these words creates that music which lifts our hearts above the earth and above time.

"But that moment never came! We had not noticed the noise coming from behind us. We didn't understand it at the beginning. It was Albert who stopped chanting when the noise was directly behind us on the deserted riverbank.

"They were seven or eight young men, totally drunk, having just come out of one of the bars that stayed open late on Saturdays. I was able to make out the faces of two students with us at the university but I didn't know the rest of them. They were singing a song that was popular at the time, changing the lyric to say, 'She is more than a woman, more than a woman. She's many whores in one.' Then they laughed and repeated it several times, their voices increasingly louder every time. I felt Albert's whole body stiffen, so I squeezed his arm as I whispered 'Let's go; they're drunk. Let's hurry away from here.' I was pulling him away from them but they advanced towards us and made a big circle around us so we couldn't escape. They began to dance keeping their legs apart, lifting their feet from the ground as much as their drunken bodies allowed them to do, imitating what they had seen in the movies about American Indians or Africans in the jungle. Albert tried to send them on their way by clapping and saying, 'Bravo! Tomorrow we'll finish this film, Tarzan,' and he pushed one of them so we could get out of the circle but they did not budge. One of them approached us, teetering, then lowered his pants and said as he felt around in his underpants, 'Look! Is the African better than this? Why do you go so far? Austrian goods are better. Come on, King Kong, let's compare,' and he reached for Albert's pants, trying to undo them. His own pants by that time had fallen to his feet. In his drunkenness he only needed one push from Albert to fall to the ground, stumbling in his undone pants. They also didn't need more than that to attack Albert with their fists and kicks and obscene insults. Albert was able to take off his belt and began to turn around himself brandishing the belt to keep them away while shouting to me, 'Run away. Call the police. Call for help.' But at that very moment while I tried to get out of the circle which had grown slightly less tight, one of them pushed me hard on the back and I fell to the ground, crying, 'Albert. Albert. They've killed my baby!' When they heard that and when they saw me writhing on the ground, with my hand between my thighs, they fell silent for a moment then they all ran away.

"But I had indeed lost my baby.

"I lost not only the baby, but Albert too. And I lost not only Albert, but myself as well. That was my 'five in the afternoon.' After the first few days at the hospital and after the police investigations, I went back home. Muller was busy organizing a demonstration and making posters on which they wrote 'The Murderers' and drew hands dripping with blood and the like. I was determined not to join that demonstration, but he took Albert with him. Afterwards Albert told me it was bigger than all Muller's previous demonstrations and that people were following its progress in silence on the sidewalks. That gave me no relief whatsoever. On the contrary I felt angry, as if I had had to lose my baby for them to feel guilty. I yelled at Albert, 'Enough already! Tell Muller to stop this nonsense. Tell him to shut up. Tell him to die!'

"That was one of the few times that I said anything at all. Those days I spent most of the time in bed, lying wide-eyed in silence with Albert there on his seat in the corner, drinking and pretending to read. Sometimes a whole day would pass without exchanging a word and without eating and without even remembering that we hadn't eaten. At that time my father came over almost every day, bringing us food and cleaning the mess that had accumulated in our room, washing the dishes and glasses and yelling at us for leaving the room without any ventilation. Letting him do whatever he wanted, we murmured apologies, 'You shouldn't have. Please don't trouble yourself. We were going to clean the house,' and so forth. He didn't pay any attention to what we said. It was he alone whose feet were firmly on the ground. He, my father, who had at the time decided to retire, was once again an angry young man, a warrior. He was determined to find the young men and to take them to court. He worked as a detective, an investigator and attorney. He asked me one day to go with him to the university to identify one of those young men whose description I had given and whom he believed he had found. I told him that I was not leaving the house and that he should calm down and leave this job to the police. I asked him if that would bring back my baby. My father slapped me in the face and carried me from the bed and forced me to change my clothes and pushed me out of the house. He was determined this time to win the case and for the first time he actually did. He was able to find them and take them all to court. His statement was strong and his argument was persuasive so they put three of them in jail, and so it was over and everyone's conscience was salved. My father also insisted at the time that we go back to our studies and take the exams. He came by every night after work in his office to make sure that we were at least opening the books and reading. I don't know how I passed my exams, but Albert flunked.

"I was almost ashamed of myself because I'd passed, ashamed because I had my father who stood by me whereas Albert was alone without family or relatives in this city that hated him. I had started to recover. No. Wrong. I never recovered. With the blood that came out between my thighs that Saturday night something else came out and has never returned. Another Brigitte appeared. I don't know exactly what was lost. Perhaps the first thing was that poetry no longer moved me. I no longer asked Albert to read to me as I used to. And he, at the same time, no longer read poetry or anything else; he just sat at home and drank. I tried everything I could. I went to his African friends and asked them to visit him and encourage him to get out of the house, to ask him to write articles against Macias as he used to. I even went to Muller and begged him to entice him back to his African society and to human rights in the hope that Albert would go back to normal. And Muller would indeed come and talk with Albert, who remained silent or laughed for no reason or argued with Muller in a mock serious tone. But once he told him, almost whispering, 'Listen, if I was not able to protect my own baby, how do you expect me to defend strangers?'

"Muller said, 'You will protect other people's babies and you will protect your next baby. We cannot change the world overnight, but we have to work. If they've insulted you, why give in?'

"Every time Muller came he harangued Albert with those hollow speeches and Albert would get up and go with him just to get him to shut up, I believe. As for the next baby that Muller talked about, it never came. Perhaps we, both of us, were anxious for it not to come.

"Then Albert obstinately dug in his heels and no longer went to Muller or anywhere else. The African friends also stopped coming. I told myself that perhaps they had grown tired of him; all he did now was to drink until he got drunk. I got a summer job so we could live and to save for the following year's tuition. Albert did not work. He paid tuition and lived on a monthly sum sent to him by his family, which had fled to Spain and had managed to smuggle out some of its money. When we started living together, he was careful that the two of us did not spend anything beyond that sum. He did not let me spend anything on the house or ask my father for help. Now, however, that sum was barely enough for one week of drinking day and night. He was no longer too ashamed to ask me for money, and when I refused to give him anything, in the hope that he would stop drinking and get a grip on himself, he cried and begged and promised that that would be the last time, that he would also look for a job the following day. But that never happened. To the contrary, I began to notice that money would disappear from my purse and when I asked him about it, he denied and swore and pretended to be angry. Once, as I was coming home from work in the evening I heard while still on the stairs many sharp and angry voices in our room. Alarmed, I went in and found all his African friends there. They were surrounding him as he sat on his chair, drunk, his head hanging down on his chest as he often was in those days. They were calling him names and did not pay any attention to me when I came in. To the contrary, one of them held him by the collar of his shirt and lifted him up a little and said to him, 'Speak!' Then they dropped him back in his place but Albert said nothing.

"'What happened? Tell me what happened,' I shouted as I tried to reach my husband. One of them, shaking with anger, replied, 'This bastard, this traitor is writing to Macias! True or not?'

"I looked at him as they all were doing. We all looked at him as he stayed silent for a while, looking at the faces around him before settling on my face for a long time, then said slowly and calmly, in Albert's old, real voice, 'I haven't betrayed anyone.'

"Once again he began to look with his red eyes at their faces, one by one, with a strange smile on his lips, before he burst out laughing as he said, 'Because you are really happy here? Answer me. Because you're really happy here, you don't want to go back there?' and he spat to one side as he said that. One of them slapped him in the face. Another, looking at me with eyes bloodshot with anger: 'This European woman is the cause!' But they pulled him away and they went out murmuring apologies. But I alone knew. I was certain that he was right. Yes, this European woman is the cause."

I lived for a long time with Brigitte's words that flowed that night in her Japanese room. When she finished it was late at night but she sat there on the floor, in the darkened room, her hair down and almost hiding her face, and her shoulders drooping. She said to me without raising her head, "How did all this talking start, anyway? Why, after accepting years of silence, do I feel I have to speak? And yet I haven't gotten rid of any burden. I feel all the old hurt coming back, so why did I have to speak now?"

Then she raised her head slowly and said, "Forgive me, but would you leave me alone?"

I left her and afterwards behaved indeed like that casual neighbor on the train to whom one revealed all one's secrets. I had met her several evenings with Ibrahim and Muller before both of them left and I made no reference at all to that night she took me into her confidence, nor did she. Those days she and I were both spending a lot of time with Ibrahim. I didn't see her with him the day he left. At the airport Ibrahim and I embraced affectionately and our eyes welled up with tears. Enmity had not only been erased, but, now that each of us had revealed his wounds to the other and seen the scars, deep affection between us grew, as if we had never harbored any enmity towards each other at any time.

From the airport I went directly to the café and I found her there. Was it a coincidence or did she know my routine and was waiting for me? I didn't ask her about that but we started meeting everyday at noon. I didn't miss a day nor did she, even during the holidays. We didn't make appointments or agree to meet or anything but after I gave her a ride to her office and before she got out of the car she'd say, "See you later," and we would both know that we would be at the café the following day at the same time.

Those first days it was I who spoke. I also didn't know why I had an overwhelming desire to talk about myself and my concerns. The first time we met she said, "This evening I want to talk," but during our noon-time meetings it was I who was overcome with the desire to talk. At the beginning I told her my story with Manar, at least what I could figure out of that story, what I was unable to tell Ibrahim or anyone else, and what was pursuing me day and night. I told it with the same simplicity with which she had told me her story. I told it all at once, without hesitation. And I also did not feel that I had gotten rid of any burden, but I had to tell it.

To assure myself that what was happening between us was not love, I told myself many things: what we shared was our own love of poetry at a time when poetry was irrelevant; that I, alone and far from home, took her as a surrogate for my children; that I pitied her because of what had happened to her; that despite the age difference we were friends united by homesickness, why not? But something unsettled deep down inside me was scoffing at all these musings.

In the course of our daily confessions there was no longer anything that we hid from each other. I asked her once about Albert and she said she no longer followed news of him after the divorce. It was he who left her and went back to Africa after all his colleagues shunned him and after he flunked repeatedly. She told me nonchalantly, "I heard that he's become his country's ambassador somewhere. Maybe now he's a minister. I don't know and I don't want to know." Then she said in a way that suggested she did not want to pursue the subject, "The world has ended what was between me and Albert."

And yet there was one thing that she never talked to me about. Perhaps she was certain I knew even though I'd said nothing. I had not alluded, directly or indirectly, to what had taken place between her and Ibrahim, and she did not say anything about it.

Then gradually we stopped talking about our personal affairs. After a while I noticed that I was the one doing the talking and that most of the time she sat in silence, listening intently as if all those meaningless stories about my travels and my childhood and my friends were things so important that she shouldn't miss a word. From time to time she would ask me to read her some poetry in Arabic and would listen, fixing her eyes on me and raising her hand if I tried to translate a poem or even just one verse. She would say, "What good would that do? Don't you understand that the more ignorant I am of the words, the more the poetry penetrates me?" Sometimes she surprised me. Once when I had finished reading a poem by Salah Abd al-Sabur she said, "What a sad rhythm! Like the rhythm of tears reluctantly dropping from the eye." Another time when I read to her part of Imru al-Qaais's famous ode, she smiled and said, "Here's a peaceful caravan, slowly making its way through the desert and suddenly the enemy horses are rushing it from every direction. Don't you hear this tumult?"

That's what she used to say before we stopped even the poetry, before my avalanche of daily chatter started, while she listened and I was afraid of being silent. I think also that I was afraid that she might get bored with me so I kept entertaining her with stories like a child. I didn't know before that time that I was capable of talking for so long or that I had such a reservoir of memories. She seemed to enjoy it as she listened. Or, I wonder, was she hoping the whole time that I would stop jabbering and shout out the truth? But how could I dare? How, when she's half my age? How, after all I have known of her life? What do I have over Albert? Am I not like him a man of color, a foreigner and an exile? I have no place here or there just as he had none. And, first of all, where do I get his youth? And what do I have over Muller? Don't I, like him, drone on and on, using big words? Sometimes I would notice. Actually it was she who drew my attention to it: whenever I slipped into talking about politics or what was happening in my county, she would interrupt me, holding her head between her hands and saying apologetically, "Let's talk about something else, please. One experience is enough."

But everything changed after what happened in Lebanon.

I was sitting at the café that morning in June, hunched over the newspapers I had bought, the Arabic, English, and French papers, trying to extract something from between the lines, to predict the change that would finally take place in Lebanon and in Egypt and everywhere in the homeland. I was agitated and enthusiastic when Brigitte came in and I didn't notice until she stood in front of me. I greeted her quickly as I gathered the newspapers to clear the table. As soon as she sat down I began to tell her of what I'd read and heard on the radio. I told her, "Israel has launched a comprehensive war on the Arabs on the strange pretext that a person or persons unknown shot its ambassador in London."

But Brigitte kept listening to me without emotion and finally as I was going full steam relating details, she interrupted me with a sullen face, "Enough already! Haven't I told you before? I don't read any newspapers and I have neither radio nor television in my house. I don't want to know anything about this world that I don't understand. Wasn't it you who told me the first time we met that this life is a lie?"

I said to her angrily, pounding the papers piled in front of me, "But this blood is very real!"

She replied calmly, "It was not we who shed this blood nor we who can stop it."

I got up, quite beside myself and said, "This is the quintessence of callousness!"

It was the first time that I had quarreled with her. I told her, as I gathered my newspapers piled on the table, that she used her personal story as an excuse for her selfishness, to live totally indifferent to everything like all the others. I told her she at least should have appreciated what war meant to me even if it did not mean anything to her.

As I was leaving, she grabbed my hand and said in a beseeching tone, "So be it. I am as you say and worse, but please don't go. Let's stay friends just as we are. I don't want to lose you too!"

However, I jerked my hand away angrily and left. In those days I stayed away from her, living at a feverish pace, cutting newspaper clippings in all languages and watching all news programs on television and writing every day a lengthy report to my newspaper in Cairo about reactions in Europe to this massacre. I translated the angry commentaries and described the demonstrations that leftist parties organized. I turned the radio dial from Morocco to Cairo to Baghdad waiting at every moment for something to happen, something other than these pictures with which television and the papers assaulted my eyes every minute. I was waiting for anything to change this humiliation.

But nothing happened.

Nothing but tanks and bombs, flying and leveling, and planes shelling, and Israel's healthy soldiers smiling at my face on the screen, raising their machine guns in victory salutes. In the refugee camps naked children and mothers wearing plastic slippers ran, slapping their own faces in the midst of huts whose roofs had slid down on their walls to create jagged piles of rubble, of dust and bricks and twisted iron rods amid black and white smoke. And Egypt expresses regret and the economics committee holds a meeting to discuss the five-year plan. And Tyre falls and Sidon falls and the Ain el-Helweh refugee camp is razed and Rashidiyyeh and Miyya-Miyya refugee camps fall and are burned down. Saudi Arabia expresses regret and announces that the new crescent moon has been verified and sends messages to the kings and presidents. Algeria denounces the war, and announces extending new incentives to foreign investors. And the planes are all over Beirut: 200 dead, 400 wounded, 90 dead, 180 wounded. Just figures reported in the news. A whole street burns down and all its buildings lose their facades after it is hit with fuel air explosives. The pictures show the remnants of life in the bare rooms: overturned tables, children's toys stained with blood, photographs, and small statues of the Virgin Mary smashed on the floor in the midst of fires and corpses lying on their backs and others doubled on their sides. A paralyzed old woman in a shelter is sitting in a wheelchair, trying to push it forward or backward in the middle of a ward that has lost its walls but the stones scattered on the floor impede her movement in any direction. She lifts the white shawl off her head and cries.

The image of that woman keeps haunting me at night as I struggle with sleep. I am haunted by the image of a terrified man running in the street amidst the din of guns, carrying a severed human arm wrapped in a newspaper dripping blood. Why is he carrying that arm? I am haunted by the image of Israeli soldiers driving before them, with rifle butts, blindfolded young men whose hands are tied behind their backs. But I tell myself that tomorrow, in the morning, everything will change. This cannot go on if Israel has done this because an ambassador, one person, was injured—a volcano of anger will erupt in us as we see and hear of hundreds dying every day. Our sense of honor could not have been lost forever; after all it is blood and not ice that runs in our veins. Anger will erupt in the morning!

But in the morning comes the second ceasefire, the third, the fifth, and the American envoy comes and the American envoy goes, the seventh ceasefire, an ambulance speeding in the burning streets, its loud siren wailing, Israel cuts off water and electricity to Beirut, a little barefoot girl with disheveled hair is using a mug to fill a jerry can with sewage water. In places other than Beirut nothing happens. The Norwegian nurse tells me that all I've seen on television and all I've read in the papers is something other than the truth.

One morning when I hadn't slept well as had been the case since the war began, Bernard called me and said, "Come right away! There's something important about Lebanon that you must hear."

I went to his café. He was waiting for me with a blonde lady, on the heavy side, about forty years old. He introduced her to me saying, "This is Marianne Eriksson, a nurse from Norway who left Lebanon yesterday. She is spending the day here en route to her country."

She said with a faint smile, "I was kicked out of Lebanon. There is a difference."

I studied her pale face and bloodshot eyes as she leaned her back to the seat languidly, her hands hanging down her sides, yet making an effort to appear awake and alert. I said to myself, this is a woman who needs to sleep, not talk.

She turned to Bernard and said with that tired smile, "Even the expulsion was a problem. Did I tell you how they expelled us? They were detaining us in the hospital after closing it and the Norwegian ambassador kept trying to get us repatriated for five days, to no avail. Each time they found an excuse for keeping us in detention: once because they didn't work on Saturdays, another time because the officer in charge of giving permits was on field furlough. The ambassador told me that their commander told him, "What's the hurry to leave? The girls are having fun . . . ""

She emitted a subdued laugh then fell silent. Bernard, who appeared unusually dejected, said, "Forgive us."

She looked at him in surprise and said, "But what did *you* do that I should forgive you?"

Then she clasped her hands on the table and said to me, "Are you going to publish what I say to you? Bernard says he'll try but he is not promising anything. Are you sure that you will publish?"

I avoided her eyes, which looked straight at me, and said, "I also am not sure but I'll try."

She asked me what newspaper I worked for and I told her, "A newspaper in Egypt."

She nodded and said, "I understand." Then she fell silent for a moment, "Or, actually, I don't understand. But where would you like me to begin?"

I said, "I'd like to know something about you first."

"You're right. I work, I mean I used to work, in the Ain al-Helweh refugee camp in the south with other foreign nurses. We were assisting the Palestinian doctors and nurses there. Do you know that refugee camp?"

"No. I visited Beirut about twenty years ago but I didn't go to the south."

"Even if you had seen it back then, I don't think you would have recognized it now, before it was destroyed by the war. I've been told that the camp had changed considerably over the last twenty years. It was no longer just a refugee camp. When I saw it the first time about two years ago it looked like a village or a small suburb of Sidon. It had about seven or eight hundred houses overcrowded with inhabitants, Palestinian and Lebanese, who had no place outside the camp." She fell silent again and Bernard intervened, saying,

"Listen, Marianne, we don't want to overburden you. I've taken down the most important points that you've mentioned to me and I can give them to my colleague . . ."

Marianne interrupted him, saying, "No, on the contrary, I am anxious that your friend also hear what happened." I took the tape recorder and placed it in front of her and said nothing after that. It was she who pointed out to me that the tape had stopped and asked me to replace it.

She said, "I will tell you only what I saw with my own eyes. When the planes appeared and the raid began on the ground floor of the clinic. I forgot to tell you that our clinic was not a war hospital. Our work ordinarily was to treat physically and mentally handicapped children, and also to provide first aid to routine cases before referring them to hospitals. We had two other nurses from Norway who were not used to the sound of bombs. I also was frightened even though I had lived through such raids before. We heard of what happened at the Rashidiyyeh refugee camp two days earlier, so we went down to the shelter, I mean the ground floor of the clinic, and quickly prepared places for the children and moved them there. I knew that such raids ended in half an hour at the most. After the raid, as usual, there were some dead and some wounded and some homes that were destroyed and a lot of shrapnel. Near the shrapnel we also found leaflets in Arabic dropped by the planes telling the inhabitants to evacuate the refugee camp because shelling would begin in a while.

"But it didn't begin in a while. It began at once, before we could even bandage the wounds of the victims of the first raid. The male nurses rushed with their stretchers carrying critical cases to the ambulances. Each one of us carried one or two of the wounded children. People were running to the shelters dug into the ground when the bombs started falling again. Those who were nearby took refuge in the clinic because it had the flags of the Red Crescent and the Red Cross and because it was distinguished from all the other buildings by its white paint and was supposed to be spared the bombing. The fact that so many people came to the clinic was not something bad; we asked those who were healthy among them to help us in preparing places for the rest of the children and women on the ground floor and we recruited some of them to help in administering first aid to the wounded who didn't stop arriving at our ill equipped clinic. We were busy working on the casualties of the air raids in the evening when we heard a new kind of shelling, preceded by a lengthy whistling sound then a muffled racket followed by successive explosions, concussions in the buildings, and earth tremors.

"Some people said in panic, 'The tanks and heavy artillery have arrived.' To our wounded were added those who were hit by flying glass from the windows that had withstood earlier raids but which were shattered in these explosions. To them were also added many more who were able to reach the clinic from neighboring houses and shelters. Some came in carrying their children or mothers or wives asking us to treat them without noticing that they themselves had bleeding heads or chests. Some rushed in screaming with their clothes and bodies on fire and many dropped dead as soon as they entered the clinic. We were unable to treat these newcomers with anything more than sedatives and ointments. We began to assist the doctors as they performed emergency operations that neither they nor we were trained to perform: amputating arms and legs, eye surgeries, head surgeries, and all kinds of other procedures. The wounded kept coming. There was no longer room to move in the clinic. Our original patients, the handicapped children, I mean those among them that were able to move, were running everywhere covering their ears with their hands and screaming, wanting to get out. Some wanted to throw themselves out of the window to escape the concussions and the racket. It was very difficult to assign one of the nurses familiar with their conditions to take care of them under such circumstances.

"At a moment when the shelling stopped, the Belgian doctor Francis Capet took a chance and said, 'I'll try something with the Israelis.' He took an ambulance and packed it with as many burn victims and critical cases as he could and he drove to the entrance of the refugee camp but he returned less than half an hour later to tell us that the Israelis refused to take the wounded and told him that they would not offer him any help unless he handed over the terrorists, meaning the Palestinian doctors and nurses who worked with us at the clinic. Doctor Capet whispered in my ear that he was barely able to get the Lebanese government hospital in Sidon to take ten of the wounded he had taken with him. He said that the hospital was also overcrowded, that the situation there was as bad as the situation here. He didn't have the time to tell me more than that nor did I have the time to listen. Our clinic ran out of medications and there was nothing left to offer by way of first aid except words and putting covers over the faces of the dead.

"In the morning everything was over. I mean everything in the refugee camp was gone: the houses, the people, everything. When I went out for a few moments at dawn I did not recognize the place. There were fires in the few houses that were still standing and flames and smoke coming out of the rubble of the houses that had been destroyed. There were a few people going through the ruins, looking for their relatives or for the bodies of their relatives. There was no other sound except the coughing and soft, muffled moaning that you didn't know whether it came from the standing houses or from the rubble. On the ground, bodies and body parts were everywhere, especially around the shelters. I'll explain something about these shelters; they were holes in the ground that were covered and lined with concrete. They worked to some extent against air raids because unless the roof was penetrated directly by the bomb, the shelter provided protection from the shrapnel. But with the heavy artillery that was blasting the houses and the land, most of these shelters turned into tombs for those who took refuge in them. Dozens of them, children, men and women had crowded into those shelters. I saw one of them that had turned into a small pond in which heads, legs and arms floated. Of the floating bodies I was able to count . . ."

I noticed that her voice was choking and that she was signaling me to stop the recording, so I pushed the button. She was overcome with tears that she couldn't stop, and she kept wiping the corners of her eyes with her finger and saying, "Please excuse me. I am a professional nurse. I've seen a lot of pain and many different things in my life and I've gotten used to it, but when I saw . . ."

I said in a weak voice, "If it gives you pain to speak, this is enough."

The intermittent whistling had started in my ear and the headache at the back of the head and I really wished she would stop but she said, "No, no matter what, I must say what I've seen and you must publish it."

Seeking his help, I turned to Bernard who was resting his chin in his hand and watching us with a slightly open mouth and he said, "Yes, Marianne. I told you I've written a summary." Then, as if talking to himself, "I thought we had made some progress since Genghis Khan."

Marianne replied, "I don't know what to tell you. I didn't have any children and I was somewhat sad on that account, but when I saw the anguish of all the mothers there and all those children . . ." Then she overcame her thoughts and said with some determination, "Let's continue. Do you want me to repeat the last part?"

I said, almost screaming, "No!"

Then I added quickly, "I mean, your voice is clear. I can understand it."

"Well then, I'll continue from where I stopped. Not much more remains in any case."

With a heavy heart I pushed the record button and Marianne continued, "I went back to the clinic, running and crying. I decided to repeat the attempt that Doctor Capet had made the day before. I knew that if a Palestinian driver drove the ambulance, the Israelis would kill him at once. So I drove the car myself and took with me a Dutch nurse and we stacked the critical cases that needed emergency aid into the ambulance. One of these cases was a woman named Khadra al-Dandashi. I knew her because she had come originally from the Rashidiyyeh refugee camp after the Israelis entered it and arrested her husband. In our camp she suffered a deep wound in her shoulder and her arm was hanging down swollen with shrapnel and clotted blood. It had to be amputated but we had no equipment and no medications. I took her with the others to the government hospital but there was no space available. I took her to a private hospital we previously had dealings with and I met the hospital owner whose name is Ghassan Mahmud.

"He took me to his office. Ghassan was polite but firm as he told me that he could not take my patients. He told me that it was a private hospital that had a reputation to protect and, "Your patients are too dirty. I must protect the reputation of the place." Nothing would make him relent so I took my patients and left them in front of the gate of the government hospital. Khadra al-Dandashi was unconscious and I don't know if she survived or not.

"When I went back the Israelis had entered the camp. They arrested all the Palestinian doctors and nurses and they took all the wounded young men, beating them and driving them by force. Doctor Francis said to them, 'Arrest the doctors and nurses here in the hospital. I have wounded and sick women and children and I need these doctors.'

One of the soldiers told him, 'Shut up, terrorist. Shut up, Baader Meinhoff. Maybe we'll come back and take you too.'"

Marianne was talking and the tape was recording but I no longer heard anything but the intermittent whistling in my ear and a few scattered words: Rashidiyyeh, Naqura, the shelters, the rubble, the Norwegian ambassador. At the end I noticed a long silence then I heard Marianne saying in a loud voice, "Do you want to ask about something specific?"

I said without thinking, "Yes; how did you get out of Lebanon?"

Marianne looked at me in surprise as she answered, "But I told you that from the beginning and I've just repeated it. I said the Norwegian ambassador in Tel Aviv intervened to get us released and repatriated after they detained us in the clinic without work."

The whistling in my ears was turning into ringing, so I said again, without thinking, "Yes. I'm sorry. But why did you go to Lebanon in the first place?"

When I noticed the look of surprise on her face begin to give way to anger, I tried to apologize. But Bernard broke the silence to tell Marianne, "My friend wants to know what made you take the risk of working in Lebanon. To be even more frank he would like to ask about your political inclinations. Isn't that so?"

I nodded, confirming what he had said, saying, "That is indeed what I wanted to ask about. Are you, for instance . . ."

Marianne interrupted me, the pitch of her voice rising a little as she said, "No, I am not, for instance. I am not anything, for instance. I am not a communist. I am not a leftist. I am not a member of the Baader Meinhoff nor the Red Army as the Israelis would call us by way of insult. I am not a member of any party or organization of any kind."

"Then why?"

"I went for the first time with my doctor husband in response to an advertisement. They needed a doctor and a nurse for the treatment of handicapped children. That is my specialization. The advertisement fit us perfectly." Then she hesitated for a moment before saying, "But I will admit that after I went there like any ordinary nurse the first time, I went afterwards because I could not believe what I saw. I could not believe that a whole people is subject to being killed at will and to having such cheap blood. I still do not believe that all those thousands are dying because one individual was shot by an unknown person in London."

After a moment of silence I found myself repeating what Bernard had said at the beginning, "Forgive us."

"What have *you* also done that I should forgive you?"

Once again I fell silent and the whistling in my ear returned. When she got up to leave I shook her hand mumbling another apology. She said impatiently, "I don't understand why you and Bernard are apologizing. But please, do something. Write the truth."

As he shook her hand, with a tired smile on his lips, Bernard said, "Write the truth? That's more difficult than saving your wounded in Lebanon, believe me. But who knows?"

We were walking in silence in the street, Bernard and I. It occurred to me for a moment that if I had helped Yusuf with the newspaper that he wanted to publish with his millionaire friend, I would have been able to write what I wanted about Marianne's testimony. I also remembered that one of my friends worked for an Arabic magazine in Paris and that he had asked me to write for that magazine.

I said out loud, "But what good would publishing in Arabic in Europe do in any case? To whom will we be speaking?"

Bernard was busy with his own thoughts and he turned to me, saying, "Sometimes we forget. But isn't our profession to tell the truth no matter what the price?"

I laughed loudly.

"What happened to you? Why are you laughing like that?" Bernard asked.

I stood there on the street and said to Bernard in shock, "You're asking me what happened to me? You're really asking me?" I remained standing for a while looking at his surprised face, then waved goodbye to him and went on my way.

When I arrived at my apartment I took two aspirins and sat at the desk right away. I put the recorder and tapes in front of me. The desk was cluttered so I spent some time organizing the piled newspapers. I threw away the papers from which I had already clipped important material and I arranged the other papers that I hadn't read or opened. Then I put the clippings on top of the papers on a corner of the desk. I tried the pencil I used for writing then sharpened several others and placed them next to the notepad.

I looked at the photo of Khalid and Hanadi on the desk then raised my eyes and looked at the smiling Abd al-Nasser and asked him, "What should I write?"

I asked him, "What should I do? I've tried everything. I wrote a story at least one half-page long with the headline, 'Europe Horrified by Beirut Massacres.' It was published in a half column with the headline, 'European Countries Criticize Israel's Stand.' In one article I quoted at length paragraphs from reports by the Red Cross and human rights groups which talked about shelling hospitals and the use of internationally banned phosphorus bombs and cluster bombs, and all of that was deleted from the article. Every time I tone down my language so that the article might be published. I quote what neutral sources say and I don't express my own opinions. I wrote of a US Congressman, an American this time, who stopped over in this city on his way back from Beirut. I wrote that he said that what was happening in Beirut was the crime of this era. I quoted him saying, 'The US pays Israel seven million dollars in aid every day. This is the money that is used to kill children and women in Beirut,' and the story was published as 'American Senator Proposes Reducing Aid to Israel!'

"What should I do? What should I write? In any case I cannot include Marianne's testimony in the monthly letter. How? 'Norwegian nurse walks on her hands for 14 hours and tells what she has seen in Beirut?' 'Norwegian nurse breaks record of counting corpses?' What should I do?"

I remained seated for a while with the pencil in my hand, then I went to the kitchen and made a cup of coffee. I doubled the amount of coffee and stood holding the little coffeepot over the very low flame carefully watching the bubbles as they made their way up to the top so that it wouldn't boil over or spill. I brought the coffee back as I thought to myself: Yes, Bernard, more difficult than saving the wounded in Beirut!

I drank the coffee quickly and my heart began to pound. But I sat at the desk and picked up the pencil and wrote a headline, "Norway's Ambassador Protests Detention of Nurses." Then I crossed it out and began to draw squares and pyramids on the paper.

I picked up the first clipping in front of me. It was from an Arabic newspaper published in Paris. The author was asking, "How long will the silence last? What happened? Didn't our blood flow in anger against the French in Damascus and in Tunis and in pursuit of independence? What happened to that blood? Where did we lose that sense of honor that made a man rise to help his brother? Forget about men! The sense of honor that made wolves in the forest get together to defend themselves against a tiger or a lion. Are we worse than wolves and beasts?"

The other clippings repeated the same question, "How? Why?" The same expressions. "Shame! Silence, conspiracy," and such.

I asked myself, "What's left to be said then?" I asked myself, "Who are these authors addressing or appealing to exactly? What sense does it make that we keep asking each other what happened? As if there were other Arabs, other than us, who are asking—Arabs who are hidden in a magical place whom we expect to appear and act on behalf of all of us!"

What should I do? I got up and began to pace the room.

Shall I make another cup of coffee? What good will it do?

The area I was moving in was very small; I walked three steps then returned to the desk. As I stood there I picked up the first newspaper under the clippings. On the first page there was a picture that I recognized. I read the news story and the severe ringing returned to my ear. I sat on the chair at once holding the paper in my trembling hands. I said to myself perhaps I didn't understand. I read the story again. No, there's no hope to unread what you have read! You've already read it and that moment at which you were still in the dark and he was still alive will never return, not ever. Yes, Khalil Hawi has shot himself in the head in Beirut. This happened. It is over. There's no hope to "unknow" it.

I left the living room and stretched out on the bed with my clothes on. I began to press my heart with my hands as if I could calm it.

So, you are fearful for your life? You fear these fast beats and the ringing in the ear? Don't be afraid. You won't die. Your stone heart will survive the story of Ain al-Helweh and the strong coffee and the death of the poet. Have no fear. If your heart were pumping real blood you would have been there now, next to him, dead, to his right. Have no fear. Nothing will happen to you.

I jumped out of bed and went to the living room and stood in front of Abd al-Nasser. I asked him why Ghassan Mahmud was alive and Khalil Hawi dead. Why do those who believed you and your vision die? He had seen us, as you yourself said, washing in the morning in the Nile, the Jordan, and the Euphrates. So why did you lie to him? Why did you raise and hold close to your bosom those who betrayed you and betrayed us? Those who sold you and sold us? Why is it that only Ghassan Mahmud stays alive? Don't defend yourself and don't argue with me! Khalil Hawi has committed suicide. Besides, what do you want to say? That we could have done something? How, when Khalil Hawi had nothing but his ribs which he made into a solid bridge from the caves of the East, from the swamp of the East to the New East? What New East when there's nothing left but the caves, the swamps, and Ghassan Mahmud? How did you want him not to shoot himself in the head? His weapon was good for nothing else. What do you think?

Don't cry! Especially, don't cry! And there's no need for that rasp in the voice or for a decree from the President of the Republic to nationalize the International Company of the Suez Canal, an Egyptian Shareholding Company, and there's no need, for a great country has come into being to protect and threaten and preserve and waste, and there's no need for that ringing in the ear because I can't stand it, you hear?

Then what's that glass shattered on the floor?

And where does that ringing come from?

Who's shouting?

What's falling?

7

Tender Night, Gentle Garden

ONE THING FOLLOWED ANOTHER.

Then came tranquility and beauty. Then the black cat was chasing the mouse and the mouse snatching the cheese. Then the cat was putting the bomb in the cheese to explode in the mouse and the mouse throwing the cheese at the cat and when it exploded the cat fell on its back but only its hair and tail burned. Then it became a cat again, chasing the mouse. Afterwards comes the fat funny man beating the thin funny man or maybe vice versa. Then comes Charlie Chaplin to say that tomorrow the sun will rise and birds will sing and flowers will bloom and to eat his shoe when he goes hungry. I smile at Charlie and when my eyes get tired I turn on the radio next to my bed and sweet music comes from it which says, "Sleep, sleep, sleep," so I go to sleep.

In the daytime I walk a little and spend some time in the lounge, watching television or watching and being watched by fellow patients with whom I exchange smiles and small talk. In the lounge the television shows the same programs as those on the small set over my bed. There are no news or other real programs, nothing that has anything to do with the real world, just cartoons and some commercials for antacids and toothpaste, screenfuls of beautiful young women flashing their white teeth and grinning from ear to ear. In that lounge of the cardiology floor we sit for hours, snug in the robes we wear over the white hospital gowns which make us feel naked, our sleepy eyes following Mickey Mouse,

Woody Woodpecker, Lazy Dog, and Laurel and Hardy, laughing in a dignified manner the whole time. Then, at six or seven, our nurses, always
quietly smiling, bring us our tranquilizers and some water. Afterwards
we go back to our rooms where happy sleep comes then we wake up in
the morning to watch the cat chasing the mouse.

The doctor told me that I was lucky and that had Bernard not brought
me to the hospital in his car at once, the attack would have killed me in a
few minutes because there was also a blood clot forming in an artery and
moving towards the heart. He told me that I should avoid stress and to eat
and drink in moderation and not to smoke. When I told him that I had quit
smoking some time ago, he replied, smiling in rebuke, "Here you are,
paying the price of the previous years!" He was a young doctor and was
said to be a genius but he didn't offer any encouragement or hope. His
most precious gift, though, was the tranquilizers. Now sleep was coming
easily and often. Bad thoughts went away as did all other thoughts.

Bernard used to visit me on his way from the day nursery where he
took his Vietnamese son, Jean-Baptiste, who was four or five. He had an
almost round mouth and his dark eyes bespoke intelligence but he clung
to Bernard and refused to speak to anyone. I knew from experience that
it was impossible to break the shell of a shy child with persistence so I
left him alone hoping that one day he would get used to me. Whenever
he came I gave him some candy from the box that Yusuf, the Egyptian,
brought on his first visit, then I talked with Bernard. I thanked him for
saving my life and he burst out laughing, saying that in fact he saved
himself because he would have felt guilty if something had happened to
me after the interview and when he called me he did not understand a
word I said but he heard a scream and the sound of the phone hitting the
floor and realized what happened. I told the story to my fellow patients
in the room or the lounge and told them that I owe him my life. Bernard
gently reminded me that I had already told them the story. Then he went

on to say that he also should try these medications that made me lose my memory and made me so polite. Bernard adamantly refused to bring me any newspapers or tell me about what was going on in Lebanon. He told me the doctor had prohibited everything that might lead to stress and had given strict orders to that effect to all visitors. I didn't feel that I had any ability to insist, so I amused myself watching him exercise the utmost effort to not introduce any subject that would prove stressful to me. In the end he limited himself to telling me his stories with Jean-Baptiste. He complained constantly that he gave him a hard time trying to get him to go to bed on time at night.

One time he told me that the previous night he had threatened to punish him if he did not sleep and Jean-Baptiste replied that he was not concerned about that because he could turn himself into a bird and fly before any punishment. Bernard sought my support for his argument that all people should sleep on time and wake up energetic in the morning. I said that he was right and added as I looked at Jean-Baptiste, "And also all the birds and all the cats and all the dogs must sleep on time at night."

He surprised me by fixing me with a defiant look from his dark eyes and asking me, "Does the fish go to sleep on time at night?"

"Yes."

"How?"

"It has a little house underwater in which it goes to sleep.'

Jean-Baptiste pursed his lips derisively and was silent for a moment then said to me, "And the goldfish that we have in the aquarium?"

I looked at Bernard to help me out. He said, laughing impatiently, "It doesn't sleep. And unless you go to bed on time you'll definitely turn into a little goldfish! You understand?"

I was not permitted to go beyond this level of conversation. Even Yusuf who visited me almost daily—I was unable to get him to tell me anything about what was going on in the world.

He had visited me the first time with his wife who, as soon as she came in, grabbed my hand with both her hands and addressed me as if talking to a child, "Poor good sir! Even though you took such good care of your health! You only drank your medical coffee!"

Yusuf, somewhat embarrassed, said, "Enough, Elaine. He's all right."

She looked at Yusuf as if accusing him of saying the wrong thing, "What do you think? The gentleman is all right, of course. He's just a little under the weather and he'll leave the hospital after he gets some rest."

Then she whispered as if revealing a secret to me, "The nurses have told me you are making phenomenal, truly phenomenal progress. Soon we will be on our feet and on our way. What do you think?"

Her husband repeated, more firmly, "Enough, Elaine!"

Afterwards, Yusuf started to come by himself. He began to talk to me like Bernard and Mickey Mouse and Charlie Chaplin about entertaining and funny matters. His favorite stories were the things that happened to him when he arrived in town and his adventures at the time to find a place to sleep. He said that when he arrived in the summer there was no problem, he was able to find an out of the way corner in one of the public parks, away from the eyes of the police. But his troubles began when the harsh winter came. At the beginning he was lucky: he discovered a cellar that the tenants in a quiet building used for storage where there was an old bed to which he sneaked at late hours and slept there until the morning. However, a tenant discovered him one night and thought he was a thief and wanted to call the police but he managed to escape. He said that he spent the night squatting in a phone booth looking for some warmth, but the air came into the booth from all directions. In the morning he was so frozen that he couldn't walk. He said another Egyptian with some experience that he had met in a public park saved his life. Yusuf had no job, had no residency papers and had run out of money and began to think of going back to Egypt. He thought going to jail was easier than his situation at the time. Then he met Mamun who had been a worker in Egypt and unemployed here. He showed him how to eat and sleep. First he introduced him to a charitable organization which doled out a simple meal for free to the poor and gave them small sums of money, just barely enough to buy something to eat in the evening. That same night he accompanied him to his secret sleeping place. They sneaked at night to the railroad yard and there were locked single cars. Mamun had a special key that he used to open a first class sleeping car where the beds were comfortable and the covers warm. He drew his attention to the first lesson to continue enjoying this boon: to make sure to get up before dawn and leave the car before the yard workers arrived. Yusuf said that they spent happy nights in that car, but one morning, after having stayed up drinking and chatting, they fell into a deep sleep and in the morning they discovered that the car was moving fast and that they were on a journey whose destination they did not know. They spent the time watching out for the train conductor and moving from one car to another. Then they got off at the first stop. There they discovered that people were speaking a strange language that neither of them knew. They stood in the station bewildered until they found a person who looked like an Arab and they asked him where they were. The man got angry and thought they were mocking him but after some explanation and persistence he told them that if they really did not know where they were then they should know they were in Milan. When the man left, Mamun asked him in puzzlement, "Where the hell is this Milan?"

When I asked Yusuf how he was able to come back here, he laughed and said, "We returned a few days later, in the same sleeping car and in the same way."

Yusuf told me about all the hard times that he had as if they were a joke but he always stopped before meeting Elaine and marrying her. Sometimes when he spoke, Pedro Ibañez came to my mind and I asked myself, was he sleeping now in a cellar or a train? Was he really better off now than he was at the settlement center?

From time to time Yusuf conveyed to me the prince's greetings and his inquiries about me. I also received, on a daily basis, a large, well-arranged bouquet of flowers with a card reading, "Greetings of Prince Hamid bin ——— and his wishes for a speedy recovery." At the end of each day I gave the bouquet to a different nurse and they were happy to receive such rare and precious flowers.

Brigitte came every day at noon, on her usual lunch break. She would come in her blue uniform carrying a small bouquet of flowers and her smile spread cheer in the room as soon as she stepped in. I felt somewhat proud when I saw the other patients' dazzled stares and their using any pretext to come close to us and speak with us. But this pride turned into a sense of shame and embarrassment when one of them said with a wink one day after she left, "Is she the reason you're here? At your age, my friend, we'd better avoid the young and pretty ones. Our hearts cannot take that anymore." I mumbled in protest and in as much anger as my medications permitted saying I did not allow him to say that, that she was just a friend, that she was my daughter's age and many such protestations. Then afterwards when she came I made sure that we sat in another hall or a different floor of the hospital, away from prying eyes. Those days she was the one who chattered, looked for amusing stories to entertain me. And, as I continued to get better and with the help of the tranquilizers, I couldn't resist laughing boisterously even at things that were not so funny. And she laughed because I was in such high spirits the whole time.

The day before my discharge from the hospital, the doctor summoned me to his office and said with the utmost seriousness that he had studied my case and found out that I was a journalist, and that line of work was not suitable for my condition now and that I must change it. I came very close to laughing at this advice but I promised him that I would do my best as soon as possible. The doctor instructed me to consume no more than two cups of coffee a day and after two weeks to stop taking the tranquilizers. As for the blood pressure and the blood thinning medications, I must understand that as of now, they were part of my daily routine. I told him I understood but he didn't seem to be quite convinced and he repeated the instructions in a different manner.

As soon as I left the hospital, I bought the day's newspapers and headed for my café on the riverbank. Walking in the streets and the fresh air seemed like a surprise after my days of confinement at the hospital. I couldn't walk fast so I began to savor my new freedom slowly. I noticed when I arrived at the café that the flowers in the flowerbeds at the entrance had changed. They were late summer, early autumn flowers with subdued colors: brown, violet and dark yellow.

I began to read the papers as I drank a glass of juice but I put them aside after a short while and began to look at the river. The headlines were the same, as were the statistics: thousands and thousands of bombs from the planes and thousands of artillery rounds on Beirut under siege. One of the newspapers made some comparisons saying that yesterday 185 thousand bombs equal to twenty-six thousand tons of explosives were dropped on Beirut. It also reported that yesterday's casualties were 280 dead and 500 wounded. There was an article in a progressive Arabic newspaper eulogizing Khalil Hawi, saying that he was a great poet but he had made a mistake when he committed suicide because a man should not collapse vis-à-vis difficult circumstances and so on.

I folded the papers and got engrossed in watching the swan formations. Near me an old man was giving his grandson small pieces of bread to throw into the river. A large flock gathered under the window, dipping their long white necks into the water and raising them at the same time, then turning on the small ducks that crowded their territory to attack them with their angry red beaks. I said to myself that that was the real Swan Dance.

I realized after a moment that Brigitte was standing near me. She knit her brow when she saw the papers folded on the table and she said somewhat reproachfully, "You're so stubborn, darling. Didn't the doctor forbid all that?"

Then she kissed me on the cheek warmly and said, "I am so happy that you're back. You don't know how much I missed sitting here with you!"

She took the folded papers and threw them on a distant seat. I said to her, "There's no need for that, Brigitte. Not on account of the doctor's orders, but I myself have decided to do like you. I've decided not to read the papers or watch the news from now on. Who needs it? You said it was not we who shed the blood or we who could stop it. We especially cannot stop it."

"Hear! Hear! Someone has regained his sanity!" Then she laughed as she added, "Even though I don't like sane people!" I bent my head resisting the tears that wanted to form in my eyes.

We started meeting and talking every day once again. However, things never returned to what they had been like before. I understood that I'd changed a little after my illness and treatment but I kept asking myself, "What has changed her? Why the silence and the long bouts of seeming distant? And why doesn't she tell me her stories with the tourists anymore?"

Another kind of change began to happen to me. Even after I got off the tranquilizers, I began to experience strange reactions. I began to notice that in the evening when I sat at home watching old Egyptian movies on video, tears came to my eyes with the utmost ease when I saw Fatin Hamama suffering the schemes of old Zaki Rustum or when Kamal al-Shinnawi deserted pregnant Shadia for no reason. I wiped the tears from my eyes, stopping the tape and trying to laugh. I remembered how, in my youth, I used to mock these films and talk about how backward the cinema in our country was and about melodrama and such things. What had happened?

Tears also came to my eyes when I listened to Khalid or Hanadi's voice on the telephone. I actually cried when Hanadi told me that she passed her exams and scored seventy percent. I asked her to inquire right away about the membership dues for the Equestrian Club and she said, "Thank you, you're the best dad ever, but are you crying or does it just sound like it?"

And when I congratulated Khalid on his passing his exams with distinction, I told him in a shaking voice that I was proud of him and that I forgave him, Khalid replied in surprise, "What are you forgiving me for, Dad?" I repeated that I forgave him and got off the phone before sobbing.

With difficulty, I also began to hold back tears in front of Brigitte, reproaching her if she came a little late to our noon meeting, and she'd have to explain and apologize while she looked in surprise at me because she saw me turning my face away and pressing it between my palms to resist crying. Ultimately I had to tell her what was happening to me. She said, "Actually I, for one, find you much better this way than you were before. I've told you that I didn't like people who are very sane. But why don't you go to the doctor if it bothers you?"

My doctor, however, didn't understand anything. He examined me carefully as usual and sent me for blood tests then after he reviewed the results said that great progress had been made, that I was almost normal. When I explained to him again how I felt and that I could no longer control my tears, he listened to me attentively and wrote me a letter of referral to an ophthalmologist saying, "After we make sure the eye itself is all right, I can refer you to a psychiatrist."

I almost swore at the doctor but I took the letter and left the clinic quickly, muttering as I went down the stairs. I felt the old stressful feelings coming back, so I stood at the entrance of the building drawing deep breaths, trying to calm down, and trying to remember where I had left my car. I was actually calmer by the time I went out to the street and felt a light, refreshing breeze.

I walked all over the long street looking for the car in vain. So I stood at the corner shading my eyes with my hand trying to make it out in the midst of the dozens of cars parked right and left. But in a moment I forgot the car and everything else and asked myself how I hadn't seen it before. How did I miss noticing it? How did this beautiful autumn, which had begun early this year, escape my eyes?

The trees on both sides of the street in this quiet neighborhood had changed colors: the green had faded and was adorned with soft, shiny yellow leaves glowing in the sun. Every tree was now a giant flower luxuriating in faded green, yellowed green, brown-yellow tinged with red— silvery colors and others that I could not describe in the midst of this autumnal festival. The wind blew some leaves that fluttered slowly like golden butterflies before resting on the ground. There they joined another sleepy swarm creating a circle around the trunk of the tree, drawing under it the echo of another yellow tree, ruffled by the wind, their chafing producing a small, coarse sound that nevertheless tickled the senses.

I stood for a long time thinking about nothing, moving my gaze between the clean blue sky and the trees shedding their ornaments on the ground. My tears streaked down without any effort on my part to resist them, as if something deep down inside me said that out of the heart of the soft, golden fire, my soul would be kindled and resurrected. I began slowly tearing up the doctor's letter and the wind carried its white snips that also fluttered around in the midst of the lost leaves.

I wonder, was it also the very same day that Brigitte said she loved me? That day that love came as a high wave to an inexperienced swimmer, engulfing him, making him gasp inside it and flailing his arms not knowing which way to go? But why lie? That day I was floating above that wave, happy and vain that I, that old man, was loved by that young beautiful woman and that, for me, her eyes filled with tears and her hand trembled when I touched her as she said in an almost inaudible whisper, "What's happening to me? And who am I to deserve all this joy?"

And I was asking myself, "Who am I to deserve all this love? Isn't it shameful to feel all this joy at this age, these days, in the midst of that war?"

But that was later, later. That time when she left me in front of the door of that café, our café, saying that she would leave me, that she was afraid that she had fallen in love with me, that time I stood in the road, planted as if I were one of those trees, hearing nothing, seeing nothing except those words, "I am afraid I have fallen in love with you," I didn't even think about what the words meant. I just let them permeate me in the hope that my dry, furrowed soul might absorb that dew that it had been denied for so long.

"I am afraid I have fallen in love with you!"

A white sail quickly passing through blue waves.

That same evening you call me. Your voice over the phone sounds small and guilty, "Can I see you?" We meet and all my calculations are gone. All the words that I had prepared to return you and myself to our senses were lost. I take you in my arms as soon as I see you. I kiss you on the mouth. I hold your arm. I embrace you. I move you away a little to be able to see your face, to make sure that you are you and that I am I, then embrace you again.

We walk in the dimly lit streets holding hands. You say, as if talking to someone else, "It was not fair. It was not fair that I met you at this age, that all this love came to me." Yet we laugh. We are surprised and we are happy. You walk fast as if you were pulling me by the hand, treading the ground lightly as usual, as if you were touching it with just your toes. We enter the garden without being aware of it and walk its paths lit only by the moon as I love you and the beautiful night like a veil enveloping us and I am around you and you are around me, your head on my chest. You feel my hand and ask me, "Are you cold," and I say, "No." You raise your head a little and mumble in confusion, "Is all this really happening? Are we not dreaming?" And I say even if it were a dream, how beautiful it is! A bird wakes up in the night and flaps its wings on a tree and a leaf falls on my head. You are delighted with it and place it on your lips and you turn towards me and I see in the moonlight your round face in the middle of the halo of your golden hair and you smile and those lines that I love appear on your chin and around your eyes and you ask me, "Why do you like to kiss me in the light?"

I say, "Because I like to see your face."

"But I see you with my eyes closed. For months I have been seeing you with my eyes closed," you say and you close your eyes and I kiss those eyes. You put your long, soft fingers around my head so I kiss you but I hear you saying apologetically, "You're hurting me." I pull back and apologize. You lean your head on my shoulder and you say, "But I want this hurt," then you kiss me quickly all over my face and my forehead and you say breathlessly, "What's happening to us?"

I say, "Look at me. I love you as if I were a boy. My life is over but I love you as if I were beginning that life."

You say with a clear laugh as you place your head on my chest, "But don't you know that all lovers are ageless children and that love is a child?" I also know that this is a lie but oh how beautiful! What a beautiful illusion! I love you and you are with me in the tender night in the gentle garden when you are young no more and I am old no more, glowing together in this silver moon, the same age, without age, in the heart of love the child, in the only eternal time. I love you and you are with me.

That was the beginning, the night we became one.

On my way back from your house on that love night when we became one, I walk in the middle of masses of stone houses pierced by the few small windows of light that have stayed up. I walk feeling cold so I put my hands in my coat pockets, walking faster, yet not wanting to go home. I don't want to be bound by any place. I wish I could soar above this thick, massive, wall-filled world, and you with me to another world, soft and transparent, unbound by bricks or appointments or newspapers or wars or hunger or death or yesterday's worries or tomorrow's surprises, a world that we make together, ageless even if short-lived, here and now, a world that rectifies all the past and erases it, a world that fixes the present, keeping nothing but joy.

Nothing but joy!

It was as if this wish were an infection that we both caught!

That night and the other nights I was amazed by your ability to love, your desire to stay up the whole night and to do everything in depth as if no tomorrow would ever come. We had to seize the moment because if we didn't now it would be lost forever. We made love and you insisted that I read poetry to you and you read to me. We would go out in the dead of the night to walk in the cold empty streets, embracing, then go back to start all over again. I didn't believe that with you I could actually be ageless but I was more anxious than you not to lose one moment of our continual nightly wedding.

You had your rituals. You liked to curl up on your side, your knees at your chest, your eyes closed, your thumb in your mouth, sucking it in a low monotonous sound. I bend over you and you pretend that you are startled and you make murmuring sounds and say incomplete, meaningless words like a baby, babbling as you extend your arm to embrace me and you say in a small voice, "Kiss me, kiss me a lot. Kiss me everywhere." I didn't need much effort to understand that you loved everything that took you back to your childhood, before the female in you awoke, complete and mature.

I understand. But how do I understand what happened to *me*? How was I able in the late autumn of my life to match your vigorous youth? To delve down with you into those nightly whirlpools without drowning or giving up? And where did the high blood pressure and the headache at the back of the head and the constant blurring of the eyes go?

I almost laughed when the doctor told me on my regular check up day, "See? You are almost totally normal. I see that you are following my instructions. No stressful situations and no excess of any kind. Right?"

I said, "Yes."

"And journalism, did you change your profession?" he asked.

"I stopped being a journalist."

"That's much better. In your condition it's best to avoid anything that raises blood pressure."

I was not lying to the doctor. I had, for quite a long time, stopped writing letters to the newspaper or even contacting it. They were happy. I was happy.

Oh, how happy I was! Suddenly, in those days, it dawned upon me that I have tried everything; to be a good son, a good husband, a loving father, a man with principles, a journalist with a conscience, and a dignified old man providing for the future of his children after he died. It dawned upon me that I have tried everything but joy, but being happy inside. So, what bliss to know in my life, even if it were just once before the end, that sacred joy that seeks nothing beyond itself! It dawned upon me that throughout those months with Brigitte, I was trying to find the way to a fact that was there the whole time, but to which I was blind: that all the time I have been playing so many roles that I myself, in the midst of all those masks, lost my own real face. Even though I didn't soar high in my play-acting, my wings also were made of wax that melted in the sun of the truth. They melted in a painfully slow way that almost killed me. So, how happy I was to have finally fallen to earth!

Who am I? Finally I know who I am. I am not important at all! I have never been important! Son of the custodian; deputy editor-in-chief; I entered Port Said; I climbed the mountains of Yemen. Screw it all! What did you do in your life after that? You lived taking pleasure in torment-ing yourself, as Ibrahim said. You didn't even do as Marianne or Ibrahim or even Muller did. You confronted the real war so you rushed to make your separate peace then you considered yourself a victim and a martyr. A martyr for what? A victim of what, other than your vanity and your weakness and your fond desire to slap the world back? But you won't ever do that except by stealing happiness. Oh what joy then that I've finally fallen! What joy to lose all the past now to find you, Brigitte!

The rest now is happiness! Nothing but happiness!

Pardon me, Prince Hamlet! I leave you alone, for "the rest is silence." Awesome silence becomes you and I was not destined to be you. I am but a deceived old man who twittered for a while, for a moment, and the words reverberated only in his own ears.

Pardon me, Prince, because for me, the rest is happiness!

And forgive me Ibrahim because she is not coming back to me at the end of life as a punishment but as a blessing.

8

Let That Day
Come Slowly

I FORGOT MANY THINGS during those days including the story about Prince Hamid. I sent him a message of thanks with Yusuf after I left the hospital, then both he and his newspaper project slipped my mind completely. But Yusuf contacted me after a while, telling me that the prince would be "delighted" to see me. I sensed some urgency in Yusuf's tone, so we made an appointment.

Yusuf accompanied me to the prince's suite in a century-old hotel overlooking the river, distinguished by wide, tall windows behind wrought iron railings in the form of small, closely arranged hearts, surrounded in the summertime by arranged flowers. As we were in the old wood elevator, slowly squeaking its way up to the third floor, I said to Yusuf, "This is a very peculiar prince. Why isn't he staying in one of the modern hotels that rich Arabs prefer?"

"You'll see him now yourself and find out what he is like," he said enigmatically.

The door was opened by a huge swarthy man with Indian features who escorted us in a dignified manner through a corridor between closed rooms to a large parlor whose window had a frontal view of the river. We waited there for a moment as another swarthy man wearing a white jacket and white gloves offered us cold drinks.

I looked at my watch. It was six o'clock sharp when the Asian guard who had escorted us opened the door and held it wide open until a man

entered followed by a blonde holding a notepad and a pen. I figured out
it was the prince as Yusuf stood up and the other man said casually,
"Hello, Yusuf."

I stood up as he came close to me, his hand fully extended, saying in
an affectionate tone, "Hello, Ustaz."

He shook my hand saying, "Thank God you are well. I was worried
about you."

I mumbled a few words of thanks as the prince sat on a couch in front
of us inviting us to sit down. As soon as we did the blonde asked us in
English what we would like to drink as she raised the notepad. The
prince told her in impeccable English as he looked at Yusuf, "Our friend
prefers your vintage wine, I think."

Yusuf nodded and the prince looked at me quizzically and I said,
"Decaffeinated coffee."

The blonde said, "And Your Highness?"

He raised his hand without looking at her and she understood he did-
n't want anything and withdrew immediately, followed by the guard who
closed the parlor door.

Prince Hamid was about thirty-five with a shaved, round face and
whitish complexion, but with eastern features accentuated by his jet
black hair and bright, amber eyes. He was wearing a dark blue suit and
a necktie with an intricate striped pattern of subdued sky-blue and yellow colors. He seemed to be on the short side but I immediately felt his
strong presence.

The prince repeated as he looked at me, "Thank God you are well. I
was actually worried about you, but Yusuf was constantly reassuring
me."

Yusuf spoke for the first time, saying enthusiastically, "I always conveyed Your Highness's greeting."

"Thank you, your Highness. You've overwhelmed me with your generosity. Those flowers brought me a message of hope every day," I said.

Leaning back on the couch with gilded arms, and taking out of his inner pocket some amber prayer beads, he said, "That's the least that one should do. I don't know if Yusuf has told you or not but I was one of your readers when I was studying at Victoria College in Egypt. I kept it up when I was studying in England but . . . "

"But there was not much to keep up with," I interjected.

Moving the prayer beads, he said, "It's regrettable that your writing is not receiving the recognition that it deserves, but we all know the circumstances."

Then he added, disdainfully as if he had remembered something, "I know your editor-in-chief well. I've known him since he was your paper's correspondent in our country. As a journalist and as a human being, he needs God's help, as you say in Egypt."

I said calmly, "He's an old colleague. I might have differences in opinion with him, but he's really a good man. He has been generous to me during the illness and after."

At that moment the guard opened the door and the servant with the white gloves came in, and after he put the drinks in front of us he left, moving with his back to the door. Prince Hamid said, "Actually, my idea as I've explained it to Yusuf is to publish a small newspaper that comprises the best Arab writers, I mean nationalist and progressive writers. I know your Nasserist inclinations of course. Anyone who thinks we were against the late Nasser would be making a mistake. On the contrary we, or at least I, know that he is the only one who tried to do something for this region. Before him nobody had heard of us, but he gave our countries stature in the world. And he learned from his mistakes. He knew very well before he died that the Soviets were deceiving him and that it was not in our interest to butt heads with America. And he was about to change and make changes but . . ."

He remembered something and laughed briefly as he said, "Finally, he, God have mercy on his soul, understood the spirit of the people. You know where we stand on visiting tombs. But I thought it was a good omen when he visited the tomb of Sayyida Zaynab after the setback, even though time didn't give him a chance." Then the prince sighed, studying his beads as if he were addressing them, "Look at where we are now. Look at our situation in Lebanon."

I said in spite of myself, "Actually I don't watch what's happening in Lebanon or elsewhere. The doctor . . . "

The prince interrupted me saying, "I know. I know. The doctor said to avoid all stressful situations, and I of course am keener than he that you do. I don't want you to expose yourself to anything that might, God forbid, bring about a setback. On the contrary, I think you need some time for convalescence. What I am thinking about now and what I told Yusuf to talk to you about is for you to participate with us at the conceptual level at this stage. I want you to think calmly, and of course to take your time, about your own conception of a nationalist newspaper at this juncture; how such a newspaper would not duplicate the other newspapers that are published here in Europe. What departments should it have? Which writers can help it come up with a new formulation of nationalist thought? What format should it be? Should it be weekly, biweekly, or even a daily?

I said cautiously, "But your Highness, you know first and foremost that a newspaper is a project that costs huge amounts of money for every issue. Before thinking about these things we should think about the size of the readership and more importantly, about advertisements because they are the primary source of financing."

The prince said curtly, "Don't worry on this account. I've asked somebody to look into the financial aspects and I know exactly the cost of printing and distribution for a weekly, and that's where I am inclined right now, or even if we can issue it as a daily. I can handle that because I am not thinking of profit, actually I expect loss. Didn't you tell him that, Yusuf?"

Yusuf was sitting in his seat leaning forward to follow our conversation attentively without saying anything and without even touching the glass of wine placed in front of him. When the prince asked him he said, "Actually, I preferred that your Highness explain the project to him yourself because you are more familiar with its facets."

Prince Hamid said disapprovingly, "You mean you did not offer him the most important thing, which is to travel for some time for convalescence after which he can think about all these matters? Didn't I assign you to do that?"

I mumbled thanks but the prince said, "This is no empty gesture on my part, Ustaz. I believe that writers, I mean real writers, are the most precious resource we have because it is they who constitute the mind and the conscience. Do you think we would have fallen so low had the nation's conscience been clean? Therefore I believe that safeguarding our writers should be one of our utmost priorities. That's why I took the liberty of urging Yusuf since you left the hospital to persuade you to go and rest anywhere you like and I took the liberty of sending him with a modest contribution for this purpose. Actually, I consider it an obligation, nothing more."

Then he turned to Yusuf reprovingly and said, "What's the meaning of this? I am quite surprised that the Ustaz is still here now, and therefore I asked to see both of you. What did you do with the assignment I gave you, Yusuf?"

Blood shot up to my head and I looked at Yusuf, who put his hand in his jacket's inner pocket and took out a long envelope which he placed on the table between us and the prince, saying, "Here's the check your Highness sent. I didn't give it to the Ustaz and I didn't cash it . . ."

But I interrupted him saying, somewhat sharply, "Thank you very much but I don't accept. I mean I don't need travel or convalescence now."

Pointing at me, Yusuf said, "For this reason I did not carry out your Highness's request. I didn't believe the Ustaz would accept it from me. I also thought it better that your Highness offer it to him."

The prince was fixing me with a probing glance almost coldly, his prayer beads rolled in his hand, then he turned to address Yusuf pointing to the white envelope with his finger, "Put that thing in your pocket first."

Prince Hamid's face quickly recovered its pleasant expression and addressed Yusuf in a friendly manner, "How then do you want to become a journalist? A journalist, Mr. Yusuf, translates people's ideas correctly. You should have told the Ustaz that this is not even a gift but a modest remuneration for his effort participating with us in planning for the paper, when his health condition allows, of course."

Yusuf said with a faint smile, "I am still a journalist in training, Your Highness."

I said, "An idea came to me as we were talking. I understand that what is needed is a newspaper that is a distinct from the newspapers published here in Europe. Right?"

"Precisely. We don't want to duplicate the newspapers in London or Paris," Prince Hamid said.

"But there are now many newspapers addressing Arabs in Europe. So what does Your Highness think of an Arab newspaper in English or French that would reflect our point of view here? This is actually what we need. A colleague who came from Lebanon recently had a hard time publishing even one news item or statement."

"That's a very good idea," the prince said. But his lukewarm voice suggested that he meant the exact opposite. He fell silent for a moment before bowing his head to address his rosary beads again, "Of course there are difficulties. To begin with, where do we get the Arab journalists who write well in foreign languages. We can of course resort to translation, but in that case would the articles retain their original power? And who will be the target audience? It will be of interest to a very few Arabs and of no interest to almost any European. It also means that we will have two teams of editors, Arabs and foreigners, and this is somewhat too much, I mean financially speaking."

I said truthfully, "Your Highness sums up matters with the utmost precision and identifies the most important problems."

He didn't seem to react, but he said as if deep in thought, "And yet, it's a very good idea as I said. We will at one time or another need to address the western audience. But let's first begin with the Arabic newspaper and when it succeeds we can publish a monthly or biweekly supplement in a foreign language." He said this as he looked at his watch. Yusuf stood up and I followed suit. The prince rose, saying, "I expect you to think about it, but not at the expense of your health, as we agreed, after you've completely rested."

"I promise you that."

He shook my hand firmly and said, "I know you keep your promises. Next time we will meet in my house here. I am not very comfortable in hotels and of course my house will be your house." Then he turned to Yusuf and said, "Your task is to keep checking on the Ustaz and Linda will contact you if I need anything from you in the coming days. Goodbye."

As we were going downstairs there was a flush of happiness on Yusuf's face. He couldn't help it as we were in the elevator: "You taught him a lesson, Ustaz."

"What do you mean?"

But instead of replying, he said with self-contentment written all over his face, "You know what he would have thought if I had not taken out the envelope when he asked me about the money, even if he wasn't sure the check was inside? But I was prepared! Don't I know him well after all this time?"

"Personally, and in all candor, I don't understand him and I don't understand you."

We began to walk along the riverbank opposite the hotel. The trees arrayed there were losing their leaves faster than the city trees so we were stepping on that spread of yellow leaves which emitted a subdued rustling sound as we trod on it. For some unknown reason I took comfort from this sound as if it were bearing a secret, delightful message. Why? I don't know! But everything in those days was bearing messages of delight. I told Yusuf, "I was afraid this meeting was going to bother me because I don't like these formal situations. But this prince is a different person; he makes you think."

Yusuf interrupted me enthusiastically, "What did I tell you? He's different. He's very sharp. But his problem is that he thinks he can buy anybody. He says each human being has a price! Do you know the amount of the check that he left for me to give to you?"

"I don't want to know."

"And yet, it's twenty thousand dollars."

I let out a faint whistle and said, "And this only for convalescence? What am I worth to the prince? And why? How important am I to him?"

Puzzled as if he had thought about it before, Yusuf said, "Frankly, I don't know. Of course this sum for him is like five cents for me. He spends that much and maybe more every day. Do you believe that this hotel suite is booked for him throughout the year even when he's out of town? In addition to rooms for the guards, employees, secretaries, and servants."

"But what exactly does he do here?"

"He has many companies. He also trades in Arabian horses and the stock market and in everything. He has companies in America and in his country and everywhere in the world."

"But a person like this, Yusuf, why does he need you or me? He can snap his fingers and find a hundred journalists, not just one. So why us?"

"I'll tell you."

But he changed his mind and said almost imploringly, "And yet I beg you to think about it. I mean, you can actually deliver such a project to him, right?"

"No problem there. I've worked in journalism all my life and I can deliver the project within days. But why? Is he indeed keen on Arabism and nationalism as he says?"

He let out an intermittent, sarcastic laugh, "Surely you didn't fall for that one, Ustaz?"

I interrupted him somewhat impatiently, "If you know something, Yusuf, why don't you say it?"

He started somewhat reluctantly, "Believe me, what I know isn't much. I know why he wants me to work for him, or I think I know. The reason is that I have legal residence status in this country and perhaps I'll get my citizenship soon and I can get a permit for the paper in my name. Second, he trusts me since I worked for him as a driver for some time and he knows me quite well. I also know approximately why he wants to publish the paper."

"Now this is it. Why? Get to the point, Yusuf."

"Prince Hamid is a younger brother of the country's ruler, but he believes that he is more entitled to be crown prince than the older brother, because the crown prince isn't educated and some people say that he's white here."

Yusuf said the last phrase while wiping his forehead with his hand. I hadn't heard that expression before but I understood what it meant and

Yusuf went on to say, "And yet the ruler fears the crown prince because he has followers and he fears to name Prince Hamid in his place . . ."

I interrupted him, laughing, "He fears that Prince Hamid would take the ruler's own place!"

"Bravo, Ustaz. And the newspaper, as far as I can tell, will be a weapon with which to fight the crown prince and pressure the ruler. That's why I almost laughed when you talked of the foreign-language paper and about publishing our problems in Europe and such. I think that he wants a strong paper indeed, one that people talk about and prominent writers write for. But all he cares about in all this is his country in the Gulf. If ten issues get in there, even smuggled, then the purpose of the paper will have been fulfilled."

I went one step ahead of Yusuf and sat on one of the benches facing the river. He came and sat next to me and said anxiously, when he noticed my silence, "Are you tired from the walking?"

"On the contrary. Walking is good for me, as the doctor said. But I'm thinking of what you said. You're smart, Yusuf, and you know every-thing, so why are you interested in this project? Is it only a matter of work and money?"

He started talking passionately, "Of course you are saying to yourself, 'A driver, a homeless man, and a cook, what does he have to do with journalism?' I . . ."

I interrupted him, "I never said any of that. All these experiences will come in handy when you write. Besides, you've told me you studied journalism at the university."

His voice full of sadness, he said, "Thank you for being so kind to me, but actually I never imagined that I'd be in such shape as I approach the age of thirty. From my early childhood I did very well in school and my father was proud of me and had great expectations for my future. I fell in love with journalism at an early age and in secondary school I was the announcer of the school broadcasting service. I used to send articles to all the papers and magazines and some of them appeared in readers' letters sections. At the university I was a straight-A student in the first and second year. The "wall magazine" that I wrote from A to Z attracted students when I hung it up on Saturday every week. Even students from other colleges came to read it. I called it *Al-Nadim* and tried to make use of the tradition that blends the serious and the comic, so the students felt it was different from the other magazines that filled the university those days in 1975 and '76. My father wrote the headlines in beautiful red calligraphy and he also shared his ideas with me in editing every issue."

He fell silent suddenly, his mind wandering far away, and after a while he said as if not talking to me, "I miss my father."

I wanted to get him out of the depression that had come over him, so I asked, "What did you write about in your magazine those days?" Life gradually came back to his voice and he said, "About everything that happened in the country. I inherited a love of Abd al-Nasser from my father. He was the director of a public sector company but he never strayed from the straight and narrow and we lived in comfort even after he retired. The pension was more than enough for us, I mean at the beginning. My love for Abd al-Nasser increased as I saw what happened to us after his death. I saw my old father struggle to make ends meet with the pension that was becoming worthless while the new thieves flourished everywhere. I wrote about that in the wall magazine. I made comparisons between simple folk, like my father and people like him, under the open-door policy. I also ran for student union and I won. I took part in all the strikes and sit-ins that took place back then. But afterwards the Islamic group members, wearing galabiyyas, were let loose upon us by the government and they tore up our magazines whenever we hung them. If we resisted they beat us with brass knuckles that they put on right in front of the university police who were protecting them only."

Sighing, I said, "So what Ibrahim al-Mehallawi said is true. We are in the same boat."

Yusuf, in his sad tone, said, "No. It's not true. We read you and we learned from you when we were young. But when push came to shove and we looked for you, you weren't there."

His words hurt me, so I said in self-defense, "What could we do? Those days in particular, that you are talking about, I wrote a book on Abd al-Nasser." I stood as I went on, "In any case I'm beginning to feel cold, and besides I promised myself some time ago not to get into any arguments, especially political ones."

Yusuf got up after me and said, "I'm sorry. I didn't intend to upset you. All I wanted was to explain to you why I'm interested in the newspaper that the prince wants to publish. I didn't suffer and leave home to end up being a cook."

We were going towards the hotel where I had parked my car when he said suddenly in a low voice, "Ustaz, I want to get rid of that woman!"

I didn't say anything. Yusuf's tone changed as if he wanted to correct himself and he said, "Please understand me. I am not a low-life, I am not one of those foreigners who marry citizens to get residence and then divorce them afterwards. Elaine is really a good woman. I mean, do you understand me? I want . . ."

But once again he burst out, "I want to get rid of that woman!"

"I'll see what I can do, Yusuf."

But at that time I was not thinking of what he'd said about Elaine. The sting of his blaming me took precedence over all else.

I didn't have a date with Brigitte that evening and I decided to call her to get together. But when I turned the key in the apartment door I heard the voice of Umm Kulthum coming from the recorder and I knew that she had come on her own. I was elated. I had many tapes of Arabic and classical music, but out of all the tapes I had she was enamored only of Umm Kulthum. As soon as I came in Brigitte rushed towards me and I hugged her closely. Actually I clung to her as if seeking her protection.

She sensed something unusual so she retreated and began to look closely at me, then in a threatening tone, wagging her finger in my face, she said, "Something happened this evening. Did you fool around? Do you deserve punishment?"

She was wearing her uniform but had taken off the jacket and kept on the light white blouse and short skirt. She had undone her braid and let it hang over her right shoulder. She stood there confronting me, pointing her finger at me. I took her extended hand and kissed it as I led her to the small sofa in the living room. She was in a good mood that night. I understood why when I saw the open wine bottle and how much had already been poured.

I told Brigitte what had happened at the meeting with the Prince, and pretending to be very sorry and hitting me on the shoulder with her fist, she said, "Are you naive or something? Why didn't you take the money? These are people who literally throw money out of the window. If I were standing under the window and someone threw me twenty thousand dollars and said, 'Take it, it's yours,' would you expect me to say no? Of course I'd take it right away and take you with me on a trip around the world."

"No matter at what price?"

"But the man did not ask for a price, as you said. He wants you to rest. He loves you because you are you, but not the way I love you."

I pressed her hand saying, "If only I could believe that to be true!"

She withdrew her hand from my grasp forcefully and said angrily, "And why would I lie to you, Your Highness, if you please? I will return to you the yacht you gave me as a gift last week."

She slid suddenly from the sofa and knelt in front of it, facing me, and placed her hand on my chest saying, "When will you stop these doubts and these stories? When will you really believe that I love you because you are you? I've grown tired of stupid hearts and greedy hearts and selfish hearts. When will you believe that I've spent my life looking for this heart?" She kissed me gently on the chest and I bent down to lift her up, saying,

"But you also know that this heart was on its way to death before it met you."

She shook her head and said, "I wouldn't have forgiven you if you'd left me! Do you believe me? I am now getting reacquainted with the first Brigitte. I am discovering her as if I were meeting an old friend."

She got up suddenly and clapped her hands and said, "Come on. We're through with this story, through with it for good. These doubts are not coming back and nothing will remain except you and me forever. So now let's have some poetry with this lady's beautiful voice."

Brigitte went to the bookshelves and pulled out "The Complete Poems of al-Mutanabbi," which she could identify by its thick yellow cover and which she knew that I liked to read from often. Then she opened the book and began to move her head quickly from right to left, her eyes wandering around the open page and saying in Arabic all the words that she had learned from me as if reading poetry: "Hello, how are you? Where are the eye glasses? You are very beautiful. Tea. Welcome, welcome."

She pushed the book towards me after she finished "reading," saying, "Come on, read that poem about the sea under the shining sun, in which the calm waves touch the beach then ebb gently as the women sit on the sand weaving fishermen's nets and the children help their mothers. And on a rock a boy stands, his hand on his head looking closely at the blue sea. When he sees the first boats on the horizon he shouts at the top of his voice and the mothers drop the nets and the weaving and run until their bare feet touch the water and their clothes get wet as they wave and shout and the children have a festival on the beach. Come on, that poem that you read to me yesterday."

I laughed, telling her, "There's not a thing of what you say in that poem. There's no sea at all. This poet didn't write anything about the sea. If you knew what it meant . . ."

She put the glass she had been drinking from on the table and put her hands over her ears, saying, "There, you've spoiled everything! You've taken away from me the sound of the waves." Then she pressed the book into my hand and said, "Come on, read, please." I opened the book at random and started reading from the page it opened to:

Until when this backwardness and laziness?
And this excess upon excess?
Distracting oneself from seeking glory,
Selling poetry in the loser's bazaar,
Spent youth cannot be recouped
Nor does a past day ever come back.

I closed the book, saying, "I don't feel like poetry tonight." She let her hands drop to her sides despondently. I drew her down to sit next to me. Umm Kulthum had finished singing her song about moonlit nights and silence filled the apartment. Brigitte leaned her head on my shoulder for a while then raised her anxious blue eyes towards me and said,

"Tell me the truth. Something else happened tonight besides meeting the prince, what is it? Why don't I feel now that you're with me as you were yesterday?"

I told her what had happened between Yusuf and me. I told her that we had talked about conditions in the country and that he told me that I had let him down, he said that he looked for me but I wasn't there. Brigitte looked at me for a moment without understanding, then she said, "But how important is that? What's the importance of anything? Haven't we agreed not to let the world defeat us again? Haven't we just agreed that there will be nothing in the world except you and me?"

As she said this she reached out and lifted my arm and placed it around her shoulder, and I reached out my other hand and hugged her closely, saying to myself: Yes, there should be nothing but her and me. The world should not defeat us again. With her face in my chest she was saying in a soft voice, "Yes, like that. This warms me, this gives me protection. I have never known this peace and serenity. Touch me. Do you feel how Brigitte has changed? Do you feel her now as a woman reborn in the peace of love?"

You used to push my hand to your chest and say in a soft, childish voice but it was also a disjointed, breathless voice, "Brigitte, sir, has never known such peace in love, so let her enjoy this peace, let her enjoy it forever." I roamed all over your face with my lips, all over your body but I didn't tell you that this old man also had been born in love only with you.

That night indeed was a night of peace.

But I have known other nights.

In our first warm, sun-filled days I used to be able to get over and transcend those nights because our nights of pure love overflowed and erased them into oblivion.

Yet from the beginning I knew your other side: when you sat on the floor next to the sofa, your hand clasping your knees close to your chest as you stared at nothing, wearing that mask on your face behind which Brigitte hid; when no talking to or begging or closeness was able to return you to our world; when you pushed me in the chest to stay away from you, to leave you alone to your own affairs about which I knew nothing as you squatted there on the floor, clinging to yourself convulsively as if you wanted to push your whole body back inside your skin again.

I learned to leave you alone at those times, and to wait. I learned not to try to speak with you or to touch you until you gradually became yourself again, until that glassy look in your eyes vanished and the blue irises regained their captivating gleam, before you asked me in a matter-of-fact tone but with some surprise, "Why don't you come and sit here next to me?"

I also knew nights of madness.

When you would jump out of bed suddenly, naked, after mumbling some sentences in German and standing in your living room pulling a book of German poetry from your bookshelves and turning its pages quickly looking for that poem that had summoned you in the middle of the night. Then you would begin to read in a loud voice that would keep getting louder and louder as if you were in an empty desert. Then I would chase you and place my hand on your mouth and you would try to break free and you would jab me with your elbow to get away from me and you would growl, wanting to continue this mad recitation undeterred by hearing the neighbors' angry knocks on the walls or by my reminding you that they could call the police about this noise at night. Then you would swear at me, the police and the neighbors in a choking voice. You would only calm down when I would suggest that we go out and that you recite the poetry on the riverbank. Then you would put on your clothes with feverish haste and hurry me up. But as soon as we would step outside you would ask me as you shivered, "Why did we go out in this cold?" But I've also learned that these moments are part of you and I learned a little later to love them because they also are you.

I did not, however, forget Prince Hamid in those days.

I kept asking myself in surprise whether I was still a journalist with a journalist's sense after all the years of unemployment in this European city, reporting bad news for a bad newspaper. What suddenly removed

the rust from my soul despite the doctor's warning and Brigitte's warning me not to take arms again against the world that has defeated me?

Something stronger than me was pushing me in those days to be the
journalist who had died and whom I had buried, something that pushed
me to research and to find out. I had no choice but to obey.

About a week after meeting the prince, I went to Elaine's café in the
morning.

She welcomed me with her professional smile and led me to a far corner in the café as she chattered, "What did I tell you? Didn't I promise
that we'd be back on our feet sooner than we imagine? And look at us
now, we are better than we were before! But, you know something?
Perhaps we should give up that medical coffee also. I read that it is
not . . . that it is not very healthy. Juice is better."

She kept talking non-stop and I mumbled, agreeing to what she was
saying, interrupting her every time she stopped talking by asking about
Yusuf. But she surprised me after I sat down by pulling up a chair and
sitting opposite me.

She kept looking at me for a while as she clasped her hands on the
table, her usual smile fading gradually, then said, "I have been waiting for
you, sir. Actually I was going to call you if you hadn't come today." The
tone of her voice changed as she spoke. The tone of chatting with a café
patron disappeared and a serious look entered her eyes as she looked at me.

Anxiously I said, "But why? Has something happened? I hope Yusuf
is all right."

"Yes, yes, definitely. But *I* am not all right."

She fell silent for a moment as if thinking how to begin, then suddenly raised two imploring eyes towards me and said, "Please don't take
Yusuf away from me!"

"Take him? How? I haven't seen him for some time and I have never
tried . . ."

She interrupted me, "I know, I know you've never tried to take him, but it is he who is trying to go with you."

"Not even that. Believe me."

Her eyelids were twitching rapidly and she said in a somewhat raspy voice, "Then he's trying to go back to the Prince. He wants to work as a journalist and he wants you to help him. Isn't that so?"

I didn't reply, so, looking me straight in the face, she said, "I know everything, sir. I know very well what Yusuf wants and if I had enough money I would publish a newspaper for him to work in as much as he likes."

She tried to smile as she said that and began to fiddle with the table with trembling fingers but that was not enough to prevent the tears from gathering in her eyes. I wanted to speak but she reached toward me as if begging me to wait, saying as she struggled with her tears, "I won't be able to stay with you long and Yusuf might come out of the kitchen at any moment. Therefore please hear me out. I love Yusuf."

"That's natural."

This time she let out a soft laugh, saying, "No. No."

After a moment, turning her face away from me, she added, "No. It is not natural and I know it. He could have been my son and I know it. He almost finished college and I am uneducated and I know it. But I love him and he accepted me. Don't ask me why he accepted. Did he accept me because he was looking for work and to settle down? Perhaps. He was going through a difficult period after the Prince left last year and he didn't have a work permit. But many worked for me before him, men younger than him, more handsome than him. Yet I hadn't thought of any man since my first husband died."

She paused for a moment then continued hesitantly, "With Yusuf, there was something . . ."

Then her voice failed again and I said, "Madam, nobody decides to love. One loves, that's all there is to it. You don't need to explain any-thing or justify anything to me. I believe you and I understand you. No one can understand you better than I."

"So you also understand my fear?"

"Definitely."

She turned her face away from me again, saying in a soft voice, "Pardon me, but I don't think you understand it fully. I know that Yusuf will leave me. I am fifty years old. I am doing all I can to remain a wife and a woman in his eyes. But how long do you think that will last? How long can it last when he is so young while I age every day? One year? Two years? A little longer, a little shorter? So be it, sir. I accept. I know it's my last happiness, so please let it continue. Yusuf will leave one day. Please let that day come slowly. Don't rush it. I know that if he worked as a journalist, if he left this café once, he would leave it forever. When he sprouts wings he will fly away for good. Am I selfish, to want him on land, to stay with me? Perhaps . . ."

I felt so sad my tongue was tied as I looked at her tormented face: is she speaking about herself now or about me? Should I confess to her that I also was afraid that that day would come soon?

She was imploring me repeatedly, almost whispering, "Please, sir. Do what you can."

She left and I don't know what I said to her but I was deep in thought when Yusuf finally came and shook my hand with his wet hand, saying, "Welcome, Ustaz. I didn't expect you to come so soon."

He sat opposite me where Elaine had been sitting. This time he had forgotten to take off the white kitchen apron. As soon as he sat down he asked me excitedly and enthusiastically, "Well sir, did you finish the project?"

I didn't respond right away. What I had come to do and what Elaine had just told me were mixed up in my mind. Yusuf noticed that my thoughts had strayed far away so he asked me, "Is the Ustaz tired?"

"A little, but that's not important. I wanted to ask you, Yusuf, and I hope you will be frank with me, did you tell me all you know about Prince Hamid?"

Yusuf placed his hand on his chest and said with a reproachful look in his eyes, "I swear by my father's life that I have not hidden from you anything important that I know. But why do you ask me this question?"

"I will tell you right away. Actually I was somewhat surprised at the prince's insistence that you and I collaborate with him. Frankly we are not exactly stars in the world of journalism. And as I told you, he can, with his money, hire whomever he wants of the big stars . . ."

"Pardon me, Ustaz, your name . . ."

I interrupted Yusuf decisively, "Nobody knows my name anymore. I don't live in an illusion or in lies. Perhaps some people knew me twenty years ago or more. But right now I am not a winning card in the game of journalism."

"But this actually is an opportunity for your star to rise again. You deserve that and more than that," Yusuf said uncertainly.

I smiled, saying, "Exactly, Yusuf. The prince must have thought that way: here's an opportunity that a lost person would not hesitate to accept. But let's leave that aside for the moment. I also want to ask you: Do you know Ishaq Davidian?"

He said sarcastically, "Of course. Who doesn't? He's one of our 'compadres' and one of the richest millionaires here. He emigrated from Egypt in 1956 and became a citizen of this country. He owns half the apartment buildings in this city." Then after a pause, laughing, "I took part in a demonstration against him."

"A demonstration against Davidian? Why?"

"The people in this neighborhood demonstrated because he buys old, low-rent houses and tears them down to build huge luxury apartment buildings in their place that rent for twice the monthly income of the people he made homeless. So where will they live? In the street?"

"I didn't know that story. What was the result of the demonstration?"

He shrugged his shoulders, saying, "Like any demonstration. We carried posters against Davidian and went to the alderman and gave him a petition. As for Davidian, he continued to buy old buildings and tear them down. Demonstrations, Ustaz, have nothing but their slogans and their loud voices, while he has the money and the law. So what can a demonstration do?"

"You're right. But did you hear or read that he donated a hundred thousand dollars to the Israeli army after the invasion of Lebanon? Did you know that?"

"I didn't know it, but it doesn't surprise me. He is one of their well-known men here. He writes to the newspapers defending them and hosts delegations that come from there, and . . ."

Then he paused for a moment before saying in surprise, "But why all these questions? What has Davidian got to do with what we are talking about?"

"Do you know what Davidian trades in, besides real estate?"

"Almost everything: hotels, banks, the stock exchange and everything."

I looked at his eyes as I said, "Don't you also know that he is Europe's biggest Arabian horse dealer? It was you who drew my attention to it when you talked about Prince Hamid's trading in horses. Actually, Yusuf, your prince is Davidian's biggest partner."

He looked at me in shock and the question was more like a scream, "Prince Hamid? No!" Then he said with disbelief in his voice, "Perhaps you're wrong. The prince is a nationalist, you heard him speak yourself. How? He has friends in all the Arab political parties, even the PLO itself!"

"Listen, Yusuf. For a week I have been doing nothing but research on the prince. I got in touch with everyone I know here, even those who work at the Arab embassies whom I tried to avoid all the time. I went to the stock exchange. I talked to financial editors in newspapers and with horse traders and even horseracing editors. If I had a scintilla of doubt, I wouldn't have spoken to you."

He remained silent for a while then said, "But why does he do that? He has all the money in the world."

A sentence Prince Hamid had uttered about Abd al-Nasser and the Americans awakened something inside me, and what I found out later confirmed my intuition. Perhaps he indeed wants the newspaper because of his ambition to rule and his desire to fight the crown Prince. And it may be bigger than that, something that neither you nor I know. He is in any case very intelligent, very rich, very ambitious, and extremely persuasive. Men like him do not escape the attention of the powers that be and their plans. But I kept it to myself and did not complete what I was thinking and instead told him, "In brief, he wants the two of us to be his pawns to do something that we know nothing about."

Yusuf was not following what I was saying, he was muttering, "The prince is Davidian's partner, so if we work for the prince we would be working for Davidian and Davidian has given money to Israel."

Then he laughed bitterly as he said, "You've closed all doors for me, Ustaz."

"God forbid—How?"

He said without turning his face towards me, as if talking to himself, "What do I do now? Stay here and live and die a cook or a waiter? Go back home and be unemployed? Here at least I am sending my father some money every month. Emigrate in God's big world? Where? Would it be different anywhere else? What should I do?"

As if defending myself, I said, "Listen, Yusuf. I didn't ask anything of you. All there is to it is that you pressed me to put together the plan for the newspaper and now I want you to know why I can't do that." Remembering something, I added, "In any case I have one request for you. As I told you, I don't know whether the prince is working alone or has an outfit behind him. All I'm asking is for this to stay between us."

I laughed briefly as I said, "I don't want a car to hit me in the street or be stabbed by an unknown person as I go back home at night."

He said perfunctorily, "God forbid!"

I added, "I'm only kidding, of course, but I mean I want this to be between us. After that it's up to you. You can continue to work for the prince if you like."

He let out a short laugh, more like a moan, "I demonstrated against Sadat and was sentenced to jail and I ran away from my country and from my family because I thought he was endangering the future of the country. And I, the poor one, lost my future for my principles while the rich and powerful . . . Hello, principles!"

As he spoke he tried to get up, with worry and defeat written all over his face. I held him by the wrist so he would remain seated and said, "Why do you give up so fast? The end of the world has not come because you won't work at the prince's newspaper. Write, if you want, and try to publish what you write in the newspapers that come out here in Europe, or also send it to the papers in the Arab countries. If you don't like to be a cook, look for another job and try to be rich and strong yourself."

I felt as I talked that I was not convincing at all, yet I went on, "Please Yusuf, don't let the world defeat you as it defeated me."

He didn't comment on my words, which had come in a quick succession, but he mumbled some conventional words of thanks as he went hurriedly towards the kitchen. Elaine looked inquisitively at me from the other end of the café but I turned my gaze away.

I left the café quickly and waved goodbye to Elaine from a distance.

There was plenty of time before meeting Brigitte at noon, so I decided to go home and rest there for a short while, but instead I drove the car to the riverbank and parked it near the café, then I began to stroll in the quiet streets near the river. It was cold and cloudy and it looked as if it was going to rain soon, but I didn't care.

I thought I was going to close the matter for good! To tell Yusuf what I'd found out, then wash my hands of the newspaper and the prince, devote myself once again to the joy that I had promised myself to experience exclusively. So why didn't that happen? So be it. I made a mistake indeed. It was not my business to interfere in Yusuf's life or Elaine's, or to concern myself with this matter. From the beginning I should have apologized to Yusuf by saying my health made work out of the question and the whole matter would have ended there. How important was that investigation that I threw myself at? What did I gain when I found out who he was? You are not going to save Lebanon from Davidian and you will not fight Israel with your discoveries. We agreed a long time ago that you are not important, so why all the games? You will not even save Yusuf. The poor man was as horrified as you were when you found out the truth. You never imagined when you began that you would reach that conclusion. All you wanted was to find out who that Prince Hamid was and all the threads led to Davidian. A nationalist and a progressive newspaper indeed! His highness planned it with great precision: first, feed him the illusion of principles, give him the hope of once again becoming a real journalist after he had become a nonentity, dazzle him with undreamt wealth, trips and dollars and endless projects, then in the end use him like a pawn and move him any which way you want. No matter how high the price, he will cost less than anyone else and will be more obedient. But why? What does he actually want from me? Why me?

My feet led me unconsciously to my little secret garden. There was nobody there. Exhausted, I sat on the nearest bench. All the trees had turned dull yellow and shed leaves covered with a brown layer, the color of rust, on the ground. I felt cold after a short while, so I got up and walked briskly on the short crisscrossing path that always led back to the starting point. Calm down. Forget this prince for good. Didn't you promise Brigitte and yourself to avoid this world? But that's what I've already done. I have withdrawn inside my skin and tried to forget everything. Even my telephone conversations with Khalid and Hanadi have become something casual in my life and I make sure they are not long. I ran away from everything that reminded me of my old conflicts and my old self. I've accepted also that I am a defeated father who shouldn't fight to regain what he had already lost. So why this bewilderment now? Why did that Prince have to appear? Should I, too, have to "wrestle horses that count Time as one of their knights"? Count Prince Hamid and Davidian as some of their knights? Arabian horses, really!

But enough of that. We've said that story was over. Let's go back as if it never was. Let the Prince and Davidian go to hell, to oblivion, which is more important. Think of the only joy that you get out of this world. Elaine said don't rush its end, so don't rush its end. Don't even think that its end will come. Brigitte is there. Flesh and blood, not a delusion or a trick of the imagination. Yes. Yes.

I was escaping from the garden, almost running on my way to the café. I stood for a moment out of breath when I saw the oval building jutting out into the river. I felt that tears were welling up in my eyes.

What a blessing that our café is still here!

What a blessing that it will give us both shelter!

What a blessing to see her there, coming from the end of the road walking as usual. She's not walking but floating on invisible ether, and I am with you, also leaving behind this earth that is full of evils, to catch up with you, your love lifting me to that ether, to that innocence to escape together to serenity and together make that joy.

9

This Cave

S HE WAS WEARING A RAINCOAT, her face hiding an anxiety that I didn't miss.

Next to our usual window I helped her take off her raincoat. She was not wearing her uniform under it, but a white blouse and a blue pullover the color of her eyes. She had pulled back her hair and plaited it in a haphazard way, and some golden strands had fallen around her face, which looked less round than usual. I asked her as we sat opposite each other, "You didn't go to work?"

She pointed at the clouds in the sky, "A tourist tour in this weather? The office called in the morning and said there were no tours today."

"So what are you going to do?"

"Pray for the sun to shine! Even though that won't do much good. The tourist season is almost over anyway, and we have to think of the future."

I knew that she had a difficult time living on the measly sum she was getting from the tourist company. She didn't have an official work permit or a contract with the owner of the company but he found work for her all the time because she was fluent in many languages and content with the low salary. The owner was also pleased that as a foreigner she didn't have rights to insurance or pension benefits so he kept her while regularly getting rid of his citizen employees before they completed six months of work so they wouldn't gain these legal rights. Ever since I knew her, Brigitte lived within her income, allowing herself no luxuries and accepting nothing from me. If I invited her to lunch one day, she would reciprocate the following day. One evening she borrowed from me a very small sum of money and the following morning I found an envelope in the mailbox with the money in it. She couldn't wait until noon when we usually met to repay the loan. Ultimately I stopped inviting her to restaurants or giving her any small gifts, to put her at ease. I know now that she will not accept any help even if she loses her job. So, what's going to happen to her, and to us?

Brigitte surprised me when she reached out to hold my hand laughing as she said, "Don't worry, you won't get rid of me easily. There must be some other solution or another job. The director of the company talked to me today about someone who wants French lessons. I think I can give lessons to beginners and foreigners."

I didn't know whether she had said that just to reassure me or if it was real. She kept holding my hand between her hands and patting it as if she were rocking a baby as she looked through the glass window. Rain was now falling in big drops on the river and waves rose to receive the drops.

Looking at me with a sly smile, Brigitte said, "See that? The sky is making love to the river and they'll give birth to new waves."

Then she began to shake my hand, saying somewhat loudly, "Hey, you! What are you thinking about?"

"I am thinking about what you just said and about things that happened today. I'm also thinking about what will happen tomorrow."

She tightened her lips, withdrawing her hand from mine, saying, "Then you'll never change. I told you several times that what happened and what will happen do not matter. All we have is the moment, here and now."

"I'm twice your age and you're teaching me lessons?" I said, joking.

"Is it my fault that you haven't learned your lesson after all these years?"

She was right! But what can I do when Elaine's picture never leaves my mind, and her sad voice, as she tries not to lose all her dignity while actually begging me, rings in my ears? What kind of harbinger is that?

Brigitte kept looking through the window in silence as a shadow of a smile appeared on her daydreaming face. It rained more profusely and black clouds took over the sky. She turned towards me, "I am from a crazy family!"

"You said it! But what reminded you of that now?"

"The rain. It reminded me of a day like today in my childhood." She knit her brow as if trying to recall the memory precisely. "Its morning, however, was sunny. I was sitting with my father in his study watching him silently as usual when he turned towards me suddenly and said, "Brigitte, do you know the names of the trees?" I didn't and he said, "It's a shame that you still don't know the names of the trees. Come on, let's do something useful today. I'll teach you their names!" At the edge of town there was a large botanical garden, almost as big as a forest. But when we arrived there the clouds hid the sun and the garden was almost dark. Then it began to rain, but none of that stopped my father. He accompanied me from tree to tree, picking a leaf from one tree to compare it to the leaf of another tree nearby. He was totally engrossed in this and told me all the details that he knew, and I followed, not wanting to miss a word. We didn't even have an umbrella to cover our heads. We ran to seek shelter under an elm or the branches of any other leafy tree, without him stopping his explanations or me missing even one moment. But when we got home, my mother screamed in dismay. She cried and yelled at my father to change his clothes quickly as she took off my wet dress and dried my hair, with tears in her eyes, muttering, "The girl will die, she will surely catch pneumonia, surely!" My father did not go to change his clothes but stood there, planted in his place and dripping and looking at me in panic as if he suddenly realized what happened, so I winked to reassure him. And, you know something? That lesson was never forgotten. In every country I have tree friends to whom I go and I share my joy with them and complain to them if I am sad. I think trees understand me, I am sure they do. What do you say we have a baby?"

At first I didn't grasp the question, but the parallel lines were now gathering next to her eyes and chin and her eyes glistened as she looked eagerly at me.

"You're kidding?"

"No, I haven't thought of a baby since, since the other one went."

"A baby? At my age, Brigitte?"

"It doesn't matter. It's never too late to give your gift to life, a baby who is you and who is me—we live in him together and we live with him far away, on an island or on a mountain top. We teach him to love trees and flowers and poetry. We teach him also how to have tree friends, listening to what their branches say and understanding the messages sent by their falling leaves. We will also teach him not to forget them in the fall. He will tell the tree that he shares its agony of death and rebirth, that he too will be reborn with it when its green leaves sprout again, that he will not forget it when it stands naked in the winter but with his love will give it warmth. Let's have that baby!"

Her cheeks were red and she was actually trembling as she shook my hand eagerly and urgently. I kept silent for a moment before telling her, "And what will happen when he gets off that mountain top or leaves that island? Will people be as kind to him as the trees?"

"But didn't I tell you that we will teach him love above all things? Love will save him as it has saved us. Isn't that so? He will be saved, always . . . always."

Some doubt crept into her voice as she murmured "always . . . always" nonstop in a soft voice as if she wanted to convince herself and me that it was true. It seemed to me now as she pursed her trembling lips that she was fighting off tears and fighting off the admission that she was pursuing a distant dream.

How do I protect her? If I only knew how to protect this woman who has given me all this love and who is now sitting in front of me, defeated, looking for an impossible baby in an impossible world! I kept patting her hand and pressing it gently, trying to convey to her without words that I understood and that I was with her at that moment of longing, to tell her, 'It was you, Brigitte who said that love saved us, who said let's live the moment we have. So why don't you do that now?' I pressed her fingers, then I raised them to my mouth and whispered to those fingers that I adored, "Just let this day slow down. I don't have impossible dreams, just let it slow down, that's all I hope for."

Suddenly, however, a wicked thought came to me so I dropped her hand and cried out, "Brigitte, are you . . . "

"No!"

"I haven't asked you anything yet."

She nodded slowly saying, "But I know your question, my friend. No, I am not pregnant. I won't do anything behind your back if that's what you're afraid of."

I remained silent and turned to the window again. The steam that had gathered on the windowpanes blocked the view of the river and the mountain. A sunset-like dusk settled on the café and when I looked at Brigitte again she was bowing her head, and her face, surrounded by unruly locks, seemed featureless, as if it were peering from behind a cloud. There was silence and dejection. Something had glowed for one moment then it went out. Throughout the rest of our meeting I didn't try to explain anything or justify anything, and neither my attempts nor her attempts managed to dispel the gloom that had settled after her answer to the question I didn't utter. We kept chattering, trying to forget the baby that was born for one moment during which he was enamored of trees, then died at the tip of a question, but we knew it was there haunting us, tormenting her with regret because she loved it, and tormenting me because I buried it alive before it was born.

Our meeting ended soon after that. I asked her to come with me but she said she had a headache and wished to rest a little. She asked me to give her a ride home, and before getting out of the car she said in a casual tone that she would call me to get together in the evening.

I also was exhausted and when I reached my house I took my mail from my mailbox and went upstairs to my apartment, then threw the newspaper on the desk, muttering, "So be it, Brigitte, so be it Elaine. Come what may!" Exhaustion had given way to indifference.

I postponed calling Khalid and Hanadi; I wasn't ready yet. I hadn't gotten rid of the unborn baby to tend to older children, so I kept pacing in the room, rearranging things aimlessly, moving the chairs, reshelving the books in the bookcase once by size, another time by subject. On one of the shelves I saw the picture of Abd al-Nasser whose glass was shattered when I fell with it to the floor. The broken glass had scraped off part of his mouth and distorted his smile, so his face looked sad. Once more, I decided to get a new frame for it. Then I stood in the middle of the little living room, looking around. Nothing remained to be done! There had been nothing to be done to begin with, so in resignation I returned to the desk, sat down and began to go through the mail.

I found some issues of my Cairene newspaper, glanced at the headlines, and put them aside. I kept the Thursday issue and opened it to page eight where Manar published her weekly column. But it was not there. Instead there was a religious article: "Between Sharia and History," so I put the paper on top of the other papers and began to dial the Cairo number, looking distractedly at the picture published with the religious article. It was a profile of the face of a veiled woman, with a white scarf covering her hair and surrounding her face. I said to myself as I kept mechanically dialing the number, "I know this face. This face is familiar."

Suddenly I put down the receiver and snatched up the newspaper.

Yes, of course. It was Manar. Yes, it's the Women's Page as usual with her name in the middle. There was a subtitle in small font under the headline: "Between Sharia and History: What Happened to Women's Rights?" I quickly scanned the article. I had correctly guessed the theme from the headline: the sharia, or canon law, preserved women's tangible and intangible rights but men throughout history have been chipping these rights away. The article was full of quotations and citations of religious reference books. It was not Manar's usual style. She had toned down her attack on men for whom she used to save words like bullets, the mildest of which were such expressions as: "man's historical tyranny," "jurists of ignorance and lies who break the neck of the texts," and the like. This time the strongest sentence in her article was something to the effect that if men had understood the sharia properly, equality would have been achieved a long time ago because in the sharia women's rights were equal to their duties. Men have additional rights because they have additional duties.

I put the newspaper down in front of me and kept staring at it.

Until last week her picture in the middle of the column was the same one that she had used for the last ten years on the Women's Page, the picture in which her smiling face appeared in the middle of the halo of her parted black hair, long and flowing on both sides of her face. In the new picture the profile of her face was grave as she stared into the distance. The old nickname they gave her when she started working at the paper came back to me. They used to make fun of her enthusiasm and call her Manar Shafiq, after Duriyya Shafiq who had formed a women's political party that Abd al-Nasser dissolved after the revolution. I remembered moments of the dialogues we had in which she defended her right to choose her line of work, to wear what she wanted, and to do exactly what I did and "don't you dare speak of man this and woman that."

And now what do you think, my friend?

Tell me what to do if you've kept writing like her for thirty years, saying the same things about the necessity of liberating women over and over again when lo and behold, women don't want to be liberated? What do you ultimately do? If you can't beat them, join them!

And yet there is a simpler answer: Manar is following the path of virtue and you are going down the slippery slope of vice.

Very simple!

I reached for the telephone to dial the Cairo number again but I put the receiver back again. What do you think of Khalid? Also very simple. As they say in the proverb: from the loins of the impious, the pious shall come.

Come on, face the truth. Yes, sometimes I am ashamed of myself because he is so young and innocent and because I, the old man, am clinging to the last drop that life can offer. I remember very well what Ibrahim said about the circumstances that make us. What then were the circumstances that made our generation see nothing shameful in living one's life? Why did we accept the fact that we were human beings who did right and wrong, and who sinned and repented, who hoped for God's mercy and who were confident that repentance would come before it was too late? Why does Khalid want to be an angel whose purity shouldn't be sullied by just one game of chess? I know that if he lived that life the way he's started to now, he would not experience the dilemma that we had, he would not try to rectify his past as Manar, in her way, was trying now and as I, in my way, was trying to do. There would not be conflict in life or a crack in the soul; everything would be clean and easy. And yet something inside me tells me that that's impossible, Khalid! It's never happened that humans sprouted angels' wings. Had you been here with me we would have talked as we used to, as friends. I would have tried to explain to you and to listen to you. But, come on! Don't delight in tormenting yourself!

I folded the paper and Manar's picture and once again dialed the number. After several attempts as usual, Khalid's voice came, "Peace be upon you."

"And upon you, Khalid. Where is Hanadi? Why didn't she answer the telephone first as she usually does?"

"She's sitting right here and will talk to you right away." Then he laughed. "She's angry."

"Angry at me?"

"No, angry at *me*."

"What did you do to her this time, Khalid? Is it the old television story?"

"No, she watches as much television as she likes. It's just . . . " His voice waned a little. "Stop it, girl! Don't snatch the receiver . . . "

Hanadi's crying voice came through, "Listen, Daddy, tell Khalid to leave me alone, otherwise I'll run away from home for good!"

"Oh my God! Run away, just like that? Why, for heaven's sake?"

"Every day he gives me a hard time and makes up a new story! Now he doesn't want me to go to the club. Even Mom told him to leave me alone but he doesn't listen to her. He doesn't let me go out and . . . " Once again her voice choked with tears.

"Calm down, Hanadi. Calm down and give Khalid the phone. You will go to the club as much as you like. But please stop crying, Sweetie, for Daddy's sake. Please!"

Her voice came through the uncontrollable crying, "Tell him . . . Tell him, Daddy."

"I will. Give me Khalid."

His voice came through, calmly, "Peace be upon you."

"We've been through that already. What's the story with your sister?"

"Well, Father, immoral things take place at the club and there are bad young men and I . . . "

"There are bad people and good people every place on earth. Let her learn on her own and protect herself."

His voice grew angry as he said, "If I, a man, have stopped going to the club, how can you expect me to let *her* go? Are you going to spoil her just as Mom does and every time she sheds two tears, you'll give her what she wants? Hanadi is no longer a little girl, and here I am in charge of her."

"Are you raising your voice at me, Khalid? And you are in charge of her? I haven't died yet, my son."

"God forbid. I didn't mean it like that. I meant . . ."

I too raised my voice, "I don't want to know what you meant! I told you to leave her alone, you understand? I've never in my life imposed an opinion on you or told you to do this or to quit doing that. I let you be free to think what you want and do what you like. Isn't that so?"

"Yes."

"So? Why is it that you want to impose your opinion on others? That's very strange! Leave Hanadi alone, free to go out and go to the club and do what she wants. You understand?"

He hesitated for a moment before saying in a low voice, "All right, so long as you are not convinced of my point of view." Then he was silent for a moment. "But I actually wanted to talk to you about something totally different."

"Okay. First, give me Hanadi."

"Yes, Father."

"Okay, Hanadi. I told Khalid that you can go out and can go to the club whenever you want, but of course you have to get your mom's permission and to tell her when you are going out and when you are coming back."

"That's what I do, I swear to God. Thank you, Daddy."

"And I also don't want you to upset your brother."

She burst out again, "Can anybody upset him? He can make life hard for a whole town as he sits as if he were a sultan and says, 'Peace be upon you.'"

She did a perfect impression of the way he spoke and I smiled involuntarily but I said, "You shouldn't do that, Hanadi, otherwise I'll be upset. He is your older brother and you should show him respect."

"Is that all? That's so easy. Bye-bye. I respect you, Khalid. Are you happy? Here, talk to Dad."

"Wait a minute, Hanadi."

"Yes, Daddy."

"Tell you what, Hanadi." I paused for a moment, then added, "Please Hanadi, stay as you are. Don't change."

"What will change me, Daddy?" she asked in surprise.

"I don't know. Many things change people, Sweetie, things outside them and things inside."

"Even though I don't understand anything of what you said, everything will be alright, God willing. Don't worry, be happy."

And for the first time since the telephone conversation began she laughed heartily as she said, "Bye-bye. Here's Khalid."

His voice came from a distance as he addressed his sister, "Please leave because I want to talk to Daddy about a private matter. Yes, Father."

I tried to get rid of my agitation as I asked him calmly, "What's happening?"

"Good things, God willing. All good things, may God enable us. I wanted to talk to you about Mother."

"What about her?"

"Well, you know."

"I don't know anything, Khalid. Tell me quick."

"I mean, Father, as you know, *of all things that God permits, divorce is the most loathsome to Him.*"

"Is that something to talk about over the telephone, Khalid?" I yelled.

"Please forgive me. I feel that God has guided Mother lately. She's completely changed."

"And *you* convinced her of this change?"

"I wish. That would have earned me merit. No, it was she. God guided her to the right path. She watched religious programs on television for some time, and then started borrowing books from me until God showed her the right way. It seems to me that if I talked to her about conciliation, I might find her ready. I was just saying . . . "

Once again I yelled, "Don't say anything, Khalid. Not on the telephone."

"Why? We are not saying anything to be ashamed of. Just listen to me, Father. I think I should try to probe Mother. She might . . ."

I made an effort not to yell again. "Don't try anything, Khalid. Thank you very much for your interest in this matter but this cannot be handled on the telephone as I told you. I'll write you a letter."

He persisted, "You've always expected us to be frank and to talk as friends, so don't be upset now when I tell you my opinion. Frankly, you are wrong because, as I told you, this is the most loathsome permissible thing and you are wrong."

"Thank you, my son. You spoke frankly and I listened but once again don't talk about it. I am sure that would also be your mother's opinion if you talked to her. Bye now."

"Peace and God's mercy be upon you."

I was shaking as I put the receiver down.

Once again I got up to pace in the small room. What will become of you, Khalid? Yes, we were always friends as you said, but we always discussed things before you expressed your opinion. Now you want to decide alone and to judge alone, and you want to carry out what you have decided for Hanadi, for your mother, and for me.

Are you going to tell me, like Yusuf, "But when I looked for you, you were not there?" No, I do not blame myself here at all. You made the choice. You were mature and you made the choice. I remember now the discussion we had once while playing chess when you were in secondary school. You had read *Macbeth* and said to me, "But Father, it's not his fault. The witches seduced him with the throne and said that he must ascend to that throne. He was predestined when he killed, so it was not his fault." I told you that day that it was Macbeth who created the witches to achieve his ambitions, that the witches were merely a figment of his imagination. Yes, but what's the importance of this story? Why is it coming to my mind now? Yes, I remember: I am thinking how gentle and sensitive you used to be, Khalid! It was difficult for you to condemn Macbeth the murderer! So where did this first gentleness go? Where did the sensitivity go? Why are you saying now with such decisiveness and such condemnation, "You are wrong?" What do you know about the experience I lived, or that your mother lived, to issue the verdict with such persistence: "You are wrong, Father"? If even now I am still trying to understand without ever condemning her, how can you condemn me so simply? Who gave you the monopoly on the truth?

I know that for some time now you have stopped reading *Macbeth* and other things. The only books you read now are those that prove to you that you are right and all others are wrong. But beware, Khalid! Beware, because all the evils that I have known in this world came out of that dark cave. It begins with an idea and ends up an evil: I am right and my opinion is better. I am better, therefore others are wrong. I am better because I am God's chosen people and the others are goyim. I am better because I am one of the Lord's children whose sins are forgiven and the others are heretics. Better because I am a Shiite and the others are Sunnis or because I am a Sunni and the others are Shiites. Better because I am white and the others are colored or because I am progressive and the others are reactionary and so on *ad infinitum*. Look, Khalid, at what's going on in the world now. Look at that war that doesn't want to end between Iraq and Iran, each side in the right, and keys to paradise are distributed to no end, and blood flows to no end. Look at that massacre in Lebanon and at God's chosen people wiping out an unchosen people and its army commander saying, "The only good Arab is a dead Arab!" All this killing because the killer is always better, more civilized. The killing machine is running the whole time to wipe out the others, the goyim, enemies of the Lord, enemies of the right doctrine, enemies of the white race, enemies of progress, always and endlessly enemies even though the only honorable war in the world is the one where you are defending your home, your family, or your land. All other wars are cowardly murders.

You will tell me, Khalid, "But I didn't do any of those things! I only spoke of divorce and the club and chess!" Yes, but be wary of that road, my son. Beware, Khalid, because it starts here and ends there. It begins with "You are wrong" and ends with "You deserve to be killed!"

I went back to the desk feverishly. Yes, I will write all this, I will write this letter to Khalid. I will write it before it's too late. I picked up the pen and paper.

But wait!

There is something missing in all of this! You want to tell him the truth, as you know it, you want to be honest with him as you've always been, but you haven't mentioned anything about Brigitte!

You didn't tell him you had a lover!

Do you dare?

You said before that you feel guilty especially when you think of

Khalid and his innocence. You also know that you can't live without Brigitte.

Your sense of guilt is true and your love is true, but the guilt does not cancel out the love, and neither does the love cancel out the guilt.

Will you write that too?

Yes, he must know everything, to know and think! To think then forgive, to think then condemn. It is important that he think.

It is more important that you know how to write to him.

A few days later, Brigitte visited me unexpectedly at my apartment at noon.

I was surprised by the long ringing of the bell accompanied by persistent knocks, and when I opened the door Brigitte rushed in like a cyclone. She stood in the small living room, her face flushed, her eyes fixed on my face then she said angrily, "What's the meaning of this? Were you behind the story of those lessons?"

"What story, Brigitte? I don't understand."

I tried to hold her hand and lead her to sit down but she jerked her hand away saying, "Where did you hear that I was looking for charity?"

"But I don't know what you're talking about! Please tell me, what's the matter?"

"And yet he mentioned your name."

"Who mentioned my name? Please calm down and tell me something I can understand instead of 'charity' and 'he mentioned your name.' What's the matter exactly?" I said somewhat angrily.

In a deliberately slow manner, putting emphasis on every word, she said, "The Arab prince who wants French lessons mentioned your name."

I was silent for a moment then said suspiciously, "A prince? Is his name Prince Hamid?"

"You can't expect me to remember these names! Maybe. I think that's his name."

I sat down quickly, trying to absorb very fast what had happened. I asked her, "But how did he reach you?"

She remained standing with an accusing look in her eyes as she said, "That's just what I'd like to know, from you. I told you before the director of the company . . ."

"Yes, yes. I remember. He suggested that you give French lessons after the decrease in tourist business. Did he mention at the time the name of the person who wanted the lessons?"

"No, he said it was a rich person, that's all."

Brigitte began to have doubts about her accusation that I was behind the matter. She took a few hesitant steps and sat next to me asking in puzzlement, "But if he speaks French fluently, why does he need lessons?"

"He speaks French also?"

"You don't know that?"

I lost my patience and said loudly, "Enough already! I told you I don't know anything at all about this. I saw this prince only once in my life and I told you about it that day."

"Yes, that's why I thought that perhaps you . . . because at the time I talked about the money that he throws away and I said I wouldn't mind."

"I'm not that stupid, Brigitte. I think I know you better than that. But what did he tell you about me? Please remember, this is important."

Brigitte remembered something else and said, "Wait a moment. If you didn't tell him about me, how did he know about our relationship?"

"Did he talk about that too?"

"Not directly. He was hinting. He's a complex person and I couldn't figure him out exactly."

Nevertheless I begged her to concentrate a little and to tell me everything that took place. I was barely able to understand what happened.

I learned from her that the prince had moved from the hotel, because she went to another address given to her by the director of the company. She said it was a huge palace on the mountain on the other bank of the river and she hadn't entered such a magnificent and spacious palace in her life. Each member of the staff escorted her to another until finally she reached the prince's office. She didn't expect to find him so young and elegant. Frankly she had expected him to be middle aged, wearing a white robe, and covering his head with that "scarf" the name of which she didn't know. She had expected that he wanted to learn a few sentences and words to get by when shopping in the stores or when going to restaurants like the thousands who visit the city in the summer. But the prince who received her very politely talked to her a little in English, explaining to her that he had decided to spend some time in this French-speaking country and therefore he wanted to practice conversation and writing. He told her, however, that he was not starting from scratch because he'd taken a few courses in French before, but he was not content with the level he had attained.

None of that really interested me, so I asked her urgently, "But what did he tell you about me? About us? That's what matters."

"I told you he spoke in a roundabout manner. He asked me if I were interested in journalism and when I said no he casually said, 'But I think we have a mutual friend who's a journalist.' I told him that our only mutual friend, as far as I knew, was the director of the company who had given him my name and given me his address. He said, 'Of course. And it is from him that I understood that you know some journalists here, among whom is my friend so and so.' I ignored that and said I preferred to start the lesson because it lasted an hour and some time had already passed. At that moment he seemed somewhat annoyed but in the rest of the hour we talked only about learning French. I treated him like any other student. I began by asking him questions in French and talked with him about grammar and discovered that he didn't need anything. It occurred to me that you were behind it and that the prince wanted me to know that when he mentioned your name, so I resented you. However, I didn't ask the prince about anything. I continued the lesson until the hour was over. He thanked me and said that he would contact me to make an appointment for the next lesson. I said goodbye without responding to that, but his secretary who accompanied me out of the office gave me a sealed white envelope. I opened it in front of her and found a check inside. Do you know for how much?"

"I hope not twenty thousand dollars!"

She laughed a little laugh and said, "For me it's more important than even twenty thousand dollars. The check was exactly my salary from the company for a whole month. I put it back in the envelope and returned it to the secretary and told her to thank the prince and to tell him that I did not deserve any fees because if he needed a lesson, I was not the right person: he is not a beginner, and French is not my native language. Who does he think I am?"

"But my friend Yusuf would have said nevertheless that you did give him a lesson!"

"Who is that?"

"It's not important. Try to remember: was that question of his all he said about me?"

"Yes, I didn't give him a chance for anything else. I wanted him to understand that I didn't want to get into anything other than the lessons and he understood. But he did anyway. What did he really want, in your opinion?"

I thought a little then said, "You didn't give him a chance to talk, so we'll never know. All we can figure out is that he wanted us to know that he knows about our relationship."

She said dismissively, "What does it matter if he knows or doesn't know? I don't mind if the whole world knows that I love you. And you?"

"You know the answer very well, Brigitte. You know that for me you are the whole world."

"So what does it matter if he lets us know or not? You know what I think? I think he is showing off his wealth, nothing more. I have to admit that something about him turned me off from the very first moment, made me regret that I had agreed to the lesson to begin with: maybe his huge palace, his obscene wealth, or his attempt to appear very diplomatic and very attractive."

"Well, actually he doesn't attempt that: he is indeed very rich and diplomatic and attractive."

"Maybe. That's the reason I didn't like him. I told you before that I don't like sane people but I prefer them nonetheless to the rich. Imagine, this whole palace, this whole entourage to serve one human being. Why? And those Arabs whose pictures in refugee camps they publish, why doesn't he live in a smaller house and give them the difference?"

I sighed, saying, "The time for this kind of talk is long gone, Brigitte, very long gone!"

"Since when?"

"Perhaps since the Spanish Civil War! Talking that way has become shameful these days if not a downright crime. Ask your father."

Brigitte smiled for the first time and said, "We seldom talk about these things. I talk with him about more serious things. He is now busy learning the calls of birds!"

Then she turned towards me and said, "Have you forgiven me for this uncalled-for anger?"

"It's you who should forgive me for getting you into these troubles," I said, genuinely sad.

She leaned her head back in the chair saying in some surprise, "Why do these things happen to me? Why me? All I want is for the world to leave me alone. Is that too much?"

After that she was totally gone. She had turned her head towards me, fixing me with her blue eyes, but I was sure she didn't see me or hear me, and that she could continue like that for a whole hour, sitting cross-legged, resting her arms on the chair, her neck turned towards me. Everything would remain like that for a long time before she'd shake her head and look around suddenly and ask me, "Pardon? What were you saying?"

But something had happened to me too. Another madness had seized me as hers had. These moments of suspended animation were the moments I revealed everything that I didn't say when she was awake. The first thing I revealed was my fears. So I whispered, "I know, Brigitte, even if you don't say anything, that something has come between us since I killed the baby your dreams had created, and that another rift has been caused by that prince. Yes, all you want is for the world to leave you alone and all I want is for you to be in this world. I know, Brigitte, that I am just a page in the book of your life, but you are my last page. If you fold it everything will be over, so let that page fold itself slowly. You said that love has saved us, so please don't let the world defeat us, get us lost again. Shall I read you some poetry, Brigitte?"

You did not stir at all but I got up and brought Pablo Neruda's poems, which I love, and sat embracing you and reading to you:

Oh rose,
O little rose,
Sometimes fragile and tiny,
Sometimes I feel that one palm
Is enough to contain you.
But suddenly my foot touches your foot
And my mouth your lips
And you grow bigger.

Your shoulders become two mountains
And your chest engulfs my chest
My hand barely encircling your little waist, like
A newborn crescent moon.
Released by love, your soul has overflowed
Waves crashing against the sky lit by your eyes.
I bend over your mouth
And I kiss the earth.

That is you, Brigitte. Neruda was describing you and nobody else!

I was whispering to you and I was screaming but the mask of your inclined face did not stir.

10

All the Children
of the World

I WAS PUZZLED. I didn't know what the prince wanted from Brigitte or from me. I remembered that recently I had been noticing a certain Indian sitting at the café when I met Brigitte, and sometimes I came across him on the street in front of the house. But I didn't give it much thought. I said to myself it might be a coincidence. Who would bother to have us under surveillance?

For days afterward I kept trying to reach the prince at the number I had gotten from Brigitte, but Linda always answered to tell me that His Highness was not there.

I was equally unsuccessful in reaching Yusuf to see if he had any news about the prince. He also was never there. Finally I went to the café, even though I was trying to avoid meeting Elaine again. I saw Bernard in his usual corner with a glass of beer in front of him. He waved to me but Elaine, who was carrying some customers' orders, signaled to me that she wanted to speak with me. She finished her job quickly and came towards me with a sullen face.

"Pardon me, but what did you tell Yusuf that day we talked? What happened to him?" she said.

"I don't understand, Elaine. What happened? Forgive me, I didn't have a chance to talk to him about you. We only talked about the newspaper and I told him that I cannot work on it."

Elaine leaned her hand on one of the tables looking at me in such a way as if accusing me of something. Then she bowed her head and said in a skeptical tone, "Is that all that took place?"

"Yes." Then after some hesitation, "We also talked about the prince."

"You told him to go back to him?"

"On the contrary. But it's not up to me to ask him to go back or not. He's free to do whatever he likes."

"And you met afterwards, right?"

"Absolutely not. I've come here today to see him. I need him for a really important matter."

"Really important! You can reach him at the prince's if you want him!" she said, laughing sardonically. She was about to leave but I grabbed her hand to stop her as I said, "Please, Elaine. What happened exactly? I swear to you I haven't seen Yusuf since the last time I was here. And he also has not contacted me. But you're telling me that something has happened. What is it?"

Elaine looked in Bernard's direction for a moment, then turned again to stare at me before she said, "I don't know, sir, about what you and Yusuf talked that day you came here, but after you left he left the kitchen and stayed in his room all day. The following morning he said he was going to the prince. Since that day I almost never see him. He gets up in the morning to go to the prince and returns only late at night."

She laughed bitterly again and said, "And can you explain to me why he no longer shaves?"

One of the customers called her at that moment, and Bernard waved to me again so I walked over and as I was sitting down he said to me,

"Was she talking to you about Yusuf?"

"Yes, but I don't understand anything. It's as if she's accusing me."

"She doesn't understand anything," he said dismissively.

"So, do *you* know something?"

In the same tone he said, "I don't understand anything, nobody in the world understands anything." I said to myself he's in one of his bad moods. His eyes were indeed redder than usual as he gulped down his drink and signaled Elaine to get him another. He leaned his chin on his hand as he studied the buxom young woman holding the bird feather in the painting, then he let out a sudden laugh before asking me, "What's the name of that doctor who advised you to quit the profession? I also want to go to him."

"You can quit the profession without the doctor's orders, Bernard, if you want to."

"Unfortunately I can't. The profession is a prison; there is insurance and all these complications. You cannot change your profession at this age without a reason."

"Are you serious? Wasn't it you who said once, when Ibrahim was here, that a journalist should be detached from his work?"

"I say many things I don't mean, exactly like my paper."

"And yet your paper is doing something good these days. As far as I know, it is the only newspaper that has launched a campaign against Israel's use of internationally banned bombs against civilians in Lebanon," I said, trying to console him.

He bowed his head and fell silent.

The small newspaper *Le Progrès* where Bernard worked was delivered to me by mail every day together with the principal newspapers here. Ordinarily I just read the headlines, but even those headlines were causing me dizziness and sometimes I felt that the old illness would come back, so I left them piled on the desk for days without looking at them. But recently my attention had been drawn to the fact that for several days *Le Progrès* had been publishing protests by many humanitarian organizations of Israel's bombing of houses, hospitals, and civilian targets in Beirut, and also of Israel's use of phosphorous bombs whose burns caused their victims horrendous pain before they killed them. They also protested the use of bombs disguised as dolls and toys to kill the children and the fuel air explosives that sucked out the air around buildings and leveled them with their inhabitants in seconds. The humanitarian organizations were protesting the use of these internationally banned weapons, but the morning newspaper I received every day made no mention whatsoever of those weapons or the protests. I said to Bernard, "And yet something is missing from your publication of these protests; you've never asked where these weapons that Israel used have come from. You didn't say a single word about America, which gave Israel these weapons to try them out in Lebanon."

Bernard looked at me and said sarcastically, "You want us to mention America too? Don't we have enough problems with the letters of protest we receive and publish every day from Israel's friends? You want a letter of protest from America itself? You want to close down the paper?"

Then he added, "Although that's a wonderful solution; if the paper is closed, I won't need a letter from the doctor!"

Something occurred to me and I asked him, "Are you the editor in charge of those news stories, Bernard?"

He didn't reply. He raised the beer glass to his mouth before discovering that it was empty. He returned it to the table and said in a grandiloquent tone. "*Le Progrès*! *Avanti*! *Avanti*! Forward! Forward! Don't you see that we are doing fantastic things? We severely attack racism in South Africa and we passionately defend women's rights all over the world and we write articles overflowing with kindness towards third-world countries. And we are indeed progressive, but try once to write a real article about our own role in the crisis of this world over which we shed tears! Try to give what's happening in Lebanon the name it deserves! Ask how this daily massacre can be a war, as if it is possible to have a real war between a massive army that has the most modern planes and drops the most deadly bombs from the air and from the sea on a city to which it lays siege, which does not have a single plane, an army, or a navy? Ask how can it be a war, when a few hundred or a few thousand men defend this city with rifles and machine guns or even with artillery and tanks? Where is the war in this daily massacre? Ask!"

"Couldn't *you* ask?"

"No, I cannot ask. Have you seen anyone in our papers that is able to ask?" he said curtly.

I didn't tell him that even in the Arab newspapers I didn't find anyone asking this question. In our papers too they were talking about the developments of the "war" and about the "peace" negotiations, and about the heroism of the steadfast freedom fighters in Beirut. They were publishing modern poems and traditional poems as if there were indeed a real war between two countries or two armies.

Elaine silently put a glass of beer in front of Bernard and asked me in a lukewarm tone what I wanted to drink and when I ordered coffee she left without a word. Bernard followed her with his eyes and said,

"Poor woman! Her husband is going through a spiritual crisis!"

"And apparently you too, Bernard! And me too," I said bitterly.

"I have been going through this crisis for the last forty years at least!" Bernard said.

"Forty years! Did you too go to the Spanish Civil War?"

His eyes glazed over for a moment and he said, "No, I was a young boy at the time. But the Spanish Civil War came to me."

I looked at him quizzically and he added, "My father was a worker and a member of the Revolutionary Workers Party, and they set up a refugee camp for the Spaniards who fled the war in our town. My father was among the volunteers who worked in that camp. I went with him sometimes. To this day, the stories I heard in the camp, the horrors of killing and torture perpetrated by the Royalists and the Republicans equally, are still etched in my mind. Perhaps that was why I never joined any political party and perhaps that was why, when I grew up, I decided to be a journalist. I said to myself it might help somewhat to tell the truth; people might learn and they might understand." He fell silent for a moment then said, "Come on, tell the truth!"

He had a big gulp of beer then said somewhat angrily, "No one will prevent you—we are a free country! But just wait and see what will happen to you! You will spend your life going from one *Le Progrès* to another, from a small newspaper to a smaller newspaper. They'll tolerate you and they'll pity you." Then he waved his finger in my face in warning, "Provided, however, that you don't go too far! You must learn where to draw the line."

"So it's like that all over the world!" I said sadly.

"I don't know the whole world. I only know myself! I know the great hopes that I started with and I know how they ended up. I know that my own son, whom I tried to teach since his childhood all that I knew of the world, whom I said I would raise on the truth, is now an arms dealer. He sells weapons to the Africans so they can kill each other while he makes hundreds of thousands, I don't know, maybe millions. I know that when I tried to prevent him he made fun of me and quarreled with me. He said that I wanted him to be a failure like me! He stopped just short of calling me an idiot. I don't even get a card from him at Christmas! And who knows what Jean-Baptiste will do when he grows up!"

He fell silent again. His words had depressed me and I wanted to leave, but when he noticed that I was about to get up, he said, "Wait, you haven't drunk your coffee yet."

At that moment Elaine was placing the coffee cup in front of me with a sullen face. Bernard told her, "This gentleman has nothing to do with what happened to your husband, Elaine."

Elaine looked at him for quite a while and he repeated definitively, "Nothing at all!"

She left without a word and I asked him in surprise, "What made you say that?"

"I know you have nothing to do with it!"

Then he regained some of his liveliness and said with his usual laugh, "She should be happy, nonetheless! She used to complain all the time that Yusuf drank wine from the time he got up in the morning until he went to bed in the evening. And now he doesn't touch the stuff. A big spiritual change."

I remained silent, hoping that he would go on, but he said,

"Don't look at me like that. I don't know anything about Yusuf or his spiritual change but I know something about the prince."

I became fully alert when he mentioned the prince but he hesitated for a moment before saying, "It is my duty to tell you. I hold myself responsible because it was I who introduced you to Yusuf and asked you to help him to work at that newspaper with this prince. And I told you that he is a progressive prince."

"So, what's new? Isn't he actually progressive?"

"That depends on what you mean when you use the word, but please don't repeat what I'm about to say; if my sources are correct, they're cooking up a big scheme for your region. What's happening in Lebanon is merely a beginning. There's a total reshuffling of the cards and secret negotiations among all the parties, negotiations among states and services and organizations, and His Highness is a major player."

I said after a short pause, "I'm not surprised."

"Did you know?"

"No, I don't know any details and I don't have sources like yours, but I had suspicions about the prince and his relations from the beginning, and I told Yusuf to be wary of him."

He looked closely at my face as he said, "You made a mistake, my friend. These people don't like to be found out and it's best that whoever finds out anything keeps it to himself."

After what I heard from Bernard I understood why my attempts to reach Prince Hamid had failed. I hid all I heard from Brigitte. I didn't mention the prince at all. I hoped she would continue in her conviction that all he had done was merely an attempt to show off his wealth. I knew that if she suspected that something else was behind it, if she found out that the prince had perhaps been probing her to find out through her what *I* knew, or to use her as a weapon against me, that would open the old wounds, the wounds that she had tried to heal by running away to this city, from which she might run away now. I knew what I was doing was not honest and I knew I was selfish, but I couldn't bear the thought of losing her.

Sensing the danger made me cling to her and sink further and further into the whirlpool that engulfed us both. The wave turned into a tempestuous deluge that inundated us night and day. We tossed in that deluge without getting lost, blending together into one wave, one inseparable drop.

Did you too, Brigitte, sense the danger? You gave of yourself unhesitatingly. Together we entered territories we had never been to before, in a fervent longing that didn't want to lose a single minute. I held you so closely and felt every part of your body as if, were my hand to let go of you, you would slip between my fingers; as if, if I didn't hold you tight in my arms, you would suddenly vanish. I felt you as if my fingers could immortalize your cheeks when they burned with desire, when those lines appeared while you were at the peak of ecstasy as if you were in unbearable pain mixed with unbearable joy. I felt the lips that parted with a moan that made your whole body tremble, and the long white neck in which one blue vein stood out when the blood of love clamored. I felt your smooth, round shoulders, as if to fix in my fingers the moment they shook, to stay alive forever. When your chest rose high and aroused as you panted, I passed my hands over your beautiful arms, over your long white legs, over those soft, delicate feet that carried you over the ground as lightly as the wings of a white dove. I passed my lips over your forehead, feeling just below the hairline the down that tickled all my senses. I kissed your eyelids and passed the side of my hand over those long soft eyelashes and watched your blue eyes when they lit up with passion and ardor.

I wanted to take you in my fingers, my hands, and my lips. At the height of love I feared loss; while we were one drop in the waves I feared separation.

Despite everything, you felt that something unusual was happening. As I was dipping my lips in the spot I loved, the gap between your neck and your shoulder, caressing the golden forest of your hair, covering my face with it, you said with a small laugh as you in turn felt my rough hair whose touch aroused you, "You've become ravenous these days! What happened to you?"

I didn't answer; I was intoxicated with love and the fragrance of your body.

You stopped laughing and said, "Not that I am any less ravenous! But I am afraid for you."

I said without raising my head, "My doctor says that I've never been better than I am now!"

"See? Haven't I told you that love has saved us? Yet we should be careful. We must be a little more sensible."

You felt my body tense a little in response to your words, so you began to pat my back and asked, "Are you angry with me?"

"Yes! Your love has waned. You are repeating words that lovers say before they separate."

And you said between kisses, "How many times did you say that? Do I look like I'm going to leave you? I would not even let you leave me if you wanted to! You are mine. I had lost you and I have found you. I want you to stay mine a long time, mine forever."

I mumbled as if repeating something from memory, "If only time would cease to be!"

But I didn't remember exactly when I had heard that sentence.

During those tumultuous days I received a kind letter from the editor-in-chief in Cairo. I had sent him the hospital bills and he wrote that the paper would pay my medical expenses, and he wished I would have a restful convalescence so that my contributions, which he "cherished," would continue. He advised me again not to work too hard and to go back to writing only when I had fully recovered. He said he had followed my advice and had not told anyone at the paper of my illness so that the news would not reach my family and children.

I was touched by the editor-in-chief's letter. We were old colleagues but had never been close friends because his idea of the press was simply that each authority in power was right until it lost power, and he placed his pen in its service until then. But he was a friendly man with his colleagues and didn't hesitate to offer simple services that he could afford in his position. I was particularly grateful for that open-ended leave that he gave me to recover, for it spared me the effort of keeping up with the newspapers and writing my monthly letters and seeking out curious news, or any other news.

But it was difficult in those days not to follow what was happening in Lebanon. The news was like successive blows to the head: the destruction of central Beirut using all kinds of bombs, 250 dead in a single raid using fuel air explosives, the agreement to evacuate Palestinian freedom-fighters from Lebanon, the arrival of an American force to supervise the evacuation of the Palestinians, and more. I was also following *Le Progrès'* campaign against Israel's violations of international war laws and its use of forbidden weapons. I also read the angry letters of protest sent by pro-Israel readers. The most virulent letter I read was signed by "I. F. Davidian, Businessman," who wrote saying that the newspaper was sliding down a slippery slope and that it was disseminating the various lies broadcast by the PLO. He said the war in Lebanon was simply to expel the saboteurs who were killing Israel's women and children in Galilee. He reminded the paper that millions of Jewish women and children had died in the camps of the criminal Nazis in Auschwitz and Buchenwald and the other camps. "Do you want the Jews to go on paying this tax forever? The Jewish people do not need lessons in morality or humanitarianism from anybody."

After I read the letter I said to myself that whoever read that letter would think that you too had paid the tax in Auschwitz, when most likely in those days you were in a big palace in the Zahir neighborhood in Cairo or in Stanley Beach in Alexandria living the life of a millionaire, thinking of banquets and deals rather than Nazi crimes.

And yet everything works: talking about Nazism, Arabian horses, tearing down poor people's homes, giving money to Israel. Everything works as long as you are successful!

The death of one child is a death to the whole world of course. And yet no one will ask you how many children died in Galilee—five or ten? And how many thousands of children did Israel exterminate in Lebanon and before that in Palestine? And why not? You are not alone!

In the morning, the news would report hundreds of dead and wounded every day in the city under siege, but in the evening the television would carry a somber ceremony full of religious rites and tears and anger for the burial of four Israeli soldiers who fell in the "war." The Arabs of course don't mourn their dead! And why not? There are real humans, and humans that are not needed at all. I had also read in *Le Progrès* a statement by Bashir Gemayel, the Lebanese presidential candidate, in which he said, "In our region there is an irrelevant people called the 'Palestinian people!'"

I got most of the news from television when Brigitte wasn't there. I followed the smiles of the US envoy to Lebanon, Philip Habib, and his statements about the success of his plans to arrange a cease-fire. I tried not to think that it was the same US, which had supplied Israel with the planes and the bombs that killed and set fire, that had also sent an envoy to arrange a cease-fire. I tried not to think that it was both the murderer and the condoler. And what good would such thoughts do now that it was the very US that also mediated the evacuations of the resistance forces from Lebanon? Now that it had decided and actually sent that force with its allies to banish the Palestinian freedom fighters and we signed the agreement and shook hands? Now that everything was over and the resistance forces had begun to leave Lebanon?

But one writer in the city couldn't take it anymore. Finally Bernard did it!

That morning the title of his column "Les Intouchables" caught my eye and I almost didn't believe my eyes when I began to read the first few sentences: "Our free country has been stricken by a strange malady these days. It has become mute and hasn't uttered a word about the crimes against human rights, so long as those crimes were committed by the Hebrew State.

"Journalists come back from Lebanon. They want to write about the atrocities they have seen; it is their profession. But what they write, no one publishes. Isn't that so, my dear Lawrence Déonna?

"You say some timid voices are raised? But wait! The answer will come immediately from the departments of 'Readers' Letters' which are wide open in our leading dailies: these courageous voices are of course anti-Semitic!

"They will brandish Hitler's gas ovens in your face. You say you had not been born yet at the time of the genocide? It doesn't matter. You are morally responsible, because Israel is taboo; Israel cannot be touched and everything that country does is good.

"But you will say, 'There are no bad atrocities or good atrocities, especially if their victims were women and children and old people and wounded on hospital beds. Then you are a leftist, an extremist, an agent provocateur, and on the payroll of the PLO."

The article went on in this angry tone, then Bernard added a P.S. after his signature which said, "I understand, of course, after writing these lines that I am an anti-Semite, so there is no need for anyone writing to draw my attention to it."

I had never before read anything like that in this country, and I said to myself that I should meet Bernard to find out exactly what had happened, and what Lawrence (Déonna), whom he had addressed in the column, had said. I thought of calling him and making an appointment, but then I remembered the experience with the Norwegian nurse Marianne, so I decided to postpone it. I had made another firm decision in those days not to watch the exodus of Palestinian freedom fighters from Beirut on television, and not to read anything about the subject. When Israel entered West Beirut after Bashir Gemayel was killed, it found only a handful of the Nasserist *Murabitun* confronting artillery and tanks with rifles, and I decided not to turn on the television at all, saying to myself that this was worse than masochism.

I wasn't able to escape for long, however. The same evening I read Bernard's column I got a telephone call that awakened me after an unrestful siesta. There was an unclear voice speaking the Lebanese dialect.

"You are Ustaz ———?

"Yes."

"I am Sami from the Lebanese Red Cross."

"Hello."

I tried to remember quickly: do I know him? But Sami said in a shaking voice, "With me here is your Egyptian friend Ustaz Ibrahim, who wants to talk with you. Please try to calm him down."

"Ibrahim," I said eagerly.

His voice came from the other end, raspy and intermittent, "Listen, there are mountains of . . . mountains!"

"Ibrahim! Speak a little louder, please. I can't hear you. How are you?"

"I'll be damned! I told you there are mountains of corpses and millions of flies. Flies still cover my eyes and the smell of death is under my skin. Write what I am saying quickly."

Mechanically I looked for a pen and paper on the desk as I shouted into the mouthpiece, "I don't understand what you're saying, Ibrahim. What do you want me to write? What flies?"

Ibrahim replied, yelling angrily, "Write what I tell you. In Sabra, mountains of flies cover mountains of corpses. No. Cross that out, cross out the flies. What's their importance? I can't think. Wait a moment. But flies are still buzzing in my ears. I'm sorry, I no longer have a place to write. After the resistance forces left they closed down all our newspapers. I want to tell you what I've seen before it's too late. You must record it. Wait a moment, wait."

There was silence for a moment before Sami's voice came through,

"I beg you to calm Ibrahim down. He's in very poor shape. We all are, after what we have seen in the Sabra and Shatila refugee camps, but

Ustaz Ibrahim is diabetic, as you know. We can lose him if he goes on like this. I am saying this loudly in front of him: we can lose him if he goes on like this."

But Ibrahim snatched the receiver and his stern voice came through. I felt he was making an effort to get a grip on himself, "Listen, there's no time. I won't even find a telephone to call you from if this opportunity is missed. What did they publish in your city about what happened in Sabra and Shatila?"

"They didn't publish anything. What happened?"

He screamed, "What are you saying? Even in Europe? For three days the massacres have been going on, ever since Israel entered Beirut the massacres have been going on. How come they haven't published anything? I have just come back from Sabra, and there . . . "

But Ibrahim did not finish. There was a long whistling sound, and then the line went dead. I kept shouting into the mouthpiece, "Ibrahim! Ibrahim! What happened? What happened?" I ran to turn on the television. The soap opera *Dallas* was on. I left the television on and turned on the radio. I turned the dial to the different stations, but there were no newscasts. There were music and songs everywhere. But while I was turning the dial quickly and incessantly, the soap opera on television was interrupted. A female announcer with an expressionless face came on: "We've just received a special report from Beirut. We advise sensitive and seriously ill people not to watch this report."

Silence. Dark screen. Without any preliminaries Jean-Pascale, an announcer I knew, came on. He was thin and on his face and in his eyes was an expression of indefinable sadness. Now his eyes were covered with a dewy film of tears. He was wearing a shirt and pants and behind him appeared the rubble of a destroyed house. It was sunny, and sweat was running down his forehead. The camera remained trained on his face for a while before he spoke. He said in a voice that he was trying to make calm, "Ladies and gentlemen, in twenty years of work this is a report I had hoped I would never make."

His voice trembles as he says, "This is the first time the camera has entered the Sabra refugee camp after the massacre of the Palestinians over the last few days."

After that the camera moves around in silence. It moves through narrow alleys in the midst of destroyed houses from which are jutting twisted steel rods and remnants of broken furniture, but there are no signs of any life or movement. Then the camera takes its time as it takes long shots:

Piles of corpses strewn over the ground.

Corpses behind corpses and corpses next to corpses.

A pile of mixed corpses of men and women lying on their faces and on their sides and on their backs.

Another pile of women and children sprawled on their backs, legs wide apart.

A third pile of men's corpses, swollen as if the skins and clothes will burst any moment.

Ponds of clotted blood under the heads and under the bodies.

Other corpses of men and children embracing each other with twisted arms.

The upper body of a corpse stuck in the rubble, hanging down with its head bowed to the ground, its neck cut widthwise from behind.

Two little girls next to each other, their upper bodies bare. Someone had tried to cover their lower bodies with a flattened tin but was not successful. The little legs protrude, wide apart.

The camera shakes as it captures them and zooms in a little. One of the girls has two holes filled with clotted blood where the eyes had been.

A pile of corpses with outstretched arms next to a destroyed wall as if they were climbing on top of each other. In the wall are bullet holes and vertical lines of blood: wounded fingers clinging before falling.

Corpses looking as if prostrating next to a white horse fallen on its side, its belly slashed open, its rump swollen, and its tail still convulsive. Next to it, an old gray-haired man, his thin legs jutting from a white galabiyya. Next to him a crutch towards which his hand is extended. In his head, a bloody hole.

Large flies on the horse, many flies on the corpses.

The telephone rings again. I don't reach for it. I am nailed in place following the images on the screen.

The short report ends. Jean-Pascale says in his trembling voice, "We were not able to show you all the pictures we have seen in Sabra and Shatila. Some of them are unbearable to human eyes." He says many things I don't absorb.

Distractedly I reach for the telephone receiver. It's Ibrahim's voice again. He says, "I'll dictate quickly. I'm afraid we might lose the connection again. Write down: In Sabra and Shatila, Israel, the Phalange and Sa'd Haddad's army killed thousands of Palestinians . . ."

I screamed, "Thousands? There are thousands of these pictures?"

Ibrahim did not hear me. He said, "Are you writing? Do you have a pen? I'll tell you the incidents and you can write them later on as you wish. When I arrived at Sabra the corpses had formed barricades in the small alleys of the camp, barricades that you had to climb over if you wanted to pass through the camp. You also had to pass through the smell of death and the vast swarms of flies. In one of the streets the ground was slippery and my feet sank. There was wet lime on the ground covering a large pit and from the pit peered smashed heads and blackened arms and legs."

"But how did they kill so many?"

"With all types of weapons: machine guns; rifles; knives; axes; swords; daggers; bulldozers that leveled houses on their inhabitants, living and dead; and with Israel's tanks that blasted the refugee camps the whole time to open the way for the butchers; death by dragging; death by mutilation . . ."

Ibrahim fell silent for a moment as if breathless. His voice moved away.

Sami said desperately, "Can't you calm him down, Ustaz? He's moving about freely but I tell you he's survived only by a miracle. Had it not been for the fact that he looked European and had a fake pass, the Israelis or the Phalangists would have killed him a long time ago. God have mercy on us! But believe him, Ustaz. What we have seen here makes John's *Revelation* look like child's play. God has been merciful to those who died in the war. I envy those who died in the war!"

Ibrahim snatched the receiver from him once again, and, trying to be calm, said, "Did you write all I told you?"

"Yes, almost all of it."

"Then write this: At the entrance of the camp is the house of an old gas station owner whom I know. His name is Miqdad. They slaughtered him and all his family: his children and grandchildren and his sons-in-law. They slit all their throats. I myself counted forty corpses in Miqdad's house. They butchered them and mutilated them and raped all the women and the girls and left them naked."

Ibrahim's voice rose. He was no longer calm as he said, "I saw Zeinab Miqdad. She was in her last month of pregnancy. They slashed her abdomen, took out the fetus, cut off its limbs and placed its legs and arms and body in a circle on its mother's chest after cutting off her breasts. They placed the fetus' head in the middle of the circle. The blood had clotted and maggots and flies were eating at the severed head . . ."

I threw up right away. Everything I had inside me came out at once.

Ibrahim heard my coughing and gasps and he burst out crying for the first time.

Sami's voice came through the receiver, reproaching me again, "I asked you to calm Ibrahim down, Ustaz. What have you done?"

From far away Ibrahim's voice as if he were chanting with a group of dervishes, "There is no God but God! There is no God but God!"

I was saying in a raspy voice through my coughs, "Ustaz Sami, give me . . . give me . . . the telephone number . . . please give me . . ."

The answer from the other end was a long whistling sound.

On television, *Dallas* was still running mutely. In my ear Ibrahim was speaking and Jean-Pascale was speaking, and I was trying to clean the floor and the desk with a towel. The doorbell was ringing persistently and when I opened it I found Brigitte.

She came in staggering with her arms outstretched in front of her as if she were blind, and her eyes were indeed dead. She said in a convulsive whisper, "Did you see? Did you see?"

She pointed to the television and said, "I was at the café nearby and I saw the pictures. Did you see?"

Then she threw herself on my chest repeating, "Did you see? They killed all the children of the world! Did you see?"

Her whole body was shaking as she leaned on my shoulder.

I was shaking too.

11

Climbing the Mountain

I TOOK DOWN EVERYTHING that Ibrahim said. I said to myself I swear to write it, I swear to write it even if it is the last thing I do in my life. If I had to I would write it on a poster and carry it through the streets.

The first thing I did in the morning was go to the Red Cross office downtown. Many had the same thought. I found the office full of Arabs. They were gathered around one official in the Information Department. I heard sobs like long, drawn-out moans coming from a corner in the room, but the crowd made it difficult to pinpoint its source. Those gathered around the official sitting behind his desk were showing him photos of women and children and trying to explain to him as he wrote and shouted, "The names! The names first!"

I saw another official standing in a corner surrounded by another group of people speaking all at once and also holding photos and sealed envelopes. He kept pointing to a sign in several languages, including Arabic, that said, "Telephone and postal communication with Beirut has been cut off. Please leave your inquiry and your telephone number and we will call you as soon as we get information."

I jostled my way through until I reached the official and gave him my press card. He raised it and looked at it, and I doubted that he understood anything in the midst of all the hubbub surrounding him, because he returned my card and just pointed to the sign, then turned to tend to someone else. But I grabbed his arm and said, "Please! Listen to me. I am a journalist and yesterday I received a call from your office in Beirut, from a person called Sami . . ."

Others were also grabbing his arm and asking him questions and he kept saying, "Right away, right away."

I said in despair, "I want to know how to get in touch with Sami in Beirut! There's a colleague, a journalist in Beirut . . ."

He replied slowly to let me know that he had followed what I was saying and said, "I understand. But I assure you, sir, all contacts with Beirut have been cut off for the last five days. Our headquarters has been contacting the United Nations and . . . and other bodies to reestablish contact with the office. You're a journalist and you can verify what I am saying. I don't know how our official contacted you from there, but please leave your friend's name and your telephone number."

He turned to tend to others. There was a stout woman covering her head with a scarf with a floral pattern, standing near me, leaning on a crutch. She asked me, "What did he tell you, my son?"

I told her and she took out from her bosom a small leather purse, which she opened and took out a worn photograph of a handsome young man, about twenty years old, who took good care of grooming his moustache, and said, "This is my son. He's in Sabra. Please ask him if they have any news about him. He's the only one left. All the others died in the war."

I repeated what the official had told me but I couldn't help asking her, "And you? What brought you here?"

She pointed to her leg. There was no leg. She said, "They brought me here to treat me. It's just my luck, just my luck if they condemn me to live and my only remaining son dies . . ."

She was not crying. She was looking at me, raising the picture to my face with a trembling hand and saying, "Just my luck." Then she fell silent, but her lips remained parted.

At that moment the voice of the woman hidden by the crowd rose as she said hoarsely in an ordinary tone with just a hint of surprise, "O, my son! O, all the young men!"

The whole office fell suddenly silent and all faces turned in the direction the voice had come from. My whole body quivered when I heard that call. The stout woman bowed her head and kept looking at the picture. Now her tears were pouring down her cheeks as she in turn mumbled in an almost inaudible voice, "O, my son! O, all the young men!"

I leaned my back on the wall feeling a faint dizziness as I looked at her face and the other faces in the office, but I came to right away. I gave my hand to the woman and helped her until we made it to the desk. I wrote down her name and the address of the hospital where she was being treated, and I gave my name and Ibrahim's name, then left the office.

That day and the following days I was reading everything in the newspapers. At the beginning, Israel said it didn't know what was going on in Sabra and Shatila but the Hebrew newspapers made fun of that stupid excuse. Then Prime Minister Begin had to say, "Goyim kill goyim and accuse Israelis!" He blamed the whole thing on the Phalangists. He said they sneaked into the refugee camps behind Israel's back and took their revenge on the Palestinians after their leader, Bashir Gemayel, was killed; nobody knew for sure who killed him. This claim also didn't stand. Defense Minister Sharon had to admit in the parliament that it was he who let the Phalangists in the camps to purge it of the "saboteurs." He said he did that because he didn't want the Israeli army to enter the camps "to preserve human lives"! He meant to preserve the lives of the Israeli soldiers, of course. But he said he didn't order the massacre or even hear about it.

No one bought that either. More facts of what Israel had done came out every day. The horror of what happened in the refugee camps removed all reservations, and newspapers began to attack Israel and accuse it unequivocally. Only one newspaper, *The Fatherland*, which had a long history of hating the Arabs, was the exception. It made light of the atrocities and the number of the dead, saying that they were part of the ongoing war between the Muslims and the Christians in Lebanon, that there was no need to exaggerate, for it was not the only massacre that had taken place there. That newspaper's defense of Israel was stronger than Begin's own defense. As for the editorials of the other newspapers, they all likened what happened in Sabra and Shatila to the crimes of the Nazis. Bernard wrote in his editorial that all the crimes that Hülagu, Attila, and Hitler had committed in years of murder, burning, rape, and torture, Israel and its allies managed to do in just forty hours.

I went every day to the airport. The journalists there set up a center for operations. We waited for every plane arriving from Damascus, Cyprus, or Athens, waited for any colleague returning from Beirut, or any diplomat or anyone who might have seen Sabra and Shatila after the massacre. We looked for anyone who heard from eyewitnesses of what took place during the three-day nightmare. Traditional journalistic rivalries disappeared; everyone who learned a news story or who made contact with a source shared the information with the rest of us. Journalists those days had sullen faces, struggling with some kind of sense of shame, as if they also had taken part in the massacre, or were responsible for it; as if they had to atone for their sin by finally speaking out and telling the whole truth that they knew. The testimonies we listened to revealed horrors that surpassed all imagination. The reporters decided, without any prior agreement, not to worry about readers' sensibilities and not to dilute the horrors to which they listened. Even the editors-in-chief left what the reporters wrote unchanged in most cases.

I wrote everything I found out and sent a letter to the newspaper in Cairo every day containing what I heard, reactions, and what the newspapers here said. For the first time I began sending articles to the Arab papers published in Europe without even bothering to follow up and find out what was published and what was not. What mattered was to write as much as possible, for ultimately something must get through.

At that improvised press center I met Antoine, president of the Palestinian Friendship Society in the country. He was a tall young man who always wore the Palestinian *kafiyya* around his neck. He told me that they were going to organize a demonstration together with some leftist parties. He asked if I could help him, saying that the demonstrations organized by those parties usually attracted a few dozen participants, but he was hoping that this demonstration would be a big one. He pointed to a whole page-wide photograph in one of the newspapers. It showed a pile of corpses of children who had been burned, their faces badly charred, amidst the rubble of a house in Shatila. He told me, "A demonstration the size of the crime!" Then he corrected himself and said, "Even if the whole town joined the demonstration, it would not be big enough." I promised Antoine to see what I could do. As an accredited correspondent I did not have the right to organize demonstrations or engage in domestic political activities, but I knew a person who was a specialist in that kind of thing.

Yusuf, however, told me almost defiantly, "I have to ask the prince first!"

I had called him before dawn to make sure that he was there, and I went to the café before it opened for business. We sat by ourselves in the empty café. His appearance had changed considerably from the last time I saw him. Now he had a straggly blond beard. He welcomed me in a somewhat lukewarm manner, but he listened to me politely. I told him that since he had told me about the demonstrations against Davidian, I understood he had some contacts in the neighborhood, and perhaps some societies, and perhaps he could help the demonstration attract the largest possible number of participants. But he surprised me by talking about the prince.

"What does the prince have to do with it?" I asked Yusuf.

He kept looking at my face, his eyelids twitching slightly and his pupils moving nervously. "Prince Hamid explained many things, Ustaz, things that were not clear to me," he said, the defiant note in his voice rising.

I didn't want to get into an argument with him. I needed his help— that was all there was to it. "Do what you like and ask the prince or any-body else. I don't think anyone will object to your taking part in a demonstration against this atrocity, or even your helping organize it. The whole world was horrified by the massacre. Even in Israel they are demonstrating against it, if you watch television," I said calmly.

He nodded in a dignified manner and waved his finger in my face,

"See, Ustaz? Even in Israel they are demonstrating against it! So what does that tell you?"

Anxious not to lose my patience, I said, "What does that tell me, Yusuf?"

"That politics, Ustaz, is a very deep sea! Israel carried out the mas-sacre and Israel is demonstrating against it. So what does that mean? Of course you are an authority on politics and I am just a novice. I was total-ly in the dark but, thank God, I have been awakened."

"What did you awaken to? And how were you awakened?"

He said, waving his hand nervously, "Awakened from ignorance, awakened from error! And it is all thanks to His Highness, the prince. He explained many things that were not clear to me. This world, Ustaz, is a jungle, full of fierce animals. The only thing that will save us is to become strong. And we will never be strong unless we use our minds and go back to our religion and to our roots."

"But if it was the prince who told you that, how come His Highness is working with Davidian?" Then I remembered something so I added, "And what about the wine that he offered you when we met him?"

Yusuf smiled pityingly as he nodded, saying, "Didn't I tell you that politics is a very deep sea? Sometimes, Ustaz, you have to work with your enemy and get very close to him to know his secret. The Prince works with Davidian and with the very devil himself to achieve our ends, God willing. And you are right, he offered me wine when I was in error. He even offers our enemies whiskey when they visit him. But he himself, praise the Lord, doesn't drink at all. Necessity, however, knows no laws."

Then he fell silent for a moment before saying with feeling, "His highness took care of me very well until he led me to repentance, thank God, then he explained to me how we can serve our cause."

Elaine had entered the café at that time and stayed away from us, arranging tables and chairs. I said to Yusuf in a casual manner, "And what you said about Elaine last time, have you decided anything?"

Yusuf sat back in his chair and yawned, saying dismissively, "What I said didn't make any sense. Back then I was in error. We have to stay together. It's very important to get citizenship to serve the cause here freely." Then once again he waved his finger in my face, saying, "Elaine also is one of the people of the book."

"Was it Prince Hamid who told you that?"

Yusuf did not reply, so I got up, saying, "Well then, ask the prince and if he tells you that the demonstration would not harm the cause, call me."

He too got up saying, "Pardon me, Ustaz. I can't act on my own in these matters as I told you. I am a humble man and the sea of politics . . ."

"Is very deep. I understand, Yusuf."

I shook his hand and started to leave but after two steps I went back and asked him,

"Listen, Yusuf. Did you tell the prince about our conversation concerning Davidian?"

"I don't hide anything from His Highness," he said in the defiant tone, his eyelids still twitching. I wanted to say something but when I saw his face and his wandering eyes, I changed my mind. A terrifying thought crossed my mind as I saw him: Is Khalid going to become like that?

At the door of the café Elaine surprised me as she whispered to me almost imploringly, "I want one final favor from you, sir."

"If I can do it."

"I just want you to tell Yusuf that I don't mind getting a divorce. I'll relinquish all rights."

"But Elaine, I have no influence on him to ask him that."

She didn't hear, however, and went on in her imploring tone, "I can also give him a small compensation to tide him over after the divorce. I want us to separate without any problems." Then she whispered in a trembling voice, "I'm afraid. I'm afraid of him now, sir."

Her lips were trembling as she spoke and she stole glances at Yusuf who was still standing, stretching with his hands at his waist. I told her, "I don't want to lie to you, Elaine. Yusuf will not listen to anything I tell him. Try in your own way."

After that meeting I went to the university where an Egyptian professor I knew introduced me to some Arab students whose enthusiasm was in stark contrast with Yusuf's lack of it. They promised to recruit their Arab friends and other students to take part in the demonstration. I also contacted some Arab embassies and they all declined, saying that taking part in demonstrations was at variance with diplomatic conventions. When I explained that I didn't want their participation, but rather their help, by giving me names of their citizens or addresses of their societies, they said that that was not within their purview.

Some of the embassies treated me with a great deal of suspicion, assuming that I was part of a scheme concocted by their Arab rivals to get them involved in suspicious activities. A press attaché said to me somewhat sarcastically, "But why is Egypt interested in this demonstration? Hasn't Egypt signed Camp David?"

"Yes. But what have those who didn't sign Camp David done?" I said.

I left his office. Actually I was almost thrown out. I didn't get into arguments with that man or anyone else. I really tried everything. One time I asked Brigitte if she knew any local members of the society that Muller presided over. She asked me in surprise, "What society?" I reminded her of the International Doctors Committee for Human Rights, and she said that society was just Dr. Muller! "Some of his doctor friends in Austria may also be members, but that's it."

I said, "So be it. Can Muller help us in any way? Does he know any doctors' organizations in the city? Can he offer this demonstration anything? He once told me that he believed this city was important because of its international character."

Brigitte shook her head emphatically, saying, "Muller doesn't take part in any activity unless he is the star."

Sunday morning, the day of the demonstration, was sunny and warm.

The demonstration was supposed to start at ten in the morning. I went on foot about an hour earlier. The police had decided to close to traffic the streets that led to the main square, the gathering point, and the other streets where the demonstration would proceed. When I arrived at the square it was already crowded with hundreds, and others kept pouring in from the side streets. Most of them were young people who surrounded the raised platform erected around the horseman's statue with Palestinian flags and posters saying, "No More Massacres in Lebanon," "Begin and Sharon Are Murderers," "We Are All Responsible for Sabra and Shatila," "The Labor Party Condemns the Killing of Palestinians," and others like that. I saw cameras surrounding the podium and photographers taking pictures, and policemen everywhere with their handheld radios.

In the square I met everyone I knew. The Arab students were handing out leaflets that they had printed at their own expense containing pictures of the massacres. I saw Bernard near the podium with some other journalists. Brigitte came with a girlfriend. I saw Yusuf who came up to me, saying excitedly,

"I have never seen such a huge demonstration in this city. I brought some friends."

"Thanks, Yusuf. Did you get the prince's permission?"

He evaded the question by pointing to a corner in the square and saying, "Do you see who's there?" He was pointing to a sidewalk far from the main body of the demonstration where some persons wearing yarmulkes and holding a poster on which they had changed Begin's quotation to say, "Arabs Kill Arabs and Accuse Israel." They were less than twenty persons and the policemen surrounding them separated them from the rest of the demonstration.

I said to Yusuf, "We have nothing to do with them. That is their demonstration and this is ours."

"But we must teach them a lesson," Yusuf said enthusiastically.

"The lesson is there already, Yusuf. Look at their number and let people be the judge. There's no need for knee-jerk reactions or for being agitated. But you haven't answered my question: Did you ask the prince's permission?"

He answered in a low voice, turning his face away from me, "Yes, but His Highness doesn't like demonstrations. He thinks they're a waste of time and interfere with working for the cause."

Then he turned towards me with a miserable look on his face, "But

I said to myself that I wouldn't lose anything if I came. The prince won't know."

"The truth is, you just love demonstrations, Yusuf!"

He left in quick steps and at that moment Bernard came over and asked me what Yusuf had said, and when I told him he said, "I understand the prince. For your information, several quarters were trying to prevent the demonstration from taking place. They went to the authorities and said it might get out of hand, that it might disrupt security."

"But why did they want to prevent it?"

"And why did they prevent demonstrations in many countries, including your Arab countries? They want it all to die in silence as many other crimes have. They want the memory to die and the anger to die so they can go on playing in secret. I understand the Prince, but I don't understand Yusuf, poor young man!"

Then he looked at his watch, saying, "I may not stay long with the demonstration. You'll let me know if something important happens?"

"Of course, but why don't you want to stay until the end?"

As he looked at his watch again, he said, "I don't want to leave Jean-Baptiste alone at home. He has a babysitter now but she leaves at noon."

He looked around and said in a whisper, "Strange things have been happening since I published the column you said you liked."

"Yes, I've been reading the angry letters they wrote in reply in the paper."

He said nonchalantly, "Forget the letters. Also forget the telephone calls and the anonymous obscene messages. None of that bothers me. What I'm concerned about is Jean-Baptiste."

"Jean-Baptiste? What does he have to do with all this?" I asked in surprise.

"That's what I'd like to know. I got a warning from the school that they saw some strangers talking with him at the door of the school before

I arrived to pick him up. You know that teachers watch the children from a distance . . . "

Once again he mechanically glanced at his watch.

To reassure him I said, "Don't exaggerate, Bernard. We're not in a jungle."

"Really? And those children who disappear and whose pictures are published in the newspapers or hang in the post office, how do they disappear?"

"You know better than I that for the most part those are crimes of sexual deviation and not political crimes."

"How do I know?" Then he added in his sarcastic tone, "You see why I need your doctor's address? And you too, my friend, be careful."

At that moment the microphone was turned on. It was the president of the Palestinian Friendship Society introducing the speakers. He told us that after listening to a few speeches, we would march to City Hall and to the American Embassy to present the statements and demands that we would agree on. Then he introduced a representative of the PLO.

The representative went to the podium. He was a thin man who wore thick prescription glasses. I knew that he had a PhD in political science and had independent views that the organization did not approve of.

He spoke in a calm voice: "The history of massacres against our people goes back a long time and has been repeated many times. I will tell you about one massacre that took place in Palestine in 1948. Those days the Arabs were fighting to stay in their land and the Israelis were fighting to evict them from that land. But the inhabitants of that village did not take part in the fighting. They told both the Arabs and the Jews that they didn't want to take part in the fighting. The Israeli Irgun gangs rewarded its peaceful inhabitants."

Thus the PLO representative started to relate the details of the Dir Yassin massacre. He told how Israel wiped out two thirds of the village inhabitants by slaughtering them and stabbing them to death. The only survivors were those who had fled before the Irgun showed up on the scene. He told how they killed the children of the village and the elders, and how they ripped open the abdomens of pregnant women. He wondered whether what happened in Sabra was any different. "Wasn't it the very same Menachem Begin who is now the prime minister of Israel? Back then there was no television to show the pictures and there were no Phalangists to give the job to. But now you have seen the massacre and you now know that those who perpetrated it were applying the methods that Israel had used earlier in Dir Yassin and in Qibya and in Ain El Helweh. And the purpose was the same every time: wiping out the Palestinians and banishing them from their land, then from any country they seek refuge in. So what is the world going to do to stop the genocide against our people? If you have forgotten all the previous massacres or haven't heard of them, this time you have seen with your own eyes and you have no excuse."

After the representative had spoken, Antoine introduced a university professor who was a socialist deputy in the country's parliament. I knew him well also. Over the years he had published books and articles about the exploitation of third-world countries by the West and its huge corporations. He always said that poor countries were paying the price of the prosperity of rich countries and proved that with figures and statistics. After the publication of each book or article the corporations sued him. I used to find unsigned flyers asking me persistently not to reelect that "traitor" to the parliament in my mailbox.

He started his speech at the demonstration also with figures. He said that about twenty thousand people had been killed and fifty thousand had been wounded so far in retaliation for the shooting of Israel's ambassador in London and to restore peace to Galilee. He said that that reminded him of what he saw in American movies when he was a child. In those films a handful of Americans killed hordes of red Indians who fell by the dozens or the hundreds, emitting fierce screams as if they were not human, as if they were committing an unforgivable crime because they fought to survive on their land. But when the American "hero" is fatally shot, the movie slows down and sad music is played as if it were the end of the world. He said he felt ashamed of himself even now because he used to be happy when the Indians were killed in the movies. It was only after he had grown up that he read how the whites in America had wiped out a people that had its own civilization, a people that when America was discovered, constituted one fifth of the world population.

The deputy ended his speech somewhat angrily, asking, "Isn't what we have seen in the movies what is actually taking place in reality now? Hasn't the US given the Arabs to Israel so it can dispose of them as red Indians? If Israel kills thousands of them, they are just numbers, but if one Israeli falls, it is a disaster and terrorism."

He fell silent for a moment before saying, "It is an insult to intelligence and to peace for Israel to call the ongoing massacre and the deluge of blood, "Peace for Galilee."

At that moment a voice said loudly, "Death to Israel! Down with America!"

I knew the voice without seeing the face. It was Yusuf. Two or three others repeated what he said but the PLO representative grabbed the microphone from the speaker and said, "There will be no shouting. Please, we would like to maintain order in the demonstration. Please help us do that."

Speeches followed by representatives of parties and trade unions and different organizations. Yusuf reacted loudly again after a speech but those around him silenced him angrily. I wanted to go over to where he stood to ask him to be quiet but at that moment someone who was speaking at the podium attracted everyone's attention. He was a tall old man with thin gray hair but his voice came out strong, incongruous with his appearance and age.

He started by saying, "My name is Ralph. I am a journalist, a Jew and an American.

"I was the first to enter Sabra after the massacre. I entered it after the last wave of slaughter. I took pictures and took down what the survivors had to say. I am not going to tell you everything I saw or heard. I am sure you know enough already. I'll tell you only a few things.

"You heard that the Phalangists and the Sa'd Haddad troops and other Christian forces committed these crimes. I tell you that it was Israel that planned and arranged this massacre and took part in it from A to Z and I will give you proof of that." Ralph then began to give his proof. He said that Israel had occupied West Beirut on Wednesday and met almost no resistance. There was nobody left to defend the camps after the evacuation of the Palestinian forces. Israel laid siege to Sabra and Shatila from all sides with tanks and artillery. On Thursday morning, the first day of the massacre, it began to shell the houses of the two camps, killing and wounding many. A delegation of old men came out of Shatila carrying white flags. They wanted to tell the Israelis that the camps were in a condition of surrender, that no one who could fight was left, that the Israelis could enter at will without fighting. But the Israelis shot them dead right away. Ralph listed those men's names and asserted that they were all over sixty. At that time no one could enter or leave the two camps except through the Israeli phalanx. On Thursday evening they let in the gangs of hired killers. Ralph said that some people might call them Phalangists or give them some other name, but he would call them nothing but professional killers who got paid and carried out the assignment. He said that their weapons were Israeli, their uniforms were Israeli, even their shoelaces were Israeli. Those gangs that entered the camps were not just a few individuals but a whole division: 1,500 criminals who kept slaughtering, raping, torturing, and dragging to death for three whole days. They would go out to get food and ammunition from the Israelis, then go back in to resume the massacre. Throughout, the Israelis were watching what was taking place from tall buildings, their binoculars trained on the two camps to make sure that the hirelings were doing the job they were hired to do. At night when they cut off electricity from all of Beirut, the Israelis lit up the sky with flares to enable their agents to carry out the slaughter. After that the Israelis gave them bulldozers to raze the houses on their occupants, dead or living, and to dig mass graves.

Ralph fell silent for a moment, trying to stay calm before saying, "I had seen such mass graves before, in the Ain El Helweh refugee camp after it fell. The Israeli forces used bulldozers to demolish all the houses in that camp, and buried the dead in deep ditches. I heard from survivors in Ain El Helweh that the bulldozers picked up some of the wounded with their sharp steel blades, who screamed that they were alive, and buried them with the dead. This is also what happened in Sabra and Shatila. The only difference is that in Sabra and Shatila they left some corpses in the street."

His voice rose a little as he said, "But did you ask yourselves why? You know the word 'corpses' is insignificant compared to what you have seen. You know that those who carried out the massacre and those who ordered it wanted to make human beings into something very repulsive. There were teams that specialized in doing that. They disfigured faces with knives and axes. They flayed the corpses of the victims and cut off the men's penises and the women's breasts, and severed fingers and hands, and deliberately left those body parts next to the corpses. Why? Even the Nazis tried to hide their crimes. Did you ask yourselves why Israel wanted to publicize this crime?"

An angry voice rose from the other sidewalk, saying, "Shut up. Shut up, traitor!"

Unperturbed, Ralph went on: "I'll tell you why they intentionally left these corpses. They wanted to create panic. Israel wanted to send a message to the Arabs and it did. It wanted to say, 'We can always do such things. What happened in Sabra and Shatila can be done elsewhere. Surrender and don't think of resistance.'" Then he paused longer than before and looked at the other sidewalk before adding, "I'll tell the person who called me a traitor because I am a Jew and because I am telling the truth about the massacre that Israel organized. I'll tell him that my own father was killed by Hitler in Auschwitz, but when I saw what happened in Sabra and Shatila I knew that he had died twice. Because those massacres in Sabra and Shatila are also six million."

The voice rose from the same corner, sarcastic this time: "A traitor and a liar!"

Ralph continued, "I'll also tell you what I've seen and what a man from the Red Cross at Sabra and Shatila told me. He said to me, 'The mass grave that we prepared was 30 feet deep, 150 feet long, and 150 feet wide.' I saw the grave myself and it was not deep enough because I could see corpses poking out of the lime they covered it with. The man said that they buried 3,000 corpses, not counting those killed by the murderers' bulldozers, those killed by Israeli shelling of the camps, nor those led outside the camps to be killed. How many thousands do you think those were? And how many millions would they be in proportion to the inhabitants of these camps?"

He looked once again at the person on the other sidewalk and said, "You are not a traitor when you tell the truth, you are a traitor when you don't." The only reply to what Ralph had said was a growl from that sidewalk, and it was the only sound that broke the utter silence in the square.

Antoine, the president of the Friendship Society, stepped forward to read out the demands that the demonstration would present, but the PLO representative whispered something in his ear. Antoine said, "There will be just one more and last comment." The PLO representative held the microphone and said, "I'd like to add one or two things to what Ralph said. Yes, Israel wanted this crime to accomplish the purpose that he mentioned, but it also wanted to accomplish something else revealed by Begin when he said, 'Goyim kill goyim.' What Begin wanted to say is: 'This is what the Arabs do to each other. They kill so savagely and with such degradation of humanity. Therefore what Israel does to them is totally justified. It is not enough to drive them out of their land, but they must be exterminated.' But we know now that that crime was not planned and carried out by goyim, but by the Israelis themselves. Hasn't it given you pause to think that Israel, which defends itself by saying that it was it that intervened to stop the massacres, has not arrested anyone, not a single one of those murderers? And those, as you've just heard from Ralph, were not just a few individuals but at least 1,500 criminals. So, where are they? You and I know the answer: they are under the protection of those who armed them and hired them. But we should not let them get away with it. Let our first demand be an investigation of the crime and apprehension of the perpetrators. If that is done we will know the whole truth."

The demonstrators agreed to the suggestion and the demonstration began to move. Antoine was in front shouting into a megaphone the slogan that was adopted and we repeated, pausing between the words: "Begin . . . Sharon . . . Murderers."

The police continued to surround the demonstration and their cars watched its flanks as it went slowly through the streets that were closed to traffic. Some passersby stood on the sidewalks watching and some asked about the reason for it. I heard a woman saying to her friend dismissively as we passed by them, "They're Arabs," and her friend said, "That's what I thought too, but there are others as well. Imagine that!"

We were passing by an open-air café on the sidewalk on that sunny day. The customers followed the progress of the demonstration in silence. Suddenly I saw someone dash out of the demonstration shouting. I saw him grab an Arab man wearing a white galabiyya with a bottle of beer in front of him by the collar and empty the beer glass on the galabiyya.

It was Yusuf. I ran to stop him.

The man got up in alarm. Yusuf was still grabbing him and cursing him, asking him how he could drink beer when the martyrs' blood had not yet dried. The man kept looking to the right and to the left, his face pale, calling someone "Raafat! Raafat!" as he patted Yusuf on the shoulder saying in Arabic, "Bravo! Bravo, brother. We are done, hero. Goodbye, goodbye, hero of the Arabs! Raafat! Where the hell are you, Raafat?"

But he did not manage to free his galabiyya from Yusuf's fist. I reached them but two policemen had beaten me to them and they held Yusuf's arms behind his back.

Raafat, whom the man was calling, arrived also at that moment from inside the café, shouting, "What happened? What happened? I was in the bathroom!"

The muscular young man looked Egyptian.

The man said to him, "Come on, pay up and let's go."

One of the two policemen was saying slowly to the man, "We have seen what happened. This man attacked you. You have the right to file a complaint against him. We are witnesses."

The man turned to Raafat and asked him what the policemen had said. When Raafat interpreted for him he raised his hand to his head as if saluting the policemen and said to Raafat, "Tell him that I forgo the complaint, that I forgive the man. I don't want a complaint or anything. Come on, let's go."

He kept pulling Raafat by the arm as he was translating for the policeman what he had said, but the policeman said insistently, "Even if he waives the complaint, he must come with us as a witness. This man committed battery and must be held accountable."

The man was agitated this time when he heard the translation. He took a red passport out of his pocket and said angrily, "Tell the policeman that the police have nothing to do with me. I have immunity. I don't want a complaint and I don't want witnesses. Come on, let's get out of here."

The policeman scrutinized the passport, then returned it after saluting and said in a stern voice to Yusuf, "Thank His Highness the Prince for waiving his right and don't do anything like that again."

Yusuf stood there dumbfounded and said nothing. After the policemen left, Raafat said to the prince, "Would you like me to teach him some manners?"

"Get the hell out. You disappear at the critical moment and now you want to act as if you were Muhammad Ali Clay! Get the hell out."

He left quickly, shaking off his galabiyya. The spectators that had gathered to watch dispersed. Many of them were participants in the demonstration, which was now moving away, still intoning, "Begin . . . Sharon . . . Murderers."

When Yusuf saw me he looked at me, his gaze shifting nervously back and forth, and I said to him calmly, "Yusuf, this is not the prince you have to settle accounts with."

He came to when I told him that. He kept staring at me for a while, then pulled me towards him and whispered in my ear, "Listen, leave this city. The prince can't stand you. The prince can do anything."

"What did you say?"

"I didn't say anything."

He let me go and left quickly. I also ran to catch up with the demonstration.

After the demonstration we walked in silence side by side, Brigitte and I.

The many jumbled feelings gave way to the fatigue and emptiness that accompanies every end. We made our way to the large park in the main square, which was crowded with visitors on that sunny holiday. At the entrance the chess players were standing around a large chess board drawn on the ground, studying the knights and castles, with their chins in their hands before one of the players stepped forward to move the piece he had decided on with both his hands. It occurred to me for a moment that if Khalid had been with me, we would have played here in this garden, that he would have been pleased with the audience. But I remembered: no, it wouldn't have pleased him. I wondered if he had received my letter. I will find out in our next conversation. Would it do any good? Is he going to turn out like Yusuf? Is there still anything I can do?

We sat on one of the benches as I said, "I didn't expect you to come to the demonstration. I know what you think of these things, but you kept shouting from the beginning and you stayed until the end. Many people left halfway."

She said absently in a low, tired voice after all the shouting, "Yes, especially after that stupid quarrel at the café. I think that person tried deliberately to ruin the demonstration. From the beginning he was shouting and making noises. Do you know him?"

I didn't answer her. The same thought had occurred to me from the beginning: that Yusuf and those with him had been sent to ruin the demonstration. But I wanted not to believe it. I told myself that he was not an evil man.

Brigitte inclined her head on my shoulder and I reached out and embraced her, and she said softly, "Thank you."

I looked at her face. She was smiling even though the distant look was still in her eyes.

"I know that you're shy, and you are embarrassed when we act like lovers in front of people, but I need you today."

Then she remembered something else and said, "I haven't changed my mind, though. He who suffers, suffers alone, and he who dies, dies alone. Our demonstration will not bring anyone who died in Beirut back to life. Do you know who I met today? Pedro Ibañez!"

"What happened to him?"

She said in a puzzled tone,

"That's what I'd like to know. He acted strange and totally ignored me when I talked to him. I was afraid that toil in the world of secret work would kill him. But it seems what happened to him was worse. Why didn't Muller leave him alone? In Canada, in Austria, in his country, anywhere?"

"What happened to him?"

But at that moment a little girl, about five years old, wearing a red dress, was approaching Brigitte and asking her in a poised manner, "What time is it, Ma'am?"

Brigitte pointed to her wrist and said, "Unfortunately, I don't have a watch."

Then she turned to me and I said, "A quarter after two."

The girl turned to leave but Brigitte asked her as she searched through her purse, "Why do you ask about the time?"

"I promised Mommy to return at two-thirty."

"So you still have some time. And since you are such a good and punctual girl I'll give you a little gift. Here, buy anything you want with this money before returning to Mommy."

She gave the girl a small coin, and she looked happy and stood on tip-toe to kiss Brigitte on the cheek before running to join the children she had been playing with. Brigitte followed her with her eyes, then began to look around at the trees. In front of us were two tall trees whose leaves had turned flaming red and stood out among the other trees, which autumn had colored yellow. She let out a faint laugh as she followed the height of the trees with her eyes.

"And yet I'll miss the height lovers!" she said.

For a long time I had been used to her sudden interjections, so I no longer asked her to explain. I knew that she would tell me what had occurred to her on her own.

She said with some puzzlement, "I don't know why they are always Asian." Then she hesitated for a moment, "No. There are other nationalities too, but only just a few."

Then she fell silent and once again had a distant look on her face.

"Who are they, Brigitte?"

She shook her head as if waking up and said, "What? What were you talking about?"

"You were talking about height lovers. Who are they?"

She laughed again dispiritedly as she said, "Ah, those? Didn't I tell you that they appeared in every tourist group? Sometimes I bring them here and tell them about these two trees that they brought from America. I tell them the history and how after many experiments it was possible for the planting of the trees to succeed. Then they surprise me by asking about their height and they write down that information in little notebooks that they carry. They also write the height of the cathedral tower. High things give them pause, as if they were in charge of keeping track of heights in the world. Do you know why?"

Her eyes were wide with surprise as if she were asking me a riddle. So I smiled as I said to her, "No, I don't know, Brigitte. But why will you miss them? The Japanese don't stop coming after the summer like the others. They come here all year round."

She repeated after me, "Yes, they come all year round."

Then she got up suddenly, saying, "I'm hungry. Do you have anything to eat at home?"

"There are things in the fridge."

"Come on then. Today I'll make you a special lunch."

Before going upstairs to my apartment I opened the mailbox in which several days worth of mail had accumulated.

There were the newspapers and the usual junk mail, and I also found a letter from Cairo with government stamps, inside a small envelope, similar to the letters of the Department of Taxes I used to receive in Cairo. Did that department still remember me after so many years abroad?

When Brigitte went to the kitchen to see what she could do for lunch, I put the newspapers aside and opened the letter. I read it as a stood there, then read it again. I couldn't seem to understand.

It was a half page of coarse yellow paper filled with signatures and stamps. At the top was "Chairman of the Board of Directors" and under it was "Mr. So and So," then, "In view of the board of directors' decision to reduce expenditures pursuant to the instructions of Mr. ———, it has been decided to abolish the post of correspondent in the city of ——— effective within one month from this date. Signed for the Chairman of the Board."

"It's not true!"

And that kind letter that the editor-in-chief had sent only a few days ago? The letter that made no mention whatsoever, implicitly or explicitly, of decisions of economy?

Brigitte appeared at the entrance and asked, "What's the matter?"

"It's not true!" I said.

But when I told her the news, she smiled sadly and said, "It's very true!"

"How? I tell you there's a mistake. Do you know things in Cairo better than I do?"

She shook her head and said, "No, I don't know about things in Cairo, but I know about things here."

I said in bafflement, "What do you know about things here? And what has it got to do with this letter?"

She came up to me calmly and said, "The director told me a few days ago that he cannot let me continue to work for the company because the police have asked him about my work permit. He also advised me not to look for other jobs in this city because there will always be somebody asking about the work permit. He told me the whole truth as the last proof of friendship, the last piece of advice."

"But why?"

She put her hand on my shoulder and pointed with the other hand at the open letter and said, almost shouting, "Try to think!"

Then she actually screamed as she buried her face in my shoulder, "This is Macias' and His Highness the Prince's world! It's no use!"

It wasn't difficult for me to understand, but I tried to remove any doubt. I failed many times to reach the editor-in-chief, who was also the chairman of the board of directors. I realized that he was avoiding talking with me. When I did finally manage to reach him, he was very apologetic, repeating, "It's not in my hands, it's not in my hands, I swear." But he refused to tell me in whose hands it was. He said he would try very hard to get me another month's renewal to complete my medical treatment.

I wasn't very anxious to stay another month in the city.

Brigitte was getting ready to leave. She had decided to go back to Austria to spend some time with her father before figuring out what she could do.

Everything was over and there was nothing left for you to do. The day did not come very slowly.

You feared the end and it came quicker than you had expected. You kept fighting your apprehensions as you imagined that end: Brigitte will leave you! She'll find a young man her own age, someone from her own country who loves dancing as she does, and like her, loves to climb mountains and to ski, and those things that she mentions casually in her conversations with you, and about which you do not know a thing. Will you wake up one day and find a farewell letter, or will you find out that she has disappeared without farewell? Will the end come when you fall again after these blocked arteries rebel and there is no reawakening and no second recovery?

Will the end come without any hubbub at all? Will love shrivel up and be killed by habit and boredom? You imagined everything during those moments you were terrified that Brigitte might disappear from your life; everything but the World, as she once put it, ending what was between you and her, other than that sword swooping down from the unknown to sever you from her. There was a cactus in which everything had dried up except the shriveled thorns that pierced its old flesh, a cactus that wasn't dead but wasn't alive either. You reached out your hand to it and its dead leaves came back to life to be one of your luxuriant trees that you loved. The branches multiplied and the flowers bloomed. And all of a sudden the sword cut off all the branches at once to uncover once again the cactus and the thorns, so that once again the open eyes stare at the dark at night.

That is what's happening. Wrestle then with these horses that come charging at you. Fight them alone or with patience or without patience. Show me what you can do.

Here is Brigitte, loving you as she has since the beginning. You feel her hand tremble between your hands as you felt it the first day. You read in her eyes that first love, constant as it has been. And there you are, still an eternal child in the heart of the child-love. When you embrace her the weight of years and the weight of worries suddenly falls off you and you float lightly in the endless ecstasy of love. Try then to capture the ether in which you swam that short moment of resurrection. Try to prevent it from dissolving or vanishing.

Tell her: Let's live in another city, let's try to work far from here. She will tell you: I am tired of running away and "they" are everywhere.

Tell her: Let's get married. She will tell you: Our ghosts are many, and they will chase us wherever we are. The most we can do, we already did; we stole from Time these moments of ours.

Tell her what you will. The cactus will return and the sands that drank up the spring will turn under your feet into sharpened, solid stones.

Make plans and solutions in the dark, and daylight will dissipate them.

Kneel down, cry, beg, show me what you can, for the last night has come.

Here you both are one afternoon like the afternoon you entered the apartment for the first time, but the curtains are drawn and the room is dark.

The room is empty. Everything is gone.

You are lying down on the hard floor, your arms around her, her arms around you, silent and spent after the wave has carried you for the last time.

She whispers to you after a while: "You don't have to come tomorrow. I can go alone."

"I know, but I'll come."

"Do you know who came today to say goodbye?" you whisper.

"The company director?"

"No. The director actually was nice and generous. He bought the few things that deserved to be bought in the apartment."

"So he came to say goodbye?"

"He came in the morning. He got in from the balcony. Nothing had been left in the apartment except what you see: the table and the two chairs."

"Who got in from the balcony, Brigitte?"

"He came in and chirped the morning greeting. He kept staring at the room. He liked the echo made by his flapping wings in the empty room, so he kept going around and around as I stood still here in my place near the window so that I wouldn't startle him. Finally he landed on the table and kept looking at me in silence, and chirped twice in a soft voice. I understood his message and I said I thanked him. He kept looking around the room. And finally he raised his thin foot and scratched his head. He looked for something else to say to me but he didn't find anything, so he went around the room once again and dashed outside. His wing touched me as he went out. Did your friend Ibrahim die?"

I sat up suddenly and cried out, "No! Why are you saying that?"

She kept staring at my face and said without moving, "I'm just asking, that's all. I am not a sorceress or a fortuneteller, and yet I saw death in his eyes the first time I met him. He attracted me and he frightened me. Once I needed to drink a lot, to lose consciousness, to get away from his pursuing of me and to save myself from his spell. But it was he who got rid of my spell. You know what was between us, don't you?"

"Yes, I know. But why did you say that now? It pains me that I know nothing about him."

"I told you I am not a fortuneteller. I also don't know anything about him."

"Did you love him?"

"No. He was full of the world."

Then she reached out her hand and pulled me to lie next to her again and said, "It was you I loved. I loved your silence and your chatter and I loved what you didn't say by silence or chatter."

She came closer to me and clung to me as she felt my face with her fingers, "I loved watching myself change with you. I loved seeing you lose years to be mine and me gaining years to be yours. There was a woman who had lost not just joy, but also sadness and pain, a woman who saw herself vanishing and when she found you, she regained herself and became bigger and bigger."

Then you said, whispering in total abandon as you stroked my hair, "And there she is, once again, vanishing."

I murmured in despair, "But there must be a way."

"Of course there must be a way," you repeated after me.

She touched my lips with her fingers saying, "But don't ask me . . ."

Then she got up and she rested her torso on top of me, her face on my face and her hair making a tent that enveloped me. Her perfume created a halo that engulfed me and she spread her arms like two wings and we soared together again, one last time.

When I went at noon of the following day to give her a ride to the airport, she was waiting for me in front of the house in a raincoat and a black hat, her long hair cascading down her back. As I put the suitcase in the trunk I saw her table and two chairs piled up in front of the entrance.

When the car moved she said, "It's still early. I don't like long waits at the airport. Let's take a ride."

"Where would you like to go?"

"Anywhere. I've fallen in love with this little city. I said to myself, here I'll forget the world and the world will forget me."

But she changed her mind right away: "No. There's no need for that. I don't like to see it so overcast the last time. It's a very sad city under these clouds."

"There is a beautiful wood on the way to the airport. Maybe, if you like, we can stay there for a moment."

"No, not even that. When the end comes it's best not to draw it out."

"As you wish."

I fell silent. I had nothing to say anymore. I wasn't me anymore. I saw myself, like her, having begun to dissolve for some time. I didn't lose only joy, I lost even sadness and pain.

Brigitte leaned her head back on the seat and said, "Where is peace, then, my friend?"

"To sleep, to dream," I said without thinking.

She sat up in her seat and cried out, "*You* said it!"

"What did I say?"

"To sleep, to dream! Didn't you say 'There must be a way?' You've just found it! 'And by a sleep to say we end / The heart-ache and the thousand natural shocks / That flesh is heir to,—'tis a consummation / Devoutly to be wished.' Weren't these the lines of poetry you were thinking about?"

"Yes."

"That is total peace! You said it, so don't hesitate, because actually, my friend, even without this poetry, who can bear this life? 'For who would bear / The oppressor's wrong, the proud man's contumely / The pangs of despis'd love, the law's delay,' the impossibility of justice, the defeat of tenderness by brute force, and all this selfishness and all this injustice. Who would bear this world? You said it!"

She unbuckled her seat belt suddenly, repeating breathlessly, almost panting, "Yes, yes, to sleep, to die. Besides, it doesn't necessarily have to be with a 'bare bodkin.' Don't you agree with me?"

Then she reached out her hand and pushed her whole body against me and began to turn the steering wheel toward the edge of the overpass as I screamed, "No! No, Brigitte. Not now! Not like that! No!"

She went on, with total conviction, "Why not? Why, my friend? Do you really enjoy this bitch of a world? What do you want out of it?"

She was pushing her foot down on my foot as I tried to push her away with my shoulder, as I tried to push her away with my body. The car was hurtling forward until it actually reached the edge of the road, and I pulled the emergency brake before it fell off the edge.

The car stopped, screeching loudly and shaking.

I was bending over the steering wheel, panting as I heard her saying breathlessly in a low voice, "See? You're not ready yet!"

Brigitte refused to let me see her off. She took out her suitcase at the airport and begged me not to go in with her. She said, "I hate farewells." She pecked me on the cheek, a casual friend's kiss, before turning around and going quickly to the glass door. I couldn't even stay one moment to watch her before she disappeared. Cars in front of the airport were honking, urging me to move on.

She was over. Everything was over. But as I drove the car I said to myself that there was one last thing I had to do in the city, one last account to settle.

I crossed the long bridge to the other bank of the river.

I was not familiar with that part of town and only rarely did I venture there. I went up the mountain roads but all the streets intersected and they looked the same. I stopped the car and checked the map I had, looking for the address I had obtained. I looked around but could find no one to ask. People don't walk in this part of town. There was nothing but the high fences of the mansions over which the tops of evergreen conifers peered.

It was cloudy and dark. I got out of the car. I wrote down the name of the street where I parked and took the map with me and said to myself that I'd start from that point. I walked with the map in my hand. The road was rising in the mountain and I began to run out of breath so I slowed my steps.

I felt tired so I sat down on the trunk of a cut-down tree. From where I sat I overlooked the city on the other bank of the river, but a thick fog enveloped the city and its buildings looked like disjointed gray blocks. It looked like a ghost of a town. As I looked at the city, a quotation that had been haunting me for some time came to me: "Time will pass and after us will come those who know why we have suffered. They will forget our faces and our voices, but they will not forget our suffering." No, that isn't exactly what Chekhov said. He put it more eloquently, saying something about happiness too. But will anyone really remember us? Will Hanadi remember me? Will our suffering give birth to that happiness? By what miracle?

I got up after resting a little. Another climb. There were small street signs and villa and mansion numbers, but no signs bearing the names of the occupants. There was a strong fragrance of flowers and trees that almost numbed me.

I was already numb without it. My head was spinning from the long climb.

According to the map, this must be the place. She said it was a huge palace but I don't see anything except the high fence and the iron gate and behind them the trees. In the middle of the trees is a straight walkway behind the gate, but it turns and disappears.

I don't see any part of that palace but at least there is a sign next to the iron gate. Yes.

I try to read. The letters are large but I have difficulty reading because my vision is blurred and because of the fog. I get very close. Again there's no occupant's name. The sign says, "Beware ferocious dogs." Under that it says, "Press the button and speak into the mouthpiece." When I press the button a deep voice with an Indian accent came through the speaker,

"Who's there?"

"I am . . . I want to see Prince Hamid."

"Do you have an appointment?"

I hesitated for a moment then said, "Yes."

"Just a moment, please."

He was gone for a long time, then I heard Linda's voice,

"Are you sure you have an appointment with His Highness the Prince?"

"He told me his house is my house. He said I could come at any time."

"Just a moment, please."

She also was gone for a long time. It was not her voice that came back but the Indian's: "His Highness says there's no appointment and that he does not wish to see anyone today."

"Tell him, however, that there's something important I want to tell him, something of great interest to the Prince."

This time, after a long silence Linda's voice came. It seemed that she was reading from a piece of paper because she spoke in a monotone: "His Highness reiterates that he does not wish to see anyone. His Highness does not wish to hear anything from you. He says that you are pestering him and he does not like those who pester him. His Highness is asking 'Why don't you leave quickly as your girlfriend did?'"

"Then tell him that I . . . "

But the intercom went dead and the barking began suddenly, vicious barking like continual howling getting close to the gate. Then a pack of snow-white dogs with long legs and long fangs appeared and began to paw the iron gate, baring their teeth and growling, staring at me with fiery eyes and jumping up and down. I moved away from the gate but the ferocious growling was rising higher and higher, matched by barking from the other mansions. All the dogs of the neighborhood joined efforts to expel the stranger, the barking followed me as I descended one road only to climb another.

So that's it then, nothing but dogs barking. You will not settle your account with the Prince, you will not settle your account with the dogs and you will not settle it with the gatekeepers. Yes, my friend, I understand it when the gatekeepers keep you out, but what about the dogs? You are not going to settle any accounts with the world. Everything is ending: you and Brigitte, you and Ibrahim and Brigitte, you and Ibrahim and Brigitte and Elaine and Yusuf, you and Khalid and Manar. Everything is ending. What are you waiting for? Why didn't you go along with Brigitte when the moment presented itself? To be together forever away from the world, away from the prince, away from the war you cannot stop, away from the blood you haven't shed but in which you are sinking. Why didn't you get up the courage? Why weren't you ready?

Once again those streets that go up and down. Once again I get lost. I've been lost for a long time. I held up the map and raised it closer to my eyes: nothing but meandering lines with black dots all over. I didn't see anything. The fog was now a curtain blocking everything, a curtain of wavy, dewy dots streaking, and behind it the mansions and trees swayed.

I descend. I cannot climb now. Forget the map and the car. Just follow all the roads leading down to the river. Continue descending! Finally I arrive at a small park on the riverbank, a deserted park in the midst of the fog and the cold. I sit breathlessly, the river before me a motionless leaden corridor and the city a gray mass of swaying dots.

But a voice pierces the silence, a voice shivering in the cold. A figure clad in an overcoat sits next to me and asks in a shivering voice, "You want?"

"Yes, I want."

"What do you want?"

"To understand. For more than fifty years I have been trying to understand. The child tried and the man tried and the child came back and the man died and all for naught. A hundred years is not enough!"

"You want for fifty or for a hundred? Hurry, not far the police."

The foreign accent and the bad grammar became clear. I said to myself: I know this voice. I've heard this voice before.

"Hurry: Moroccan hashish or Afghan? For fifty or a hundred? Hurry, not far police. I have it. Come with me . . . "

I turned my face but I didn't see him. The face also was swaying. I saw a face of streaking dots with thick eyebrows under the cap. I said in a weak voice, "Pedro!"

Was it really Pedro? Before I finished saying the name, he had gotten up and run, disappeared.

I shouted but my voice came out weak, "Wait! Wait!"

He came back. He came back slowly as I was sliding onto the bench with an irresistible desire to stretch out on it.

I raised my eyes but it wasn't Pedro. It was a policeman and he too was turning into streaking, wavy dots that kept getting smaller and disappearing.

The voice was coming from far away: "Sir, sir, are you alright?"

I wasn't tired. I was sliding into a calm sea, carried on my back by a soft wave and the melody of a pleasant flute.

I said to myself, "Is this the end? How beautiful!"

The voice was coming from far away, saying, "Sir, sir!" but it kept getting lower as the sound of the flute kept rising.

The wave was carrying me away.

It was undulating slowly and rocking me. The flute was accompanying me, with its long, plaintive melody, to peace and tranquility.

Author's Note

THIS IS A NOVEL based on imaginary characters and events. There are however, some exceptions.

In the first chapter: The story of the torture of Pedro Ibañez and the killing of his brother Freddie in Chile: the names are real and the events are real with some emendation.

In the sixth chapter: The Norwegian nurse's testimony on what took place at the Ain el Helweh refugee camp is real. It is a blending of published testimony and a personal interview of her conducted by the author. Her name has been changed.

In the tenth chapter: The column attributed to Bernard, the fictional character, is the text of an actual, published column.

In the last chapter: The testimony of Ralph, the American journalist, is real. The name is real and the events are real.

That, and the blood of the martyrs.

Bahaa Taher
Geneva 1995

Glossary

15th of May Revolution: Sadat's 1971 preemptive counter–coup d'etat in which he rounded up his political opponents, accusing them of constituting "power centers" against the government.

Abd al-Sabur, Salah (1931–81): Major Egyptian poet who was a pioneer of the "new poetry" movement.

Arab Socialist Union: Egyptian political organization formed under Gamal Abd al-Nasser in the early 1960s to pave the way for Egypt's transition to socialism. For the rest of Nasser's life and a few years into Sadat's rule, it was the only organization in Egypt permitted to engage in political activity.

Buhayrid, Jamila: Algerian woman, fighter for the Front for the National Liberation of Algeria, who was arrested, tortured, and condemned to death by the French. Strong protest in various parts of the world, including France, resulted in a suspension of the verdict. Her name became the symbol for Algeria's fight for liberation.

Haddad, Saad: Lebanese Greek Catholic leader of the Israeli-supported militia in southern Lebanon (South Lebanese Army) created by Israel in 1978.

Hamama, Fatin: One of Egypt's most beloved leading ladies in film.

hanim: Formal title of respect for a woman, such as "Lady" or "Madame."

Hawi, George: Former secretary general of the Lebanese Communist Party [1979–92].

Hawi, Khalil (1919–82): Lebanese poet whose despondency over the Israeli invasion of Lebanon drove him to commit suicide.

Jemayel, Bashir (1947–82): President-elect of Lebanon, August 1982; assassinated September 1982.

Kafur (d. 968): A ruler of Egypt made famous by the poems, first praising then lampooning him, written by al-Mutanabbi.

March 30 Declaration (1968): A political statement by Nasser, seen by many at the time as signaling a move to the right.

Murabitun: Military arm of the Independent Nasserite Movement, the largest Sunni Muslim militia in West Beirut from the beginning of Lebanon's civil war in 1975 until Israel's invasion of Lebanon in 1982.

al-Mutanabbi (915–65): Almost universally acknowledged as the greatest Arab poet of all time.

al-Nadim, Abd Allah (1845–96): Orator of the Urabi revolution; also famous for experiments and innovation in Arabic literary prose style.

Nkrumah, Kwame (1909–72): The first president of independent Ghana, famous for his advocacy of African unity.

Open-door policy: Sadat's policy moving Egypt's economy away from socialism (or state capitalism) toward an open market model.

People of the book: Christians and Jews as designated the Qur'an.

Phalangists: Hard-line Maronite Christian militia implicated in several massacres, most notably those in Sabra and Shatila under Israeli supervision.

al-Qays, Imru: Pre-Islamic Arabian poet.

Qibya: Site of a massacre of Palestinian civilians in 1955 in the course of which buildings were blown up while their occupants were still inside. The massacre was perpetrated by Unit 101 of the Israeli army, established by Gen. Ariel Sharon.

Rustum, Zaki: Egyptian character actor who appeared in numerous films often playing a villainous old man.

Sayf al-Dawla (916–67): Ruler of Aleppo and northern Syria whose fame and military prowess have been immortalized, in part, by the poetry of al-Mutanabbi.

Shadia: Egyptian singer and leading lady in film.

Sharia: Islamic canon law.

al-Shinnawi, Kamal: Egyptian movie actor and former leading man.

Si: A contraction of "Sayyid," i.e., "master."

Tell al-Zaatar: A Palestinian refugee camp in Lebanon, the site of a 1976 massacre perpetrated by the Phalangists and witnessed by two Israeli Defense Forces liaison officers.

Tarafa ibn al-Abd: A pre-Islamic Arabian poet.

Umm Kulthum (1904–75): The most famous Egyptian (and Arab) singer of the twentieth Century.

Uprising of January 18 and 19: Large-scale riots in major Egyptian cities in 1977 protesting the cut of state subsidies on basic foodstuffs.

Ustaz: Title of respect, usually addressed to intellectuals or scholars.

Verification of the new crescent moon: Made to determine the beginning of a lunar Islamic month for observance of religious duties such as fasting during the month of Ramadan.

"Wrestle horses that count Time as one of their knights . . . .": A quotation from al-Mutanabbi.